Presented by

J. Ellington Ashton Press

www.jellingtonashton.com

&

Hold the Line

D.A. ROBERTS

THE
LAKEVIEW MAN:
BY

D.A.
ROBERTS
THE END IS ONLY
THE BEGINNING

HAG
HORROR
AUTHORS
GUILD
MEMBER

D.A. ROBERTS

Edited by: J. Ellington Ashton Press Staff

Cover Art by: Michael "Fish" Fisher

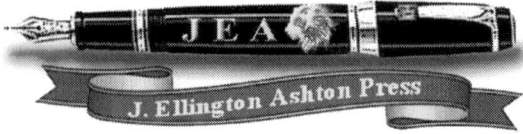

http://jellingtonashton.com/

ISBN: 9798640123838

To my friends Tyler C. and Steve M.
Your input made all the difference.
Thank you.

Thank you to Dark Angel Medical and Guncrafter
Industries for your amazing gear.

D.A. ROBERTS

Author's Note

Lakeview Man inadvertently became part of a much larger universe. It was while I was working on this book that the idea began to form for another series. A series that would launch from this book. It wasn't something I had envisioned when I first started this project, but it just seemed to make sense as the story unfolded.

From what I thought would be background characters emerged something I hadn't anticipated. It occurred to me that teams that reacted to events like the ones in this book might have stories to tell, all their own.

Then I started bouncing ideas off my friend Steve. Thank you, Steve. You really got me to thinking outside the book, so to speak. From our conversation came the concept that would take this story in an entirely new direction. New meaning was given to characters that I intended to merely write off in the background.

So, enjoy the pages that are to follow. Watch the background characters and see the idea evolve. Clark is a fun character to write and I found that the more I wrote, the more I enjoyed his company.

I thank you, the reader, for taking the time to read this book. After all, writing is and always will be a journey that we take together. Thank you for coming along for the ride.

D.A. Roberts

April 2020

Table of Contents

D.A. ROBERTS

Chapter One
A Ruined Meal

"Monsters are real, and ghosts are real too.
They live inside us, and sometimes, they win."
Stephen King

The sun was low in the sky as Deputy Daniel Clark parked his grey Ford Explorer in the parking lot of Pop's Dairy Dell in the tiny town of Reeds Spring, Missouri. Although it wouldn't be full dark for at least two more hours. The decals on the sides of the vehicle bore the insignia of the Sloan County Sheriff's Office.

The air conditioning was going full-blast due to the sweltering heat on this Saturday evening. In Missouri in August, it's not the heat that will get you, it's the humidity. Despite the air blowing on him, Clark could feel the sweat pooling beneath his body armor. If his dark hair hadn't been kept cut close to the scalp, it would likely have been plastered to his head with sweat.

"125," he said, keying up the mic on his radio.

"125, go ahead," replied the female dispatcher.

"Can you show me out at 22527 Main in Reeds Spring," he said, "I'm going to grab some lunch while I can."

"Copy, 125," replied the bored sounding dispatcher.

Clark exited the vehicle and felt the heat and humidity immediately try to kill him. He learned years before in the Army that age-old mantra of "Hydrate, Hydrate, Hydrate." It proved true in the plains of Afghanistan and it holds true back home in Missouri. The heat could and would kill you if you didn't stay hydrated. Especially when you were wearing body armor and thirty pounds of gear.

There wasn't a line at the walk-up window to Pop's, so he headed over to place his order. A young girl that looked about sixteen was leaning on the inside counter playing with her phone and didn't immediately notice him standing there.

11

He didn't say anything and tried to keep his face neutral. In his mind, he was beating on the glass and yelling for her to put the damned phone down and pay attention. But he remained calm and waited patiently.

"Hey, Brooklyn!" yelled a voice of an older male from the back. "You've got a customer!"

The girl looked up with a start and flashed red in her cheeks. She was embarrassed to be caught not paying attention. She also gave Clark a winning smile and immediately put her phone away.

"I'm sorry, deputy," she said. "I hope you weren't waiting too long."

"No problem," he replied with a smile of his own. "Just got here."

"What can we get for you today?" she asked, still smiling.

"Can I get a double cheeseburger with fries?" he asked, returning the smile. "And toss some bacon on that."

"No problem," she said. "What to drink?"

"I'll have the largest cup you have full of ice water," he said.

"Is that for here or to go?" she asked, still scribbling on the order pad.

"The burger and fries are to go," he said, grinning, "the ice water you can just dump down the back of my body armor."

She looked up, a look of confusion on her face.

"Sir," she began, "I'm not sure we can do that."

"That's fine," he said, chuckling. "I was just kidding. It's about a million degrees out here."

"Oh," she said, still confused. "Oh! I get it. Sorry."

"All of it to go," he added.

"I'll bring that right up for you," she said.

She turned to begin ringing up the total on the register when the older man from the back walked up.

"Hang on a sec," he said, stepping up next to the girl. "This one's on the house."

"You don't have to do that, sir," said Clark.

"I know I don't," replied the man. "You're out there risking your ass to protect all of us. The least I can do is give you something to eat."

"Thank you, sir," said Clark. "I appreciate that."

"Anytime," said the man. "Tell your other deputies that if they need to eat while on duty, send 'em to me. I'll feed 'em. No charge."

Returning to the grill, the man started putting together Clark's order while the girl filled a large Styrofoam cup with ice water. While they were filling his order, Clark positioned himself where he could watch every angle of approach. Constantly checking for any signs of potential danger.

"Here ya go," said Brooklyn, handing his order to him.

It consisted of one white paper bag with the food and the large styro cup of water.

"Come back and see us," she said.

"Will do," Clark replied. "Thank you very much."

Clark was almost back to the vehicle when he realized that the bag seemed unusually heavy. Glancing in, he saw three wrapped burgers and two orders of large fries. Thinking it was a mistake, he turned to go back to the window.

"The rest is for later," called the man from the window. "Enjoy!"

Clark smiled and raised his cup to the man, then hit the unlock button on the key fob. Sliding back in behind the wheel, he carefully sat the food in the passenger seat and stuck the water in the cupholder.

He'd left the engine running so the air conditioning would keep the interior of the vehicle cool. Reaching into the bag, he pulled out a long crinkle-cut French fry and popped it into his mouth.

"Shit," he hissed. "That's hot!"

Chewing quickly, he swallowed and chased it down with a large gulp of the ice water.

"Whew," he breathed. "Better let those bastards cool."

"125," said the radio.

"Shit," he swore. "What now?"

He grabbed the mic and pulled it up close to his mouth.

"125, go ahead," he replied.

"125," said dispatch, "we have a report of a missing child at 182 Lakeview Road in Kimberling City. Coachlight Village Mobile Home Park."

"125 copies," he said, "show me in route."

Buckling on his seatbelt, Clark checked his blind spots and mirrors. Finding no traffic in any direction, he backed out into the road quickly, engaged his lights, and sped off down the street.

Glancing down at his MDT[1], he saw a text message appear from Deputy Willy Konrad, radio 136. Konrad was on duty today as well but on the far side of the county.

"So much for your lunch," the message said.

"Yeah, no shit," Clark said aloud. He didn't want to risk taking his hands off the wheel to respond.

The distance between Reeds Spring and Kimberling City is usually about a fifteen-minute drive under normal traffic conditions. Clark made the drive in less than ten. Once he crossed the bridge over

---

[1] MDT – mobile data terminal.

Table Rock Lake at Kimberling City, he started slowing down. His turn was coming up rapidly.

Turning right into the Mobile Home Park, he turned again onto Lakeview Road and started checking addresses. Although he had GPS navigation in the vehicle, all of the twists and turns at the Lake tended to render it almost useless for navigation.

The intended address was at the end of the road, near the trees. Slowing down, he came to a stop at the end of the driveway. Shutting down his lights, he put the vehicle in park and glanced hungrily at the food. Ignoring it, he grabbed the mic and keyed up.

"125," he said, "show me on-scene."

"Copy 125," replied dispatch.

Getting out of the vehicle, he saw three young children all sitting on the porch to the trailer. Two boys about four years of age and looking like twins. The other was a little girl of about six. Walking towards them, he saw that they all were barefoot and the boys weren't wearing shirts. None of them looked like they had eaten recently. You could see the ribs on all three of them.

"Hi," said Clark as he walked towards the porch.

The kids looked at him but said nothing.

"Where are your parents?" he asked.

"*Intide*," said one of the boys.

Clark noted a speech impediment and wondered what caused it. Stepping past the kids and onto the porch, Clark knocked on the door of the trailer.

"Play outside!" he heard a shrill male voice yell.

Clark took a moment to push down his rising anger.

"Sloan County Sheriff's Office!" Clark yelled while knocking again.

He could hear the male trying to speak quietly but failing.

"Aw, shit," he hissed at someone else in the house. "Why the fuck are cops at the door?"

Before the other person could answer, the male yelled through the door at Clark.

"If you ain't got a fuckin' search warrant," he said, "then fuck off."

"We received a report of a missing child," replied Clark.

There was silence for a moment, then a woman's voice said, "Just a minute."

After a few minutes of someone moving franticly around inside, the door opened about six inches. Instantly, Clark was hit with the obvious odor of marijuana.

At the door was a skinny white male wearing a white tank top and jean shorts. He wasn't wearing any shoes and had an ankle monitor on his left leg. His hair was long and stringy in the back and thin to the point of near baldness on top. More of a *skullet* than a mullet.

He had numerous tattoos, most of which looked like they were done in prison. Across the front of his neck was tattooed the words "High Lyfe" with a pot leaf on each end. He also had fresh sores down both arms and some on his legs.

"Meth-head," Clark immediately thought.

"I didn't call you," said the male.

"Never said you did," replied Clark. "Someone did, though. This is the correct address."

"I called," said a female voice somewhere behind the male. "My daughter is missing."

"She's prob'ly up the road at yer damned mother's trailer," said the male, over his shoulder.

"She ain't there," said the woman, starting to sob. "I called and asked."

Glancing out the door, the male did a quick headcount of the children on the porch.

"Well, fuck," he said. "I guess we are down one, but three outta four ain't bad. Don't be callin' the cops down here, dumbass."

"Kayden is missing," sobbed the woman.

"Well, fuck," said the male, opening the door. "I guess we did fuckin' call you."

Clark bit his lip to avoid saying something he'd regret. He needed to find the missing child. He could bust this meth-head afterward. With the door open, he could smell the strong odor of both marijuana and ammonia. A clear sign they were making meth. He was already making mental notes of who to contact for a search warrant, who to call at Probation and Parole concerning one of their ankle monitors, and what he was going to say when he called Child Protective Services.

Behind the male was a morbidly obese female with glassy eyes and sores on her arms and legs. She was wearing a white t-shirt with a logo from some band he'd never hear of and yoga pants stretched so tight you could partially see through them. There were needle tracks in the crook of both of her arms.

"When was the last time you saw the child?" asked Clark, trying to keep them on task.

"She was out playing with the other kids," said the woman. "About an hour ago."

"Ok," said Clark. "What does she look like?"

"She got red hair," began the woman, "and was wearin' a one-piece swimsuit. It was purple, I think."

"When did you realize she was missing?" asked Clark, pulling out his pocket notebook and scribbling notes.

"The kids came to the door and said that a big man tried to grab them," she said, pulling out a cigarette and lighting it up with shaking hands.

"Fuck," thought Clark. "This isn't a missing child. This is an abduction."

His mind immediately went into near panic mode, mentally recalling all the exits and possible directions of travel that an abductor could have taken.

"Did you see the big man?" asked Clark.

"No, but the kids did," explained the woman.

"What are their names?" asked Clark.

The two boys are Brayden and Hayden," she said. "They're twins. The two girls are Kayden and Ayden. They ain't twins."

Clark fought down the urge to slap her.

"Can I get your names?" Clark asked, pointing towards the adults with his pen. "For the report."

"I'm Courtney Reynolds," she answered.

"Are the children's last names Reynolds, as well?" asked Clark.

"No," answered Courtney. "The boys' last name is Gomez. Ayden's last name is Johnson and Hayden's is Marcum."

Clark fought back his instinct to shake his head in disgust, then looked at the male.

"You don't need my name," he said defensively.

"Yes, I do," replied Clark. "You can tell me or I can just call your Probation Officer and ask them. I'll make sure to tell them you refused to cooperate."

"Fine!" he snapped. "Tyger Morton. Tyger with a y."

"Tyger?" asked Clark, a note of disbelief in his voice.

"Yeah," said Tyger. "I ain't got a license to show you."

"Do you have any ID at all?" asked Clark.

Digging into his pocket, he pulled out a laminated card with his picture on it. Clark took it and looked it over. His name was actually Tyger Scott Morton. The ID was a Missouri Department of Corrections Inmate ID.

Handing him the ID, Clark stepped back and keyed up his mic.

"125," he said.

"125, go ahead," said dispatch.

"Can you start me additional units," he said. "This is looking like an abduction case."

"Copy," said dispatch. "Starting additional."

Turning back to speak with the woman, Clark heard radio traffic that 136 and 155 were responding. That was good. He trusted Konrad and 155 was Corporal Amanda Sanchez. She was the shift supervisor on duty, and she would be in charge of running an abduction case.

She and Clark had dated a few months back and things were going well. He'd planned to ask her to marry him when she unexpectedly broke it off without explanation. They still worked well together as friends, but he couldn't bring himself to ask her why, although he thought about her often.

"Is it ok if I speak with your children?" asked Clark.

"Yeah," replied Courtney.

Kneeling by the kids, Clark tried to act friendly to not scare them.

"Can you tell me what you saw?" asked Clark.

The two boys stared blankly at him without answering.

"They won't answer you," said Tyger. "She drank too goddamned much when she was pregnant. Fucked 'em up pretty good."

"You shut yer mouth," she screamed and started crying.

It hit Clark suddenly why the boys didn't react. They both had Fetal Alcohol Syndrome. Clark's anger was beginning to rise and he fought to control it. He was going to get these kids away from these two morons if it was the last thing he did.

"I *sawd* the big hairy man," said the little girl.

"Did he put your sister in his car?" asked Clark.

"No," she said, shaking her head. "He *pickted* her up and *tookt* her in the woods."

"Can you show me where?" asked Clark.

The little girl stood up and held out her hand. Clark took her tiny hand in his and let her lead him away. As they headed towards the trees, Clark saw Konrad's Charger pulling into the driveway.

Konrad followed Clark and the little girl to the edge of the trees. She stopped and wouldn't go any farther.

"Is this where you saw the big man?" asked Clark.

The girl nodded and pointed into the trees.

"He was back *dere* in the *bushies*," she said. "He was watchin' us playin' back *dere*. We didn't see him 'til he *grabbded* Kayden."

Clark noticed that she was now trembling with fear.

"It's ok," Clark reassured her. "You don't have to go in there. Thank you for your help."

She let go of Clark's hand and sprinted back to the trailer.

"Whatever she saw sure scared the hell out of her," said Konrad.

Clark stepped into the trees and proceeded towards the bushes that she had pointed out.

"Want me to come with you?" asked Konrad.

"Not yet," said Clark. "No sense both of us getting covered in ticks until we have more to go on."

Moving around the bushes, he could see where the grass had been matted down from someone crouching there. They must have moved around a lot because the grass was crushed in a large area. There was no sign of tracks and no trace of the little girl. The ground was hard-packed and it hadn't rained in weeks. Finding a track in this was going to be almost impossible. There was a lingering smell there, of something rancid. Like urine and something else. It burned his nostrils and left a sickly feeling in his stomach. Whatever it was, it was fading fast.

"Hey, Konrad," yelled Clark.

"What?" he replied.

"Get ahold of dispatch and tell them to send a dog," said Clark. "We're going to have to track them."

Looking around the heavily wooded area, Clark didn't see any sign of movement or trails. It was almost as if they had just vanished into thin air.

Clark walked out of the woods and waited for Konrad to get off the phone. Konrad mouthed "twenty minutes out" to him and kept listening to the phone.

Down the road, Clark saw 155 pulling in. That was Sanchez. She got out of her car and headed directly towards Clark and Konrad. Clark had to fight down the smile that threatened to light up his face when he saw her. Her long black hair was pulled back into a bun and her shapely body was impossible to hide, even with body armor.

Once Konrad hung up, Clark quickly brought them up to speed on everything he had found out so far. He couldn't hide his contempt for the drug-addled parents. He made it clear that no matter the outcome today, he wasn't leaving here until they took custody of all of the children.

Sanchez looked at Clark and said, "It's your scene. Want to start trying to find the tracks?"

"I already had a look," answered Clark. "The ground is too hard. I thought it best to wait for the dog so I don't confuse the scent."

"Good idea," said Konrad. "Kimberling City is sending a K9 unit to start the track. Be here in a few minutes. What do you want us to do until then?"

"Keep an eye on the parents while I call Child Protective Services," said Clark. "Those two have no business whatsoever raising children. They're both high enough to hunt ducks with a rake, right now. I've got something to do before I make that call."

"By the way," said Sanchez. "Your search warrant should be here in fifteen minutes."

Clark lost the battle and smiled at her. It took a second, but he regained his composure. It took all he had to resist the urge to pull her into his arms and kiss her.

"You're the best," he said, with a wink.

Returning to his SUV, Clark took out the bag of burgers and fries. Heading over where the children were still playing on the porch.

"Here you go," he said, taking out the burgers and handing each one.

He rolled the bag down and set the fries between them. The children acted as if they had just been given the Holy Grail and began digging into the food. Konrad came up and set three bottles of Gatorade in front of the kids.

"That was sweet," said Sanchez as Clark walked back to his car.

"Might as well let them have a decent meal," he said with a grin. "I figured I wasn't going to get to eat it anyway."

Chapter Two
Running a Track

"Wisdom is knowing the right path to take.
Integrity is taking it."
M.H. McKee

Clark went over to the back of his patrol vehicle and opened the hatch. Grabbing his go-bag, he unzipped a side pouch and took out a green bottle of Deet and started spraying the legs of his pants and the tops of his boots. Konrad took the bottle when he was done and did the same.

Next Clark grabbed his external plate carrier and slipped it on over his uniform. It was Olive Drab Green with Deputy Sheriff emblazoned on the front and back. Pulling the Velcro flaps into place, he adjusted the fit until it was comfortable. Attached to the MOLLE tabs on the front were mag pouches and a D.A.R.K. Medical[2] kit for emergency trauma wounds.

Next, he took his patrol rifle out of its case and hooked the single point strap in place. The custom Black Rain Ordinance Spec15 Series was chambered in 300 Blackout instead of the usual 5.56mm, which gave the weapon more power and punch. It was outfitted with an EOTech XPS3 Optic with MagPul flip sights as backups.

Next, he put six magazines for the AR in the pouches attached to the vest. Then he pulled out a Camelback pouch and started filling it with bottles of water.

With that shouldered over his armor, he did a few knee bends to adjust to the weight. The last was an LED headlamp that he slipped on and adjusted. Konrad was doing the same at the trunk of his Charger. Konrad's rifle was a Ruger AR556 with an ACOG optic.

"You two planning on going with the dog?" asked Sanchez.

---

[2] D.A.R.K. Medical Kit – stands for Direct Action Response Kit from Dark Angel Medical. A company that specializes in emergency kits for law enforcement, military and first responders.

"That's the plan," said Clark.

"Ok," she replied. "I'll take over as Incident Commander and coordinate things from here."

Clark heard another vehicle approaching and saw a Kimberling City Police K9 SUV pulling in. An officer that Clark and Konrad both knew stepped out. Officer Brice Meadows exited the vehicle and went to the back to start grabbing gear.

In minutes, Meadows had his armor in place and his rifle slung. His was a customized Springfield Arms SAINT chambered in 5.56mm with the same Eotech optic that Clark used. Opening the back door, he took the lead and gave a command.

"Rocco," said Meadows, "*Hopp[3]!*"

K9 Rocco, a four-year-old German Shepard, jumped out of the back of the SUV. Once on the ground, Meadows gave another command.

"*Sitz[4]!*" commanded Meadows, hooking up the long lead.

Rocco sat without hesitation. Clark and Konrad were happy to see Meadows. They had both worked with Rocco and knew he was damned good at tracking.

"Let's go," said Clark.

Sanchez handed Meadows a tiny t-shirt.

"This belongs to our missing child," she said.

"Excellent," said Meadows, holding the shirt down so Rocco could get the scent.

The streetlights were starting to flicker on as full darkness was finally setting in. There was clear visibility with plenty of starlight. The moon was only a sliver on the horizon.

---

[3] Hopp – pronounced "Hop" - German command for Jump
[4] Sitz – pronounced "Zitz" - German command for Sit

"Let's get moving," said Meadows. "That trail isn't getting any warmer."

"Lead the way," said Clark.

"Rocco," said Meadows, "*Such!*[5]"

Clicking on their headlamps, they headed for the trees with Rocco pulling at the leash to go faster. Rocco's high-pitched short barks indicated he was excited and ready to run.

As soon as they hit the trees, Rocco had the scent. He was barking and lunging against the leash, running straight for the bushes where Clark had found the matted down grass.

As they rounded the bushes and Rocco found the spot, he quit barking and stopped dead in his tracks. With his tail between his legs, Rocco began whimpering like a scared puppy, refusing to go any further. Meadows looked shocked as Rocco started to shake with fear and urinated on himself. Clark immediately thought of the urine-like smell, although it was gone and he couldn't smell it anymore. However, that didn't mean the dog couldn't.

"What the fuck is wrong with your dog?" asked Konrad.

"I don't know," said Meadows, in surprise. "I've never seen him do this before."

Rocco started whining and tried to run back the way he came, towards the vehicles.

"Rocco," called Meadows, "*Such!*"

Rocco refused to obey and tried to pull away.

"Something scares the shit out of your dog," said Konrad. "That's predator behavior. I've seen dogs do that around bears and mountain lions. Any chance this was an animal that took the kid?"

"The kids said it was a "hairy man"," said Clark, doubt beginning to form in his mind about the identity of the suspect.

---

[5] Such – pronounced "Sook" – German command for Track

"Probably some homeless dude with a taste for the kiddies," said Konrad.

"No fucking way," said Meadows. "I've never seen Rocco back down from anyone."

"Then it has to be some type of animal," said Konrad. "That's the only thing that makes sense."

"Nothing about this makes sense," said Clark, looking around nervously.

"So, what do we do now?" asked Konrad, shaking his head.

"You two can go back if you want," said Clark. "I'm going to look around for a while and try to find something that might lead us in the right direction."

"Not without me," said Konrad.

"I'll be at my vehicle if you need me," said Meadows. "I've got to try and calm Rocco down and figure out just what the hell went wrong."

After Meadows had walked away, Konrad turned to Clark and shook his head.

"What the fuck?" he said. "That's crazy. I thought those dogs weren't afraid of anything."

"God knows," answered Clark. "The kids said "Hairy Man" but the dog acts like it's some kind of predator. This entire situation keeps getting weirder by the minute."

Shining the light from his headlamp into the area of matted down grass, Clark started searching the ground for anything that could help. Kneeling, he detected a faint odor from the grass. It smelled like rotten meat mixed with Sulphur. It was almost nauseating to smell. Now that he was close, it smelled different compared to the last time. More 'wet dog and rotten meat' than just urine.

"Whatever was here really stinks," said Clark, wrinkling his nose. "I don't think it's human. I've arrested homeless people that never bathe or change their clothes and it's nowhere near this smell."

"Think that's what put the dog off?" asked Konrad.

"Maybe," said Clark, "but has to be some kind of animal. It's bad."

At the edge of the matted grass, Clark noticed a faint impression in the dirt. He focused his headlamp on that area and noticed what could have been a footprint. The only thing was that if it was a footprint, it was massive.

In the direction it pointed, Clark began searching for the next track. When he found the next partial print, it was more than six feet away from the first one.

"This can't be right," Clark said, thinking out loud.

"What can't be right?" asked Konrad.

"The stride length on these tracks," said Clark. "It's huge."

"Maybe they were running," said Konrad. "Or maybe you just couldn't find the tracks between the two you did find."

Clark used his fingers to outline the edges of the track impression, then looked up at Konrad.

"Look at the size of this goddamned footprint," said Clark. "It's on two feet, so that says it's a man. But it's bigger than any print I've ever seen."

"It's not really a print," said Konrad. "Maybe he's dragging his feet or trying to conceal them. I saw a guy once who put gunny sacks over his feet to disguise the tracks. Filled them with all kinds of crap to throw off tracking dogs."

Clark didn't say anything. He just followed the direction of travel and right at the expected length, he found another impression. He didn't say anything to Konrad, but whoever made these tracks had to be very tall. He wasn't buying the gunny sack excuse.

"I'm five feet eight inches," thought Clark, "and I can't come close to duplicating that stride."

Once he established a direction of travel, he just watched for the tracks and started moving quickly in that direction. After about twenty minutes, the tracks changed direction. They appeared to be following the shoreline of the lake, heading towards deeper woods. Clark was starting to notice traces of the scent on the air.

Over their radios, they heard the voice of Corporal Sanchez issuing an Amber Alert and giving a description of the little girl and what she was last seen wearing. Clark knew that in minutes, their cell phones were going to start chiming with the Amber Alert.

"Shut your phone off," whispered Clark. "When that alert goes out, your phone is going to start shrieking. I don't want them to hear us coming."

"Got it," whispered Konrad.

Clark shut down his phone and calmly went back to tracking. Konrad kept pace but watched their surroundings. They were moving deeper into the woods and well away from residential areas. Soon they'd be getting close to a marina, then nothing but undeveloped forest beyond that. Neither of them would admit it but the farther they got into the woods, the more the feeling of dread began to come over them.

"Hang on a sec," whispered Konrad.

Clark stopped and glanced at Konrad, crouching down and bringing his rifle into high ready.

"Do you hear that?" asked Konrad in a hushed tone.

"Hear what?" Clark said softly, glancing around.

"Exactly," whispered Konrad. "There isn't a single sound. No bugs, no animals. Nothing. It's goddamned eerie."

Clark glanced around nervously. Konrad was right. It was deathly quiet. Tightening his grip on his AR, Clark looked around slowly, letting the light from his headlamp cut through the darkness. He couldn't see anything out of place, but the feeling of dread continued to grow. He could feel his stomach beginning to feel sour.

About fifty yards away, he saw green eyeshine from an animal. It took Clark a moment to realize that the eyes had to be well over ten feet off the ground. Whatever it was, it was outside the limit of the headlamp but picking up enough to reflect from the eyes. It blinked slowly and continued to stare at them without moving.

"Probably an owl," he thought.

He didn't point it out to Konrad. No sense getting him worked up over nothing. While he was watching, the eyes blinked twice more, then disappeared. He thought for a moment, he heard footsteps in the distance, but then they were gone.

The tracks were heading roughly in the direction of the eyeshine. They walked in silence until they found a massive oak tree that Clark was certain had been the one the eyes had been at. There were no branches low enough that it could have been a perched owl. When they rounded the tree, they both froze in their tracks.

"Holy shit!" said Konrad in a whisper. "Please tell me that isn't what I think it is."

"Fuck," hissed Clark.

There on the ground was a purple child's bathing suit. It had been ripped to pieces. The bathing suit and the ground around it were covered in fresh blood. The only thing remaining was a child's skull that had been broken apart so the contents could be eaten. There were teeth marks on the surface of the skull. No other bones could be found.

"I think we can safely cancel the Amber Alert," whispered Konrad.

"What the fuck did this?" asked Clark quietly, with tears in his eyes. "This wasn't done by a human."

"I have no idea," whispered Konrad. "Something is definitely not right."

"I'll stay here and guard the scene," said Clark, keeping his voice barely audible. "You go back and get a detective and the crime scene team out here. I don't want to touch any of this until they can process it properly."

"Why not just radio it in?" whispered Konrad.

"Let's keep this off the radio," replied Clark, shaking his head. "Too many ears."

"I'll be back as quick as I can," said Konrad softly, turning and heading off into the woods at a trot.

They didn't call it on the radio, because they didn't want to announce it. Everyone in the area seemed to have a police scanner these days. They would cancel the Amber Alert later with a statement that the body had been found. Only there wasn't a body. Only enough blood to safely say she was dead and most of a child's skull.

Konrad had no sooner disappeared into the dark woods when Clark heard heavy footsteps coming towards him. Pulling the charging handle to chamber a round, Clark brought the rifle up to his shoulder. Then he aimed in the direction of the footsteps as he thumbed the safety off. His headlamp illuminated an area in a wide arc out to about forty yards.

"Sloan County Sheriff's Office!" he shouted. "Step out with your hands up."

Instantly, the footsteps stopped. The woods were dead silent. This was summer in the Ozarks. There should be a lot of night sounds. Bugs, frogs, coyotes, and owls just to name a few. There was absolutely nothing. Dead silence. Clark began to get a feeling that he was being stalked.

Then he heard a sound that gave him chill down his spine. It was the sound of a very large animal taking a deep breath and releasing it slowly. Something with tremendous lung capacity. Then all was quiet again.

"Step out where I can see you!" Clark instructed. "Keep your hands where I can see them or I will shoot."

He began advancing towards the spot where he believed the breathing had come from. It was a large walnut tree with poison ivy growing around the base of it. The rotten smell was hanging in the air, thick and oily in nasal passages.

Stepping wide to avoid the poison ivy, Clark watched as his light lit up the area behind the tree. There was nothing there. Clark released the breath he hadn't realized he was holding and began sweeping the area with the rifle at the ready.

Then he heard a stick break from back near the crime scene. Turning back, he moved quickly back to the spot. There was nothing there, either. However, that wasn't what bothered him. Although nothing else seemed out of place, one thing was missing. The skull was gone.

"Goddamn it!" hissed Clark, spinning around and scanning the area.

Something had drawn him away from the scene only to sneak past him and take the skull. The terrifying part was that he never saw a thing. If it could do that, then it could have taken him out, as well. Probably could have killed him before he knew it was there.

On the side of the rifle was mounted a Surefire M600 Scout tactical light. While the headlamp was better for an area search, the tac light was better for distance. Activating the light, he began sweeping the area.

There was a flash of movement about fifty yards away. Something big and covered in black fur or hair ducked behind a tree. Gauging the size by the trees around it, Clark estimated it to be well over ten feet tall. He got a decent look at the arm and shoulder, but the face was already obscured because it held up a massive five-fingered hand to keep the light out of its eyes.

"There you are you son of a bitch," he said and kept the rifle trained on that area while he advanced rapidly.

Then he started to hear the large footsteps again, moving rapidly away from him, towards the lake. Moving as fast as he could safely go without tripping on the undergrowth and downed limbs, Clark pursued the source of the footsteps. No matter how fast he went, they seemed to maintain the same distance away. He couldn't close the distance. He could have followed it in the dark, just from the smell.

Just as he was beginning to see the water through the trees, he heard a huge splash. Emerging from the undergrowth, he stopped to find he was on top of a bluff that was about thirty feet above the surface of the lake. He could still see the water rippling from whatever had hit it, but there was nothing there. He scanned all around the water but saw nothing. Whatever it had been, it was gone now, vanished into the dark waters of Table Rock Lake.

Checking the ground at his feet, Clark froze when he saw one perfectly clear track in the soft ground near the edge of the bluff. It looked like a bare human footprint, only it was much larger. There were small indentations in the dirt just beyond the toes that he knew had to be claws of some sort.

"What the fuck?" he said, softly.

Kneeling to inspect the track, he took out three of his MagPul P-Mag magazines for his rifle. He knew from experience that each magazine was seven and a half inches long. The track was just over two and a half of the magazines long. Taking out his cell phone, he took several pictures with the magazines in them for size reference.

Doing some quick addition, Clark blew out his breath in one long, slow exhale as he shook his head in disbelief. No one was going to believe him if he told them what he saw. Even the pictures wouldn't be enough to prove it. Changing the settings on the camera on his phone, he set it to its highest resolution and took several more pictures before picking up the magazines and putting them back in the pouch.

Looking around, he could hear the sounds of the night beginning to return. Tree frogs began their song and the insects joined in the symphony of a Missouri forest. Whatever that thing was, it was gone and the animals in the area knew it. The scent was already fading away on the gentle August breeze.

Looking back down at the track, Clark stared in disbelief. Placing his size nine boot next to the track, he put his entire body weight on one foot. Pulling it away from the soft ground, he noted that his track hadn't come anywhere near the depth of the track of the creature.

Based on his knowledge of tracking and what he had seen, Clark knew the creature was over ten feet tall and had to weigh close to eight hundred pounds. Possibly more.

"That track is damned near nineteen inches long," he said, under his breath. "What the fuck is going on here?"

D.A. ROBERTS

Chapter Three
Winding Down

The oldest and strongest emotion of mankind is fear,
and the oldest and strongest kind of fear is fear of the unknown.
H. P. Lovecraft

It was well after midnight by the time Clark and Konrad cleared the scene. Their shifts were supposed to have ended at 22:00 hours, but that wasn't all that uncommon. Especially in law enforcement. You didn't just punch out at the designated end of your shift and toss the keys to the next guy. You worked your call until it was done, period.

By the time Clark made it back to the trailer park, he saw Sanchez putting the mother of the missing child in the back of her car, in handcuffs. The sheriff, himself was putting the father or boyfriend or whatever the hell he was, in his car. Tyger was also in cuffs. Motioning Clark over to him, the Sheriff leaned against the side of his car.

"Are you alright, Danny?" he asked, seeming genuinely concerned.

He hated being called Danny. Most people called him Clark, or rarely Daniel but never Danny. He could tell instantly how he knew someone by what they called him. The people he had grown up with called him Daniel. The people he'd known in the Army and again as a cop all called him Clark.

Sheriff Jacob "JJ" Prescott wasn't exactly one of Clark's favorite people, and he was pretty sure the feeling was mutual. Clark didn't have much respect for him because the only time he ever came to a crime scene was to take the credit in front of the cameras.

"I'm ok, sir," replied Clark.

"I've seen the pictures of the scene," said Prescott. "That was a bad one."

"Yes, sir," agreed Clark.

"Well, I'll be taking this one to the jail personally," said Prescott. "I've called a press conference. That search warrant yielded a working meth lab. This is a good bust."

"What about the other children?" asked Clark.

"Child Services took them a couple of hours ago," said Prescott. "Looks like their junky parents will be going away for a long time. No chance that either of them will get custody back before they turn eighteen."

"Well, at least that's good news," said Clark.

"This news story will be the talk of southern Missouri," said Prescott. "It couldn't have come at a better time."

"What?" asked Clark, his temper threatening to override his mouth. "What did you just say?"

Ignoring the tone, Prescott continued, "This is an election year, Danny. Voters will remember this one."

Clark bit his lip to keep from losing his job. Whatever minimal amount of respect he had for Prescott just vanished like smoke in the wind. He held his tongue in check, but only just.

"Nice work, Danny," said Prescott, patting Clark on the shoulder. "And make sure you file your report before you go home."

"Yes, *sir*," said Clark.

He might have said "sir" but that wasn't what he meant.

"Oh yeah," added Prescott as he got into his car, "make sure you watch the news. I'll be sure to mention all your hard work."

Clark just stood there and said nothing as Prescott backed out of the driveway and drove off. Sanchez stopped her car next to Clark and rolled down her window.

"You ok?" she asked.

"Yeah," he said, forcing himself to relax. "Just tired, I guess."

"I've got to go book this one," she said, jerking her thumb towards the back seat. "Want to meet up at IHOP in Branson after?

"Sure," he said. "I've got to write a report. I should be there in about an hour."

"I should be done by then," she replied. "See you there."

With that, she drove off heading for the Sloan County Jail in Galena. Clark watched her drive away until he could no longer see the headlights. When he turned to head for his vehicle, Konrad was waiting for him. He was leaning up against Clark's SUV holding two bottles of red Gatorade.

Tossing one to Clark as he walked up, Konrad smiled and said, "I'm proud of you, asshole."

"Proud of me?" said Clark. "For what?"

"I thought for certain you would feed Prescott his teeth," said Konrad.

"It was a near thing," Clark replied as he twisted the cap off the bottle. "I just kept telling myself I need this job."

Taking a long pull, Clark smiled and sighed.

"Thanks," he said. "I needed that."

"No," replied Konrad. "It should have been whiskey, but we're still on duty. This was one shitshow of a day. Glad you dragged me along."

"Thanks, by the way," said Clark.

"For what?" asked Konrad.

"For not mentioning the missing skull," said Clark.

"No problem," he said. "You think that whatever killed her circled back and took it?"

"Yeah, I do," said Clark, taking another pull from the Gatorade. "That's the only thing I can think of. I didn't see any other animals in the area. They were all just gone."

"I've never heard of anything that would do that," said Konrad.

"Me neither," said Clark. "Something really fucking weird is going on."

"That's a fact," replied Konrad, shaking his head. "This whole thing is fucking bizarre."

"I've got to go write my report," said Clark.

"Are you going back to the office to do it?" asked Konrad.

"No," said Clark. "I think I'll just find a quiet place to park and bang it out on the MDT."

"Alright, my brother," said Konrad, heading for his vehicle. "I'll see you later tonight."

"See you then," answered Clark, getting into his vehicle.

The HAZMAT[6] team was still processing the meth lab in the trailer as Clark backed out and headed back across the Kimberling City Bridge. The images kept flashing through his mind of the footprint and the hairy shape that ducked behind a tree at the edge of his light.

"I'm losing my goddamned mind," he muttered to himself.

Glancing over at the passenger seat, he remembered the lunch he never got to eat. He felt good that the kids got it. It was obvious that they hadn't been eating well. That thought would hold him, for now. At least the car smelled like hamburgers and fries. Now his stomach was rumbling.

Taking out his cell phone, he sent a text to Meadows.

"Hey, are you still on duty?" read the text.

"Yeah," was the reply. "I'm at the office."

"Be there in five," he sent back.

[6] HAZMAT – Hazardous Material

"Coffee?" asked Meadows.

"Maybe," Clark replied. "How old is it?"

"Made sometime this month," replied Meadows. "I think."

"Keep it hot, I'm on my way."

By the time Clark pulled into the parking lot of the Kimberling City Police Department, he felt like he could eat a dead rhinoceros. His stomach was rumbling.

Disconnecting his MDT, he got out of the vehicle and headed for the back door of the police station. Tapping out a quick shave and a haircut knock, he chuckled as Meadows opened it almost instantly.

"Come on in, dude," said Meadows. "Get inside before the goddamned mosquitos kill us both."

Clark slipped in and headed towards the desk with a dog-bed next to it. Rocco was sound asleep, snoring softly.

"Did you ever figure out what spooked him?" asked Clark, taking a seat at the desk next to Meadows.

"No," said Meadows. "That's the crazy part. Once we cleared the area and he calmed down, he went right back to acting like himself. I have no idea what could've scared him like that."

Clark did. The image of the large hairy thing ran through his mind. Although he refused to say the word even in his mind, he had a bad feeling he knew what that thing was.

"God knows," said Clark.

"So, what brings you to Casa del KCPD?" asked Meadows, chuckling.

"I came to steal your Wi-Fi," said Clark, pointing at the MDT.

"Ahh," said Meadows. "Got to do some reports."

"Yep," said Clark, opening the MDT and logging in.

"You know," said Meadows, jokingly. "I gotta start charging you for the Wi-Fi."

"Send the bill to Prescott," said Clark, chuckling.

After it booted up, he opened the reporting software and logged in his credentials. Once in, he started filling in information from the notes he took in his notepad.

Meadows set a styro cup of steaming coffee next to Clark then sat down at his computer. Then he held out a box with several donuts still in it.

"*Badge-table?*" he asked with a wry smile.

"Ahh, cop veggies," said Clark, taking one and immediately taking a bite.

"Goddamned paperwork is the worst part of this job," said Meadows.

"Just be glad we weren't cops back when they had to do everything on paper and with a typewriter," said Clark, still chewing the first bite. "Like my dad used to do."

"Fuck that," said Meadows, leaning out from behind his monitor. "This shit sucks bad enough."

Sipping his coffee, Clark began the narrative portion of his report. It took him about half an hour and two donuts to write the entire thing out. Once he finished, he reviewed it for grammar and punctuation. While it looked fine, he hesitated on the part where he mentioned the black shape that ducked behind the trees. After a moment's reflection, he highlighted that section and deleted it.

"Better leave that part out," he thought. "Otherwise I'll be going for a psych eval by Monday."

Once he was satisfied, he saved the report and forwarded it along with the case notes to the lead detective and the sheriff. Exiting the program, he shut down the MDT and downed the rest of his coffee.

"All done," he said.

"Good for you," said Meadows. "I've got four more to write. Want to take a couple of them?"

"I'll pass," replied Clark with a laugh, "but thanks for the offer. My shift ended well over an hour ago."

"You heading out?" asked Meadows.

"Yeah," said Clark. "Gonna meet someone for a late breakfast."

"Sounds fun," said Meadows. "Enjoy. Lucky bastard."

"Catch you later," said Clark as he headed out the door.

Just as he was getting in the vehicle, he got a text from Sanchez. "I just left Galena. Give me about half an hour and I'll be there."

"See you there," texted Clark.

Forty-five minutes later, they were eating their food. Sanchez sat right across from him so they could each watch a different entrance while watching each other's backs.

"How bad was it inside the trailer?" asked Clark.

"Oh my God," she said. "We found the meth lab set up in the same room where the kids all slept. It was hidden in their closet. There was a shitload of finished product bagged and ready to distribute. Close to twenty pounds. Close to forty pounds of marijuana, as well. We're pretty sure they have a grow somewhere near that trailer. There was enough heroin to make a felony case, too."

"You're one-stop drug shop," said Clark. "They were dealing almost everything. I'm glad we got the kids out of that environment. I feel sorry for them."

"Well, they'll be adults before those two get out of jail," said Sanchez. "With that much product, someone isn't going to be very happy that it's all been taken into evidence."

"Good," said Clark.

He sat there for a long moment in silence. She saw the look on his face but gave him some time to process what he was thinking.

41

"Wanna talk about it?" she asked after a few minutes.

"Only if you promise not to laugh," said Clark.

"You can tell me anything," she said. "No judgments."

Clark sighed and considered his words before he spoke. Hesitantly at first, but soon the words just poured out. He told her the entire story. Even the parts he left out of the report. He watched her face when he mentioned the large dark figure behind the tree. He was fully expecting her to laugh or make fun of him.

"No wonder you're so quiet tonight," she said. "It's ok."

"You believe me?" he asked, incredulously.

"Clark," she said, "you are a lot of things, but a liar isn't one of them. Of course, I believe you. What do you think it was?"

"I have no idea," he said. "It just completely freaks me out."

"I can see why," she said. "What else is bothering you?"

"Isn't that enough?" he asked, trying to smile.

She just looked at him and raised one delicate eyebrow.

With a sigh, he shook his head and told her about the entire conversation with Sheriff Prescott.

"I take it you haven't seen the press conference?" she said.

"No," replied Clark. "I refused to watch that asshat on TV. Should I have?"

"You wouldn't have liked it," she replied. "He said it was a team effort but still managed to take all the credit. He didn't even show up until I called for the HAZMAT team."

"Why am I not surprised," said Clark.

"I know you hate him," she added. "Why don't you work for another agency?"

"I've got my application in with Highway Patrol," he said. "If they accept me, I'll be going to the Academy in January."

"That's good," she said. "I think you would do well."

"Yeah, but I like being a deputy," he said. "HyPo[7] does all the accidents and traffic shit. I hate that part."

"But the money is good," she said, smiling.

"Yeah," he said. "But the money isn't everything. Plus, there's the fact that they can move me anywhere in the state. I don't want to move."

As the waitress came back to the table with the check, Clark handed her his credit card.

"Both on my ticket," he said.

"Yes sir," said the waitress.

"I better head home and try to get some sleep," said Clark, tossing a ten on the table for the tip. "We're back on duty at 14:00 hours. I seriously doubt I'm going to be able to sleep, though."

"Maybe I can help with that," said Sanchez, smiling demurely.

Clark was a bit surprised by the comment.

"Really?" he said, with a smile.

"Really," she replied. "I mean, if you can't sleep anyway, you might as well enjoy yourself."

---

[7] HyPo – slang for Highway Patrol

D.A. ROBERTS

Chapter Four
Joe Bald

"Courage is resistance to fear,
mastery of fear, not absence of fear."
Mark Twain

Clark awoke to his alarm going off at noon. Amanda was lying naked, sprawled across him with her head on his chest. Looking down at her raven black hair and perfect skin, he didn't want to wake her up. Unfortunately, they both had a shift today.

Brushing her hair gently away from her face, he just watched her for a few minutes, not wanting to move. The bedsheet was all that covered them and it was mostly kicked off, leaving nothing hidden.

"Well, are you going to say something," she said without opening her eyes, "or just stare at my body, you pervert?"

"Guilty," he said, not looking away. "Can you blame me? You're hot."

"Thanks for noticing," she said, slowly opening her dark brown eyes and smiling.

"Oh, my pleasure," he said, returning the smile.

"Pervert," she said, giggling.

"Want to get some breakfast before we get ready for work?" he asked.

"Hmmm..." she mused. "If we skip breakfast, we've got some time to kill before we get in the shower."

"I like how you think," he replied, reaching for her.

She grabbed his wrists in mock resistance, laughing as she pushed him back. Clark rolled with her push and pulled her up on top of him.

"Just where I wanted to be," she said, kissing him.

Later, they were sharing the big mirror in the bathroom. She was wrapped in a big, fluffy, white towel while Clark stood next to her in his boxers. After wiping the mirror, Clark started lathering up the shaving cream. Once he had a good amount on his face, he reached for his razor.

"Hang on a second there, cowboy," she said, snatching the razor before he could grab it.

"What are you doing?" he asked, grinning.

"Just wait," she said, walking out of the room.

She returned with one of the wooden kitchen chairs and sat it in the middle of the bathroom.

"Have a seat," she said.

"Why?" he asked, wrinkling his brow.

"Just do it," she said.

With a shrug, he did as instructed. Once seated, she took off her towel and straddled him while facing him.

"What the hell are you doing?" he asked, looking right at her breasts.

"I've always wanted to do this," she said.

"Do what?" he asked, not sure what was about to happen.

Reaching over, she turned on the hot water in the sink and rinsed the razor.

"I'm going to give you a shave," she said, in mock seriousness.

Clark thought about it for a moment and decided that he wasn't going to argue considering what was right in front of him.

"Ok," he said, "just don't cut me."

Afterward, he was surprised at how good of a job she had done.

"I've always wanted to do that," she said, smiling.

"Well," he said, "gotta say, I'm a big fan. Best shave of my life."

Returning the razor to the shelf next to the sink, she took a damp towel and cleaned off his face.

"There," she said, admiring her handiwork.

Clark grabbed her by both hips and pulled her closer to him.

"I thought you didn't want this," he said. "I thought you didn't want to be a couple anymore."

"I've been thinking about it a lot lately," she said. "I wasn't sure what I wanted. The only thing I knew for certain is that I'm happy when I'm with you. I want this. I want this all the time. Then I saw you with those kids last night and remembered I love that part of you. You're a good man."

"Fine by me," he answered. "I want you here with me."

"It's settled then," she said. "I want us to be together."

"Do you want to move in," he said before he even thought about it.

It was too late. It came out of his mouth so fast he didn't consider it. He didn't want to make her think he was rushing her. Before she could answer, Clark's cellphone rang.

"Hold that thought," he said. "It's dispatch. I have to answer it."

She only nodded but didn't move. Clark was glad she didn't.

"This is Clark," he said, putting the phone to his ear.

"Clark," said a voice, "this is Tiffany with dispatch. Would you mind going in-service right now?"

"Why?" he asked, his tone shifting to all business. "What's going on?"

Sanchez recognized the look on his face and tried to hear the conversation from the phone.

"Jacobson won't answer his radio," said Tiffany. "I can't reach him by phone either."

"Who else is on duty?" asked Clark.

"Bradford and Massey," she said, "but they're at the other end of the county working a nasty domestic. Your house is only a couple of miles away from Jacobson's last known location."

"Send all the info to my MDT," said Clark. "And log me active. I'll head that way as soon as I can get dressed. I just got out of the shower."

"Thank you," said Tiffany. "I'm starting to get worried."

"Where was his last known location?" he asked.

"He was checking something down in the old abandoned Joe Bald Campground," she said, concern in her tone.

"I'll head over there and find him for you," said Clark. "Relax and calm down. You can't get cell reception down there. He's probably just parked and doing his reports. I think all of us have done that from time to time. It's quiet down there."

"I hope you're right," Tiffany said. "Please hurry."

"I will," said Clark, and hung up the phone.

"Well," said Sanchez, "it's a good thing I keep a clean uniform in my bag. I'm going with you."

"Let's get going," he said as she stood up. "We can continue this conversation later."

"No problem," she said, smiling.

They both quickly got into armor and uniform, then adjusted their duty belts. Once it was all in place, they headed for the front door.

Clark's house was an old log cabin that his grandfather had built. When his grandfather died, he left it to Clark. It wasn't very big, but it was comfortably away from people. It sat off the road bout fifty yards. When the leaves were down in the fall, you could see the lake from the back porch.

Clark's Chevy Tahoe SUV and Sanchez' Dodge Charger were both parked nearby in the driveway. Next to the small workshop, Clark's old Jeep sat waiting for him to drive it on his days off.

After a quick kiss, Sanchez headed for her car while Clark got in and started his. He immediately keyed up the radio.

"125," he said.

"Go ahead, 125," said dispatch.

It was Tiffany's voice.

"Show me active and responding to the Joe Bald Recreation Area."

"Copy 125," replied Tiffany. "Thank you."

"155," said Sanchez over the radio,

"Go ahead 155," said Tiffany.

"Show me active and responding with 125."

"Copy," said Tiffany.

Clark backed into the yard and turned around, heading down the driveway. He saw Sanchez do the same and follow behind him. Since he didn't have a reason to respond running code, he just accelerated onto the state highway and kept his speed less than ten over the posted speed limit. Sanchez stayed right on his bumper.

"I'm a dumbass," he muttered to himself. "Why did I ask her that? What if that scares her off?"

Up ahead, he saw the turnoff leading to the old abandoned campground. The Army Corps of Engineers had shut down the old Joe Bald Recreation Area back in the early 2000s without any explanation. Each time someone tried to get it reopened, the Army Corps shut them down. No one knew why. Although Clark was still a kid when it closed, he remembered that it was a great place to camp and fish.

All of the buildings and electrical hookups had been removed when they closed it down, but they never gated it off. It was still open for lake access for fishermen, but camping was strictly forbidden. Now that it was all overgrown and wild, no one would want to camp there. It was still a shame, though. It was a beautiful park, once upon a time.

Turning into the access road, Clark grabbed his mic, "125 and 155 arriving on scene. Will advise when contact is established."

"Copy 125," said dispatch.

Clark detected a note of relief in her voice. Pulling to the right of the road, he rolled down his window and motioned for Sanchez to pull up next to him. She drove up and rolled down her passenger window.

"What's the plan?" she asked.

"This place is just one big circle through the woods," he said. "The roads lead to the same place. I'll take the right side and you take the left. If you see him, radio me and I'll meet up with you. I'll do the same."

"Do you think he's ok?" she asked, sounding worried.

"I bet he's asleep," said Clark. "Jacobson's a lazy bastard and probably turned off his radio so he wouldn't have to respond to anything."

"Let's hope so," said Sanchez, pulling away and turning down the left side road.

Clark headed to the right and drove slowly so he could look back into the camping spots. If he was planning on sleeping, he wouldn't park where he could be found easily.

The sun was bright and the temperature was already in the upper nineties. Visibility was good, despite the overgrowth. Clark could see the occasional concrete picnic table still sitting there waiting for campers that would never return. Even in broad daylight, the place just felt eerie.

"155, status check," Clark said.

"Nothing yet," she replied.

"Copy," said Clark.

Creeping slowly down the road, Clark saw no signs of anyone or anything. No birds, no deer, no possums or armadillos. It was odd to not see some type of wildlife wandering around in a heavily wooded area like this.

Rounding a corner in the road, Clark saw a flash of dark grey paint. As he got closer, he saw the Sloan County logo on the side of a Dodge Charger.

"There you are," he said, reaching for the mic. "125 to 155."

"Go ahead," said Sanchez.

"I've located the vehicle," he replied.

"I'm in route," she replied.

Clark pulled off the cracked pavement and into the gravel of the old parking lot near the boat ramp. He didn't see anyone in the car. Coming to a stop, he put his SUV in park and climbed out. Immediately the heat hit him in the face like a wet slap. Sweat immediately beaded upon his face and arms.

"Goddamn you, Jacobson," he muttered to himself. "We have to report this, now. You probably just got yourself fired."

Behind him, he heard the crunch of tires on the gravel. Sanchez pulled up right behind him and exited her vehicle. Clark waited for her to catch up before he proceeded.

"Something isn't right," she said as she walked up. "This feels bad."

"I think so, too," he said. "Dumbass is probably gonna get fired for this."

"That's not what I meant," said Sanchez, looking at him with a serious expression. "I mean something feels wrong. Something bad happened here."

"He's probably asleep in the back seat," said Clark, but put his hand on his pistol.

Sanchez did the same, going so far as to unlatch the hood that covered the pistol so she could draw quickly. Clark could see the seriousness of her expression and realized she sensed something he hadn't.

Drawing his pistol, he nodded at her and pointed toward the passenger side of Jacobson's car. The pistol was a Para-Ordnance P14-45 .45 ACP double stack in black nitride with Trijicon Night Sights and a TLR-1HL tactical light.

She drew her pistol and headed that way, cautiously. Clark headed for the driver's side, advancing slowly. Sanchez carried a department-issued Glock 19 with the TLR-1HL tac light.

As he rounded the back bumper, he saw that the driver's door was open and the engine was still running. Lying on the ground ten feet from the door was a department issue Glock 19. He also caught a hint of a familiar rotten odor.

"Goddamn it," he whispered and started glancing around nervously.

He didn't see anything moving in the trees or any sign of Jacobson.

"I've got a gun over here," he called.

"I've got blood over here," she replied.

"Well fuck," he said. "How much blood?"

"A lot," she replied. "There are drag marks over here in the gravel."

"Son of a bitch," said Clark.

Picking up the pistol, he dropped the magazine and checked the rounds. It was still full. Jacobson had drawn his weapon but didn't fire it.

"The gun's fully loaded," he said, replacing the magazine. "He didn't fire at whatever got him."

52

"I think this blood belonged to Jacobson," she said.

"That's what I was afraid of," he replied.

Clark headed around the car as quickly as he dared on the loose gravel. He could see Sanchez standing next to a large pool of blood that had already congealed. There were bloody castoffs down the side of the car, indicating that the blood had been slung from a knife or similar weapon.

"What makes you think it's Jacobson's blood?" Clark asked as he approached her.

"Because of this," she said and pointed at a Sloan County Deputy's badge with dried blood on it.

"Shit," said Clark. "I think we can confirm that theory."

"155," said Sanchez into her radio mic.

"Go ahead 155," said dispatch.

"Contact available supervisors and notify the sheriff," she said. "We've got a crime scene. We have an officer down."

"Officer Down, copy," said dispatch. "Do you need EMS[8]?"

"Negative," replied Sanchez. "Have them stage nearby."

"Copy that," said dispatch.

They both heard Tiffany's voice break with emotion. She knew that having the EMS stage nearby was code for saying they weren't likely to be needed and Jacobson was already dead.

Clark kept his weapon out and began following the drag marks in the gravel. You could see the occasional smear of blood, but not many. Most of the blood had been emptied near the car. The drag marks led directly towards the lake.

Clark followed right up to the edge of the water. The ground was very rocky, so there was no sign of any tracks but he was fairly certain he already knew what had done this.

---

[8] EMS – Emergency Medical Services - Ambulance

When he reached the edge of the water where soft sand and silt had built up over the rocks, he found what he had dreaded to find. One complete and one partial nearly nineteen-inch human-looking footprints. The indentations at the ends of the toes were more clearly defined in the sand. It was some type of claws.

Taking out his phone, he photographed the prints with one of his Glock Magazines in the image for size reference. There would be no keeping this out of the report, this time. Now an officer had been taken and all eyes would now be on finding the killer.

Even Clark was reluctant to believe it, despite what he had seen in the woods last night. No one was going to believe it, but two deaths in two days could not be ignored. However, no one was going to believe it was Bigfoot.

Chapter Five
Securing the Scene

"How often have I said to you that when you have eliminated the impossible, whatever remains, however improbable, must be the truth?"
Sherlock Holmes

"Don't touch anything until the detectives get here," said Sanchez. "Let's get some tape around the area."

"I already touched the pistol that was on the ground," replied Clark. "Did you touch the badge?"

"No," she said. "Let's not touch anything else."

"Gotcha," said Clark. "I'll go get a roll of tape out of the truck."

Once at the back of the truck, Clark sprayed his legs and boots with Deet and slipped into his external plate carrier, velcroing it into place and adjusting it for fit. Next, he grabbed the extra magazines for the AR, then slipped the strap of the AR over his head.

Quickly adjusting the single point sling, he left the rifle hanging in the middle of his chest. The camelback still had water in it, so he threw that on, as well. Grabbing two rolls of crime scene tape, he went to the driver's door and opened it.

Shutting the engine down, he grabbed a pair of Oakley sunglasses and slipped them on. Then, he grabbed a ball cap that had the word SHERIFF emblazoned in gold across the front and Clark embroidered across the back. Slipping that on, he shut and locked the vehicle. When he headed back to Sanchez, she saw what he'd done and nodded.

"I probably better do that too," she said. "Do you have an extra hat? I don't have one. I never wear them."

"Yeah," he said, tossing her his key fob. "There's another pair of Oakley's and another cap in the duffle bag in the back. Help yourself."

"Thanks," she said, heading for the SUV.

"Hey," he called after her, "you might want to shut your engine off. We're going to be here a while and you don't want to overheat."

"Gotcha," she said as she walked away.

Clark started putting out the yellow crime scene tape, making sure to keep the blood inside the taped off area. It took almost a full roll, but he covered the entire area. Just as he was finishing, Sanchez returned wearing her plate carrier and carrying her patrol rifle. The Oakley's and ball cap fit her well. He had to smile at the name Clark emblazoned across the back of her cap.

Staging so they could watch both directions on the only road leading to this area, they waited for the crime scene people to arrive. Falling back on military training, Clark began pacing the area with his weapon at low ready. Sanchez watched him without saying anything.

A few minutes later, they heard the sound of approaching vehicles running code. The officer down call would bring everyone who could get there as fast as they could go.

The first vehicle was an unmarked detective's vehicle. It parked next to Clark's SUV. Detective Mike Blanchard exited the vehicle. Clark didn't know him that well. He was only recently brought in the department as a detective. He had been a Lacland County Detective and came highly recommended. All he knew about Blanchard was that he left Lacland after a bad injury.

"What have you got?" asked Blanchard as he walked up carrying an evidence collection kit.

"A shitload of blood and an empty cruiser," said Clark.

"Where's the body?" asked Blanchard.

"From what we can tell, it was dragged off towards the lake," said Clark. "I followed the drag marks but they vanish in the water."

The color drained out of Blanchard's face.

"Did you say the body had been dragged off?" said Blanchard. "All you found was a big bloody spot on the ground?"

"Yeah," said Clark. "We also found his service weapon and badge. There was dried blood on the badge."

"Let me guess," said Blanchard. "The slide locked back and empty."

"No," said Clark, "he never got off a shot."

Taking a deep breath to steady himself, Blanchard looked like he was going to pass out. The color drained out of his face and he put his hand on the side of Clark's SUV to steady himself.

"Are you alright, detective?" asked Sanchez.

"Aw, fuck, uh..." stammered Blanchard. "Yeah. I'm fucking fabulous. Did you find any strange tracks?"

"How did you know that?" asked Clark.

Ignoring the question, Blanchard said, "Let me guess. Giant wolf tracks."

"No," said Clark looking at Blanchard like he was crazy. "They were human-looking. Just fucking huge. Like nineteen inches long."

"Oh, thank God," said Blanchard, then stopped. "Wait? What? Did you fuckin' say they were nineteen goddamned inches long? Who the fuck dragged him off, Shaquille O'Neil?"

"I think he's got an alibi," said Clark. "He lives in Florida."

"No fuckin' shit, smartass," said Blanchard. "Do yourself a favor, don't go telling people about those big footprints."

"Bigfoot," said Clark. "That's kinda what I thought, too."

"I didn't say Bigfoot, dumbass," snapped Blanchard. "I said BIG FOOT. Two words, not one."

"Alright, I'll put a BOLO[9] on Shaq," said Clark.

Blanchard shook his head and muttered to himself as he walked towards the vehicle.

"Don't tell me those goddamned things are real, too," mumbled Blanchard.

---

[9] BOLO – Be On the Look Out

"What did he say?" asked Sanchez.

"I don't know," said Clark. "I think he's off his meds or something."

After walking in a wide circle around the edge of the tape, Blanchard came back and lit a cigarette.

"Looks like something came out of the trees over there," said Blanchard. "No prints, just big impressions, and a long stride. Whatever it was, it's goddamned tall. We're dealing with something out of the ordinary here, folks."

"I didn't see the trail," said Clark. "I must have missed it."

"That's why I'm a detective," said Blanchard. "I look for little shit like that."

"So, what do we say when the others get here?" asked Sanchez.

"Good question," he said. "Do yourself a favor and keep the Bigfoot talk to a minimum unless you want to get sent in for a psych eval."

Clark just nodded.

"Where did you see those big prints?" asked Blanchard.

"Down by the edge of the water," said Clark.

"Show me," said Blanchard.

Just then, two more vehicles arrived. The sheriff's car and the crime scene van. More sirens could be heard approaching.

"We'll talk more later," said Blanchard. "Do yourself and your career a favor and keep your damned mouth shut about those prints. Let me have a look at them and I'll take the sheriff with me. Let him see them and draw his own conclusions. Keep all mention of this shit out of your reports."

"Got it," said Clark.

The sheriff walked up with two other deputies.

"Alright," said Prescott, "this is my crime scene now. Fill me in."

Since she was a corporal, Clark let Sanchez brief the sheriff. He just kept his mouth shut and watched the area. He did note that she kept the briefing to just the facts, leaving out the prints and what they believed had happened.

"Did anyone think to follow these drag marks?" asked the Sheriff, condescendingly.

"No sir," said Clark. "We secured the scene and waited for backup. Great idea, though."

Sanchez gave Clark a smirk. She knew him well enough to catch the subtle sarcasm that the sheriff completely missed.

"That's why I make the big bucks, son," said Prescott. "Blanchard, you start processing the scene, I'll take the drag marks."

"Yes, sir," said Blanchard.

"You two," said Prescott to Clark and Sanchez. "We have the scene. You can put on the log that you responded and I took over the scene. Nothing more. No report is needed from either of you. You can go back to patrol. Let the pro's handle it from here."

Clark just smiled and said, "Yes, *sir*."

Once the sheriff walked away with the other deputies, Blanchard handed Clark a business card with his name on it.

"Here's my number," he said. "Call me once this scene is cleared. We need to talk."

"Sounds like a great time," said Clark, turning to walk off.

"Listen to me, deputy," said Blanchard. "Something is going on here that you have no fucking clue about. Call me and we need to talk. You too, Sanchez."

"Yes, sir," said Clark.

"Until then," cautioned Blanchard, "keep this shit to yourselves. And for fuck's sake, stay out of the woods."

59

Chapter Six
Dead in the Water

*"He had been suddenly jerked from the heart of civilization
and flung into the heart of things primordial."*
Jack London

"125 back in service," said Clark as he pulled out of the lot.

"155 back in service," said Sanchez, following right behind him.

"Copy 125 and 155," said dispatch. "We show you both back in service."

Clark headed out of the Joe Bald area and towards Kimberling City. Sanchez followed right behind him. Other vehicles were arriving and shutting off access to the area. They drove through the roadblock and back into town. Pulling into the parking lot of a convenience store, Clark stopped and parked. Sanchez pulled and parked beside him.

Clark got out and walked around the vehicle to speak with her. She rolled down her window and waited for him to approach.

"Why did he just kick us off the crime scene?" she asked.

"Death of a deputy," said Clark. "He wants to take all the credit and make it look good for the election."

"Now I think I understand why you hate him," she replied. "What are you going to do?"

"Nothing I can do," replied Clark. "He's the sheriff. I have to keep my mouth shut or lose my job."

"Both of our jobs," she said, anger in her voice. "No way I'd let you go alone."

"For now, we just do our jobs and keep our mouths shut," said Clark. "I'll call Blanchard after I hear them clear the scene and figure out what's going on."

"Blanchard knows something," she said. "He looked like he was about to faint when you told him about the scene."

61

"Do you think this is the same thing that took the little girl?" asked Sanchez.

"There's no doubt," replied Clark. "The two crime scenes aren't that far apart if you go across the lake. I know I heard that thing hit the water. It took Jacobson into the water. It's using the lake to get around and avoid being seen. Plus, I could smell the same disgusting odor at both scenes."

"So, it could be anywhere," she said, frowning.

"Anywhere on the lake," agreed Clark, "and it's a huge damned lake."

"Do you think there will be others?" she asked.

"Yeah," said Clark. "I don't think this thing is going to stop unless we stop it."

"Do you really think we can?" she asked. "I mean if it's as big as you say, how do we stop it?"

"One thing's for certain," said Clark, "I'm going to need a bigger gun."

"Now we know why the dog wouldn't track it," she added. "Some primitive part of his brain warned him this was some kind of monster."

"Exactly," said Clark.

"125," chirped the radio.

Clark rolled his eyes.

"125, go ahead," he replied.

"Request for a deputy to respond to the Aunt's Creek Campground," said dispatch. "Report of a possible drowning victim near the boat launch area."

"Have you notified the State Water Patrol?" he asked.

"Water Patrol is unavailable," replied dispatch. "They're assisting with another call near the dam. They're too far away."

"Copy, show me in route," said Clark.

"Clear," said dispatch. "Showing you responding."

"Do you need my help?" asked Sanchez.

"Not for a floater," he said. "No sense in making yourself sick. They're never pretty. I'll take care of it and maybe we can meet for lunch later."

"I'll text you," she said and headed out of the parking lot.

Clark climbed back into his vehicle and headed for Aunt's Creek. He wasn't running code.

"125," he said into the mic.

"125," said dispatch.

"Can you get EMS in route," he said, "just in case."

"Copy," said dispatch. "I'll get them in route to you."

Turning on the road for Aunt's Creek, Clark realized something. From the lake, Aunt's Creek and Joe Bald aren't very far away from each other.

"What are the odds?" he asked himself, then began accelerating down the road.

A few minutes later, he pulled into Aunt's Creek Campground. It was the complete opposite of Joe Bald. The grass was well cut, no overgrowth, and the trees were kept pruned back to keep them out of the way of campers. It was also full of people enjoying the lake.

. "125," he said into the mic.

"125, go ahead," said dispatch.

"Show me out at the location," said Clark. "Will advise when I have more information."

"Copy 125," said dispatch. "Showing you out at Aunt's Creek."

Following the signs that led down to the boat launch area, he pulled into the parking lot and exited the vehicle. A woman with khaki shorts and a green polo shirt came walking out to him.

"Thank you for coming, officer," she said. "You got here really fast."

"I was in the neighborhood," said Clark with a sardonic smile.

"If you'll follow me," she said and led him down towards the floating port.

There were other people in the area wearing the same outfit as hers. They were all park employees. One of them was pointing down at the dock.

"It's this way," said the woman, leading him down the walkway.

As Clark neared the end of the dock, he saw something floating about a hundred and fifty yards off the end.

"We've kept campground guests away from the area after we spotted it," she said. "I haven't seen any boat traffic in the area recently. I hope it's not one of our campers."

"Do you have a boat I can use?" asked Clark.

"Absolutely," she replied, pulling out a small walkie-talkie from her cargo pocket. "Ashley to Eddie, can you bring the boat to the dock?"

"On my way," replied a voice.

Clark continued to watch what certainly looked like a body bobbing in the water for any sign of movement or confirmation. After a few minutes, a pontoon boat came around the end of the cove and idled up to the dock.

"Somebody call for a boat?" asked the stoner in a park uniform.

When he saw Clark in uniform, he widened his eyes and looked nervous.

"Uh…" he stammered, "good afternoon, officer."

Without preamble, Clark stepped onto the boat.

He looked at the stoner and said, "Relax, kid. I'm not here for you."

"Uh…" he said again, "how can I help you?"

Clark just pointed at the body and said, "Take me out there."

"Yessir," the kid said, and idled the boat away from the dock.

Bringing the boat around, he angled away from the dock and headed directly towards the body.

"Is that a dead guy?"

"I don't know yet," said Clark. "We're about to find out."

"Dude," said the kid, "I'm gonna be sick!"

"That's fine," said Clark, "just get me out there first. You can puke all you want once I'm done."

A nagging suspicion was growing in the back of his mind. The closer he got, the worse it became. When they got close enough to start seeing details, Clark noted the color of the shirt was identical to the tan uniform he was wearing. A bit closer and he saw a duty belt.

"Oh, fuck," whispered Clark. "That's Jacobson."

Slowing the boat and coming to a stop right by the body, Clark leaned down and grabbed the back of the duty belt.

"Give me a hand here, kid," he said.

With a shaking hand, stoner-boy handed Clark the rope that attaches to the life preserver that they would throw to a swimmer. Then he ran back to the back of the boat.

"Goddamn it," muttered Clark as he reached down and looped the rope around the torso and under the arms.

Using the railing of the pontoon boat as a makeshift pulley, Clark strained and started pulling. It took him a few minutes working alone, but he was able to drag the body onto the boat.

Rolling him over onto his back, Clark saw that the lower abdomen had been ripped open and the internal organs were missing. The only reason the body hadn't sunk like a stone was all of the air trapped inside the chest cavity. It also looked like his neck had been broken.

Looking into the eyes that had already turned milky, Clark confirmed his suspicion. He was looking into the dead eyes of Deputy Brad Jacobson. The nameplate was still on the uniform.

"Well, fuck," said Clark. "The sheriff isn't gonna like this."

"What now," said stoner-boy, looking like he was about to throw up.

"Take us back to the dock," said Clark.

Taking a quick look at the wounds to the abdomen, Clark could see individual marks of fingers digging into the damage. Taking a series of pictures with his phone, he knew that this would be his only chance to do it. Once he was done, he stood up and reached for his radio.

"125," he said.

"125, go ahead," said dispatch.

"Notify the sheriff," he said, "I have located our missing subject. He's J4[10]."

Silence from the radio. After a long moment, he heard Tiffany's voice breaking with emotion.

"Understood," she said. "I'll notify everyone."

Once they reached the dock, stoner-boy tied off the line to keep the boat from drifting away and ran off down the dock, heading for the port-a-potties near the parking lot.

Clark opened the deck box on the boat and started rummaging around. He found a yellow slicker raincoat and took it out. Gently, he covered Jacobson's body with it to both protect it from further contamination and to prevent onlookers or the press from getting

---

[10] J4 – radio code for a dead body

photos. Once that was done, he headed back onto the dock and motioned for the employees to come over.

"Ladies and gentlemen," he said, looking at each of them in turn. "I need all of your attention. That body out there is a deputy from my department. We've been looking for him for hours. Please do not speak with anyone in the press. I'm afraid I can't allow any of you to go back out to the boat. If you would please fan out and help me keep people out of the area until EMS and more deputies arrive, I would greatly appreciate it. Thank you."

No one questioned his request. They all did as he asked and stayed clear of the dock. Once they were all positioned to prevent anyone from approaching, he reached into his pocket and fished out a can of Skoal long-cut wintergreen and put in a dip.

He listened to the radio as units chimed in, they were responding to his call. He ignored all of them except two. He smiled when he heard Konrad and Sanchez join the responders.

"And now we wait," he muttered and spit tobacco juice into the water.

Clark was sitting on the edge of the dock when the first vehicles pulled into the parking lot. First on the scene was Sanchez. She jumped out of her vehicle and started walking towards him.

"Is it really him?" she asked, dreading the answer.

"Yeah," he said, "confirmed."

"Who's going to tell his family?" she asked.

"Probably the Sheriff or the Captain," said Clark. "I wouldn't want to be the one to do it."

More vehicles were entering the parking lot. Clark recognized the sheriff's car. There were also two Kimberling City PD vehicles and one Missouri State Highway Patrolman.

As the sheriff walked up, he looked angry.

"How the hell is it that you keep turning up at these things?" asked the sheriff acidly.

"Ask dispatch, sir," said Clark. "I just go where they send me."

"Smartass," said the sheriff. "Are you certain it's Jacobson?"

"Yes sir," said Clark, "he's still in uniform."

The sheriff looked like he wanted to say something else, but caught himself when the KCPD and the Highway Patrolman walked up.

"We're here to help," said Meadows. "What do you guys need?"

Clark noted he wasn't talking to the sheriff. He was looking directly at him.

"Did you collect any evidence?" asked the sheriff.

"No dumbass," thought Clark, "what was I supposed to do, drain the fucking lake?"

Instead, he said, "No sir, he was in the water. I pulled him onto the boat and covered him so you and the detectives could have the first look."

"How did he die?" asked the sheriff.

"Well," said Clark, "I don't know what the cause of death was, but it looks like he has a broken neck and he's been completely gutted. Most of the internal organs are gone. So, dealer's choice sir. An autopsy will determine which one was fatal."

"Holy shit," said Meadows, looking at Clark. "What gutted him?"

"*WE* have no idea," interjected the sheriff before Clark could say anything.

The Highway Patrolman said nothing, but gave the sheriff a look of contempt and stepped away to make a phone call. If Prescott noticed, he didn't show it.

"Why don't you two set up at the edge of the parking lot and keep the onlookers back," Clark said to Meadows and the other KCPD officer, McNamara was his name. Although Clark had seen him before, they hadn't worked any cases together.

"That's a good idea," said Meadows. "We'll take care of it."

"Thank you for coming," said Clark. "I'll buy you both a cup of coffee later."

They both turned and walked away talking quietly among themselves. Prescott headed down the dock and onto the boat without saying another word to Clark. Sanchez looked at Clark, but he just shrugged. There was nothing they could do.

"Just watch," said Clark, nodding towards Prescott.

Prescott lifted the raincoat and stared down at the body. Seconds later, he dropped the raincoat and ran to the back of the boat and began throwing up into the water.

"You knew that would happen," said Sanchez, "didn't you?"

"I suspected," said Clark, with a small smile. "He's been administration his entire career. I don't know if he ever worked patrol. At least, that's what I hear. I didn't think he'd react well to his first official J4 call."

"You realize that he's going to freeze you out of the investigation so he can take all the credit?" said Sanchez.

"That's why I took lots of pictures," he replied, smiling serenely.

"How long has he been in the water?" she asked.

"I couldn't say," answered Clark with a shrug, "but it couldn't have been more than a couple of hours. I'd bet he was dragged into the water when that thing heard our cars approaching."

"How could it have floated this far so quickly?" she said, frowning. "There isn't any current in this area."

Clark got a dark look on his face.

"He wouldn't have," he said. "That thing must have brought the body down this way. That means it's probably not far from here."

They both began looking around, scanning the area, and watching the trees across the cove. Although they couldn't see anything, Clark had a feeling it was watching them from a safe distance. Watching and waiting for them to leave the area.

It only had time to remove the organs. That means that there was a lot of meat on the body that it never had the chance to eat. Now it wouldn't get that chance at all. It would still be hungry. That meant it was going to strike again, soon. Probably once the sun goes down.

"I have a bad feeling we will be getting another missing person tonight," said Clark.

"And this campground is full of people," she said, looking back at the tents and campers in the campground.

Chapter Seven
Easy Prey

"He was a killer, a thing that preyed, living on the things that lived, unaided, alone, by virtue of his own strength and prowess, surviving triumphantly in a hostile environment where only the strong survive."
Jack London

Between calls for service, Clark and Sanchez tried to stay as close to the Aunt's Creek area that they could. They were afraid that another person would be taken.

At 21:30 hours, the met at McDonald's in Branson West. Konrad met them there, as well. Konrad lost the rock, paper, scissors duel and went through the drive-through to get their food. They met at the back of the parking lot to eat on the hood of Clark's SUV and talk.

"I hate to say it," began Konrad, "but nothing happened tonight. I know we're not finished with the shift, but I've only had like three calls all shift. Maybe nothing's gonna happen."

Clark took a bite of his burger and furrowed his brow, thinking while he chewed. Sanchez reached over and wiped a bit of ketchup off his lip with her finger, then licked it off.

"Oh, fuck," said Konrad, grinning. "You two are together again."

"Nothing gets past you, asshole," said Clark.

"When did this happen?" asked Konrad with a grin.

"Last night," said Clark.

"Actually," Sanchez said with a grin over the top of her cup of soda, "it was twice last night, and once this morning."

"Technically," said Clark, with a smile, "that shaving thing should count as four."

"What shaving thing?" asked Konrad.

"The shaving thing doesn't count," added Sanchez, smiling wickedly.

"It would have," said Clark. "Besides, it was fucking hot."

"What shaving thing?!" demanded Konrad.

"Yeah, it was pretty hot," said Sanchez, softly. "I guess it's four then."

"TELL ME ABOUT THE SHAVING THING, GODDAMNIT!"

"Definitely four," said Clark, taking a bite out of his burger.

Konrad just stared at them with his mouth hanging open, glaring back and forth between the two of them. Sanchez just smiled sweetly and took another sip from her soda.

"When were you gonna tell me?" Konrad said, shaking his head. "And I better hear the story about the shaving thing. Details people. I need details."

"This is the first time we've had a chance to sit and talk since it happened," said Clark.

"So," said Konrad, "is it serious this time or you two gonna keep playing cat and mouse."

Neither Sanchez nor Clark said anything but exchanged a glance.

"I hate you both," said Konrad, stuffing French fries in his mouth.

"I love you too," said Clark, winking at Konrad.

Sanchez pointed at Konrad and was about to say something when the radio went off.

"125," said dispatch.

"Duty calls," said Clark, reaching for his mic. "125, go ahead."

"125," said dispatch, "we have a caller on the line who's asking for a unit to respond. Caller states there is a prowler in her backyard who was attempting to enter her house."

"Copy," said Clark. "What's the address?"

"53-87 Memory Road, Galena address," said dispatch.

"I know that area," said Konrad. "Isn't that just across the cove from Aunt's Creek?"

"Fuck," said Clark, then keyed his mic. "Copy, show 125, 155, and 136 responding."

"Copy," said dispatch, "125, 155, and 136 responding."

They all dove in their respective vehicles and headed out of the parking lot with lights and sirens activated. Clark took lead with the other two vehicles right behind him. Activating his GPS unit, he fed the address in and looked for the fastest route.

"ETA, twelve minutes," said the female voice from the GPS unit.

"I'll take that as a challenge," said Clark, accelerating.

Nine minutes later, Clark killed the lights and siren when he turned onto the road leading to the house. The other two followed suit and pulled to the side of the road as they reached their destination.

Clark was the first out of his vehicle, stepping out and going to the back of the SUV to retrieve his patrol rifle. Not wanting to waste time with the additional armor, Clark shoved four magazines into his right cargo pocket and threw the sling over his head.

Konrad was digging in his trunk doing the same thing Clark had done. Sanchez stepped out of her car with her patrol shotgun, a Remington 870 Police Magnum, and waited for them to get ready.

"I'll go around the right side," said Clark, "you two go left."

Without hesitation, they headed off to the left as Clark headed around the side of the house. Activating his tac light, he lit up the area at the side of the house and began sweeping the trees. The big backyard was not fenced and had two houses behind it. One shed and a kid's playhouse/swing set were all that was in the back yard.

Sweeping his light along the back of the house, Clark saw a white male in dark clothing with his face pressed against a window. He had his penis out and was masturbating. Clark lit him up with the light and put the sights on him.

73

"Sheriff's Office!" he bellowed. "Show me your fucking hands! Do it now!"

The man froze and turned to face him, raising his hands and leaving his still erect penis pointing directly at Clark. Either fear or excitement or both caused the man to ejaculate just at that moment.

"I'm not armed!" the man yelled. "Don't shoot!"

Konrad and Sanchez came running around the corner with their weapons at the ready, lighting the man up with their flashlights.

"What the fuck!" shouted Konrad. "For fuck's sake, put your dick away, asshole. For fuck's sake, he spooged everywhere!"

Sanchez didn't say anything, just burst out laughing. Clark had to stop himself from laughing as the man looked like he was going to cry.

"I can't," he whined. "He told me to put my hands up!"

"Wipe it off and put it away," said Clark, "then put your hands back up."

Sanchez was doubled over with one hand on her knee, laughing out loud. Konrad started giggling and shaking his head. Clark lowered his weapon as the man shook his now flaccid penis and stuffed it back into his pants. Before Clark could bring the light back on him, the man turned and sprinted across the backyard towards the other houses.

"Goddamn it," hissed Clark, sprinting after him. "He's running!"

It took Konrad and Sanchez only seconds to leap into the pursuit as well. To give him credit, the man could run. Although he wasn't wearing thirty pounds of duty gear. Clark was steadily gaining on the man as he ran between the two houses, heading towards the trees at the edge of the lake.

"Stop," yelled Clark. "You're gonna get tased!"

The man never broke stride. He ran headlong into the trees and kept running through the underbrush. Clark slowed down and brought up his flashlight. Konrad and Sanchez did the same as they fanned out.

Up ahead, they all could see the man running between trees when suddenly a massive black, hairy arm shot out and grabbed the man by the head. The humongous hand wrapped completely around his head with a sickening crunch. The man never had a chance to scream.

With a quick motion, the arm and the man disappeared behind the tree and into the darkness. Clark lit up the area with his flashlight, but all he could hear was branches breaking as whatever it was moved off through the trees at an incredible speed. It sounded like a truck smashing through the underbrush without the engine noises.

"What the fuck was that?!" screamed Konrad, coming to a stop and gulping for air. "What the fuck was that!"

Sanchez looked terrified and just started in the direction of the rapidly fading sound of a massive animal tearing through the underbrush. Clark came to a stop beside her and watched the darkness as the sound faded and was gone.

"What the fuck just happened?" asked Konrad, breathing heavily. "What the fuck!"

"Do we put *that* in the report?" Sanchez asked, turning to face Clark.

Clark just continued to stare off into the darkness. He moved up slowly until he was standing directly next to the tree where the arm had emerged. There was a large crushed down area in the grass and leaves, but no noticeable prints. The air was thick with the rotten meat and urine smell. Turning slowly around, he returned to the others and stood there for a moment before speaking.

"I think it's time to call Blanchard and find out what he knows," said Clark softly.

After checking with the RP[11], they learned that the man was looking into the bedroom of a four-year-old girl. They assured the woman that the man was long gone and would not be returning.

---

[11] RP – Reporting Party

Meeting by the cars, Clark waited for Konrad and Sanchez to finish talking before he said anything. They were discussing how to log the call.

"HBO[12] the call," said Clark, flatly. "No report needed. Then we can just say the subject fled the scene before we arrived. No report means no lying in a report."

"I think that's probably for the best," said Sanchez.

"What about the dude that thing took?" asked Konrad. "What about that poor bastard?"

"There's nothing we can do for him, now," said Sanchez. "We couldn't catch that thing. And if we put that all in the report, we'll all be on psych leave."

"Don't ask me to get too broken up over a dead kiddie-diddler," said Clark. "If you ask me that was justice."

"Dude," said Konrad with a chuckle. "You're lucky you weren't standing closer. That fucker would have nutted all over your pants."

"Fuck you, Konrad," said Clark with a smirk.

"You know," said Sanchez, "this would be a funny story if it hadn't ended the way it did. I kinda feel sorry for that guy."

"What now?" asked Konrad.

"First, we clear the call," said Clark. "Then I'm going to head around the lake in the direction that thing was running. Maybe I'll get lucky and find it."

"Are you sure you want to find that thing?" asked Konrad. "I don't. I don't think I could stop it. Besides that, I don't think there are any roads that direction."

"Why don't we call Blanchard and meet up to hear what he has to say," said Sanchez.

---

[12] HBO – Handled By Officer

"Alright," agreed Clark. "Let's go."

"125," said Clark, heading to put away his rifle.

"125, go," said dispatch.

"Show me, 136 and 155 back in service," he said. "Log us HBO. The subject was GOA[13]. Show us all back in service."

"Copy," said dispatch. "Call is HBO, back in service."

Setting behind the wheel, Clark pulled out the card that Blanchard had given him, then dialed the number. It rang twice before it was picked up.

"Blanchard," he answered.

"Detective," began Clark, "this is Deputy Clark. We met earlier at the crime scene."

"Yeah, the smartass," said Blanchard. "I remember."

"I think we need to meet and talk?" asked Clark.

"Agreed," said Blanchard. "Now is as good a time as any. My place is safe to talk. I live alone. I'll text you the address."

"Alright," said Clark. "We'll see you soon."

The address was for an apartment complex in Branson West. Clark was familiar with the area and headed right for it. Sanchez and Konrad followed behind him. It was only about a fifteen-minute drive. Pulling in, they all proceeded to apartment E5. Blanchard opened the door before they even knocked.

"Come in before you scare the shit out of my neighbors," said Blanchard.

They filed in and glanced around. Although comfortably furnished, there weren't many decorating touches that made it feel occupied. Konrad grabbed a wooden kitchen chair, turned it around backward, and straddled it, then folded his arms across the back of the chair.

---

[13] GOA – Gone On Arrival

Clark sat in an overstuffed chair and Sanchez sat on the arm of the chair next to him. Blanchard dropped onto the big couch with case notes and files sitting on the coffee table in front of him.

"How much do you know about the crime scene today?" asked Blanchard.

"I got a good look at it before everyone showed up," answered Clark. "Unless I missed something."

"Well," began Blanchard, "have you seen the official report?"

"No, sir," said Clark.

"Well, its pure bullshit," said Blanchard. "Sheriff Prescott is a fucking idiot. I honestly regret coming down and working for him."

"Well, that's something we both agree on," said Clark. "What did he do this time?"

"See for yourself," said Blanchard, handing Clark a printout.

Clark began reading it while Sanchez read over his shoulder. There was no mention of footprints and it listed the official cause of death as natural causes.

"Natural causes, my ass," said Clark, angrily. "How the fuck does he explain the broken neck and missing organs! And there's no mention of the drag marks or footprints."

"That's because he erased the tracks," said Blanchard. "I went down to take a look at them and could see where the area had been dragged over with boots, but the tracks were completely gone."

"Not completely," said Clark, taking out his phone.

Pulling up the pics, he showed them to Blanchard.

"Holy shit," said Blanchard. "That's a big bastard. Did you see the thing?"

"Not there," answered Clark.

"What do you mean 'there'?" asked Blanchard.

"I got a pretty good look at it last night," said Clark. "While we were looking for the missing girl."

"Shit," said Blanchard, "that was the same thing?"

"Yeah," said Sanchez. "And there's more."

They told him the entire story right up to the thing grabbing the prowler and running off into the woods. Blanchard sat and listened to their story without comment.

"So, you all three saw this thing?" he asked.

"I didn't see anything last night," said Konrad. "But I did have the feeling that we were being watched. I saw the thing's arm tonight and that's fucking plenty. I don't want to see the rest of it. The arm was more than enough for me to know I don't want to fuck with it."

"Have you dealt with these things before?" asked Clark.

"Not the same things," said Blanchard. "Something just as fucking bad. Look at this."

Blanchard lifted his t-shirt to reveal massive purple scars all down his chest and abdomen. It was clear that it was from claws. Sanchez gasped in astonishment.

"Damn!" said Konrad.

"What the fuck did that?" asked Clark.

"The Native Americans call it the *Oolonga-Doglalla*," said Blanchard. "It means long dogs. Some people call them Dogmen. They're fucking werewolves."

"Bullshit," said Konrad. "They don't exist. Do they? God, I hope they don't."

"Believe me," said Blanchard, "I wish they didn't."

"Is that why you left Lacland County?" asked Sanchez.

"Yeah," admitted Blanchard. "My wife thought I was crazy and left me. After that, I had to get out of there. I needed a change of scenery. I just figured this was far enough. Now we got a fucking

79

killer Bigfoot eating motherfuckers around here. Fuck, now I'm gonna have to move to Florida or some shit."

"So how do we fight it?" asked Clark. "And more importantly, how do we kill it?

"I don't know," said Blanchard. "But I know who to ask."

"My shift ends in a few minutes," said Clark. "Can we go see them then?"

"They live way back in the hillbilly-assed woods in Lacland County," said Blanchard. "I'll give them a call in the morning. What's your shift tomorrow?"

"I'm weekend evening shift," said Clark. "I work Thursday through Sunday, 14:00 to midnight. I'm off the next three days."

"Same here," said Konrad.

"Me too," said Sanchez.

"Good," said Blanchard. "I'll call you when I have time to meet up. Now you all better get the hell out of here before someone calls the department wanting to know why three of our cruisers are parked at an apartment complex."

"Why is the sheriff covering this up?" asked Clark.

"I wish I fucking knew," answered Blanchard shaking his head, "but there's more going on here than we know."

Chapter Eight
White Bear

"The aim of life was meat. Life itself was meat.
Life lived on life. There were the eaters and the eaten."
Jack London

Clark awoke to the sun streaming through his bedroom window. The alarm was going to go off in a few minutes but he didn't want to move. Sanchez was asleep on his arm, cuddled up against him.

They still hadn't discussed him asking her to move in. He wasn't sure if that was a good thing or a bad thing. He wasn't sure if he should bring it up or wait for her to mention it.

Stroking her hair gently, he brushed a long strand back away from her face. She looked so peaceful, sleeping there on his shoulder. He didn't want to wake her. He never wanted this moment to end, but it always would. Life was about the moments you embrace, and he was embracing this one. Slowly, she began to stir and opened her eyes.

"Good morning, beautiful," he said, smiling.

"Morning," she said, smiling up at him.

Kissing her softly, she melted into his arms. It was the perfect way to wake up. Rolling towards her, they kissed again. He felt himself beginning to stir. When she smiled, he knew she had noticed.

"Hey," she said, "before we get crazy. Can we talk?"

"Of course," he said. "Is something wrong?"

"I don't know," she said. "Maybe."

"Maybe?" he asked, frowning.

"I mean," she said, "yesterday, you asked me to move in with you. Did you mean it or was it one of those spur of the moment, regret it later questions?"

"I absolutely meant it," he said. "I love waking up next to you."

"You're sure?" she asked, cocking her head to the side as if scrutinizing his answer.

"I absolutely meant it," he said without hesitation.

"Yesterday you kind of had this look right after you asked me," she said. "I thought you might have blurted it out without really thinking about it."

"I did just say it without thinking," he said, "but that look was me being afraid you would think I was pushing or moving too fast. That's all."

"Alright," she said, narrowing her eyes, "if you're sure."

"Oh, I'm sure," he said, pulling her to him.

She giggled as he started kissing her neck and shoulders. He was kissing his way towards other areas when the phone rang.

"Goddamn it," he said, looking up.

"You keep kissing," she said. "I'll check the phone."

He was just reaching her left nipple when she stopped him.

"It's Blanchard," she said, handing him the phone.

"Fuck," he said, hitting the talk button. "Clark."

"Hey," said Blanchard. "My friends are here. They want to meet where you found that deputy's car. Down in that creepy-assed campground. How soon can you be there?"

"Give me thirty minutes," he said, frowning.

Sanchez lifted her left breast at him and pointed at the nipple.

"Uh," stammered Clark. "Can we make that an hour?"

"Sure," said Blanchard. "See you then."

Clark hung up the phone and sat it on the nightstand.

"You are evil," he said as he picked up where he left off.

"You have no idea," she replied, grabbing the back of his head.

After they exhausted themselves and took a quick shower, Clark put on a pair of cargo shorts and started putting on a belt.

"Why do you wear a belt with shorts?" asked Sanchez.

He slipped a magazine pouch through the belt on his left, then a molded Kydex holster on his right.

"Oh, that's why," she said, staring.

"Don't you carry off duty?" he asked.

"Not usually," she said.

"I always do," he said, "especially with a goddamned ten-foot hairy bastard out there eating people."

"Good point," she said. "I don't have a conceal holster."

Clark walked over to his closet and pulled out a footlocker. Digging around, he tossed her another molded Kydex holster and a mag pouch.

"There," he said. "That should fit your Glock 19."

"Why do you have so much tactical gear?" she asked.

"Never too much gear," he said. "You never know what you'll need. Like, for example, I now need to factor in ten-foot monsters into my preparedness."

Sanchez was wearing short cutoff jeans that left just the right amount of ass hanging out of the back and a black lacy bra. Clark found a belt that would fit her and she buckled on her ammo pouch and holster.

"Put your badge next to the gun," said Clark. "That way if any civilian sees your gun, they don't freak out."

Slipping a baggy shirt over his head, Clark checked to make sure the shirt covered the holster well. Satisfied, he grabbed his Para-Ordnance and slid it into the holster. Three additional mags went into the mag pouch.

Sanchez went to the closet and snagged one of his black Underarmor t-shirts and slipped it on. It covered the gun and still left enough of the shorts visible for the right look.

"How do I look?" she asked, turning her back to Clark for full effect.

"Like you're going to make us late if you don't stop," he said reaching out to touch her butt.

"Easy there," she said. "Don't start something we don't have time to finish."

"Promises, promises," said Clark, grabbing his OD green backpack.

"What's in the bag?" she asked.

"The usual," he said. "Med kit, extra ammo, backup gun, a handful of granola bars, emergency kit, and fire-starting supplies. The basics."

"We're going down the road," she said, "not into the wilds of Alaska."

"I know," he replied, "that's a bigger bag."

"Did anyone call Konrad?" she asked.

"I don't know," replied Clark. "I hope so. I was a bit preoccupied at the time."

"Excuses, excuses," she said heading into the living room.

Looking around the little cabin, she smiled.

"I like this place," she said. "It's really homey. I could be comfortable here."

"I certainly hope so," said Clark.

Opening the front door to head outside, Clark froze in his tracks.

His hand went instantly to his holster.

"What's going on?" asked Sanchez, suddenly serious.

"Wait here," he said, drawing his pistol.

"Not a chance, cowboy," she said, drawing her pistol. "I'm coming with you."

Stepping out onto the porch, Clark kept his pistol at high ready and moved towards the steps. Sanchez followed behind him, her pistol at low ready.

"I don't see anything," said Sanchez.

"Look at my patrol cruiser," he said, gesturing.

Laying on the hood of his patrol cruiser was the head of a deer. It was sat so it was looking directly at the front door of the house. As he approached, he continually swept the area but saw no other signs of movement.

Getting close, he could see that the head had been torn from the body, not cut. The wound was ragged and bloody. Blood had pooled on the hood and dripped down onto the bumper.

"What the hell?" said Sanchez as she came up next to him.

"I think this is a message," said Clark.

"What kind of message?" she asked, looking around the area.

"It knows where I live," he said, "and it wanted me to know that it knows."

"It's just a big animal," she said. "How can it be smart enough to do that?"

"I think that there's a lot we don't know," said Clark.

He grabbed the deer head and pulled it off the hood of his SUV. Holding it by the antlers, he carried it over and tossed it into the woods. As he was starting to turn around to head back, he had a distinct feeling that he was being watched.

Backing away slowly, he drew his pistol and kept it at the ready. Although he couldn't see anything, he knew it was somewhere close, watching his every move.

"I hope the blood will wash off," said Sanchez, looking at the hood of the SUV.

"Forget the blood," said Clark. "It'll come off. We have bigger problems."

"What?" she asked, looking around.

"It's here," he said. "Watching us."

Going around to the back of the SUV, Clark unlocked it and took out his Black Rain Ordnance Rifle and the ammo. Taking it over to his jeep, he lifted the back seat and unlocked the lockbox he'd welded into the jeep and hid under the backseat.

Sanchez came around and got into the passenger side. The top and doors were already off, leaving the jeep open to the air. Clark slid into the driver's seat and started the engine.

"You have a hand grenade as a gear shifter," said Sanchez.

"It's inert," said Clark. "I bought it at Army Surplus and drilled it out. I wanted something unique."

"That's definitely unique," she agreed.

"Buckle up," he said, shifting into first gear.

Seconds later, he was heading down the driveway. He drove faster than he normally did because the trees were very close to the side of the driveway. He didn't want to let that thing get an easy swipe at one of them.

Slowing down at the end of the driveway, Clark glanced both ways and shot straight out onto the highway. Accelerating, he ran the gears quickly and hit seventy miles an hour.

"Catch me now," said Clark, "you son-of-a-bitch."

As he approached the entrance to the Joe Bald Campground, he saw Konrad's blue F150 Raptor pickup just pulling in.

"I guess Blanchard called him," said Sanchez.

"Good," said Clark.

Pulling in behind Konrad, they followed him down to the parking area. All evidence of the incident was gone completely. Even the blood had been washed away. Blanchard was sitting on the tailgate of a red Toyota pickup parked in the gravel. Beside him were two men, both Native American.

Clark pulled in beside the pickup and shut off the engine. Setting the parking brake, he climbed out and headed around to the back of the vehicle. Sanchez joined him and they headed towards Blanchard.

Konrad pulled in right behind them and got out of his truck. He was wearing jean shorts with a red St. Louis Cardinals jersey with the name Molina on the back. Sanchez could tell at a glance that he had a pistol on under the jersey.

Blanchard jumped down from the tailgate and shook Clark's hand, then Sanchez and Konrad.

"Folks," he began, "let me introduce you. This is Jay *Matoskah* and Jason *Otaktay*. I hope I said that right."

Handshakes were exchanged and greetings were given. Jason was dressed in black tactical pants tucked into black moccasin boots with a tactical belt holding four magazines and a holster with a large automatic pistol. His long black hair was in a ponytail and he wore a plain black t-shirt.

The other man, *Matoskah* had long white hair pulled into a long braid. He wore a white button-up shirt with a brown leather vest. He also wore blue jeans that were tucked into brown leather moccasin boots. Around his waist was a gun-belt that held an old Colt revolver. Extra cartridges were in loops around the belt, Old West style.

"You may call me Jay or White Bear," said Jay. "*Matoskah* means White Bear. I understand you are having a problem with the *Chiye-Tanka*."

"What's that?" asked Konrad.

"That's the Lakota word for what you white-folks call Bigfoot," said Jason.

"Although," said Jay, "this isn't typical behavior for them. You might have a different type on your hands."

"There's more than one type?" asked Clark, incredulously.

"There are many," said Jay. "Most encounters with the *Chiye-Tanka* are peaceful. They tend to shy away from humans. They resemble the classic image of bigfoot. Like a gigantic man-ape covered with dark fur or hair. They are less aggressive unless threatened and tend to eat an omnivorous diet of meat, berries, roots, and wild vegetables. The face looks mostly human with a wider nose."

"Not this guy," said Clark. "He seems to find us tasty."

"What you might have on your hands is called a *Gugwe*," said Jay. "It's a more aggressive strain. Looks a bit different too. Have you seen its face?"

"Not clearly," answered Clark. "However, there is a new development. I think it followed me home. There was a deer's head on the hood of my patrol car when I came outside today."

"Too bad you haven't seen it clearly," said Jay. "I could give you better information. If it left a deer's head on your vehicle, it's sending you a message. It knows who you are and where you live. That's a threat or possibly a territorial marker."

"That doesn't sound good," said Konrad, shaking his head.

"I'd say you've got a *Gugwe*," said Jay. "That sounds like their behavior. Be very careful. They are a dangerous foe. Some have a short snout, not unlike a baboon but with massive canine teeth. It is clear from its appearance and demeanor that it's primarily a meat-eater. The name *Gugwe* means face eater."

"Well, shit," said Clark. "That doesn't sound good. I need a bigger gun."

"There are other types," said Jay, "but it is very unlikely to find them in this area. The more aggressive ones live far to the north. They prefer colder climates."

"There are others?" asked Konrad. "That's the last time I go camping."

"Make no mistake," said Jay. "This thing must be stopped. It has no fear of man. It will continue to kill until you kill it. It is staking out hunting grounds here. Once established, it will not leave."

"Any advice on how to kill one?" asked Konrad.

"Well," said Jason, "big bullets, and a lot of them generally does the trick. But I'd say aim for big arteries. The upper arm, thigh, neck. Headshot if you've got armor-piercing bullets. Their bones are very dense. Bullets rarely penetrate them."

"Be especially careful with this young lady," said Jay. "There are lots of tales of these creatures carrying off women to mate with."

Clark looked at Sanchez and she looked around the woods nervously.

"How do I keep it away from my house?" asked Clark.

"There are ways that will discourage it from coming back to your place," said Jay, "but I know nothing that will stop it completely. If it truly means to come after you, I fear that there is nothing to do but be prepared to fight."

"Then I definitely need a bigger gun," said Clark. "Probably more than one."

"You most certainly do," agreed Jay.

Clark took out his cellphone and pulled up the pictures of the tracks that he took and showed them to Jay *Matoskah* and Jason. After a few moments, they handed back the phone.

"For one thing," said Jason, "that's a big bastard. Gotta be pushing a thousand pounds of muscle, bone, and teeth."

"It is a *Gugwe*," added Jay. "You can tell by the indentions of claws at the ends of the toes. *Chiye-Tanka* does not have that."

"Why is it so interested in finding me?" asked Clark.

"Because it keeps finding your scent near its kill sites," said Jay *Matoskah*. "It knows you are hunting it."

"But how did it find my house?" asked Clark. "How could it have tracked me when I was in a car?"

"They are amazing trackers," said Jay. "It can pick out the scent of your vehicle among the scents of others. It can smell the faint traces of your scent, even from a vehicle. The elders used to say that once it knows you, it can follow you anywhere. That it knows your mind."

"So, was that deer head a threat or a warning?" asked Sanchez.

"Probably both," said Jason. "Likely a warning to show what it can do and letting you know that it can find you anytime it wants."

"Yeah," said Clark, "I don't like that."

"Can't say that I blame you," said Jay. "Be cautious but understand, it doesn't normally go after prey that it thinks can hurt it. No animal in the animal kingdom will be willing to fight its prey. They prefer easy kills. It expends less energy and requires less risk. If you project strength, it will make it think before it attacks. It likely will still attack, but you might make it think twice. It is very difficult to drive them away from its hunting grounds."

"Maybe if I can hurt it?" asked Clark. "Or better yet, kill it?"

"Then you will be one of very few hunters to do so," replied Jay. "These creatures are extremely dangerous and efficient killers. It has been at the top of the food chain since our people were learning to make fire."

"They're the original boogeyman," said Jason. "They're why we have an ingrained fear of the dark wired into our DNA. Those damned things were hunting our people back in the stone age."

"Great," answered Clark. "We have to stop it."

"Or it will keep killing," said Blanchard.

"Are you going to help?" Konrad asked Blanchard.

"Look man," said Blanchard. "I damned near died last time I faced something like that. I'll carry the scars for the rest of my life. I don't think I could do it again. I'm still struggling with the nightmares from my last encounter with the shit that goes bump in the night."

"It's ok," said Clark. "I understand. You came here not expecting to have to deal with another monster. I'd be gun-shy too if I nearly got my chest ripped open."

"Oh, it was completely open," said Blanchard. "I was extremely lucky that one of the best medics in the business was there when it happened. He saved my life then drove me to the hospital."

"Unfortunately," said Jay, "I cannot stay to help you fight this battle. I'm afraid that there are pressing matters that I must attend to back at home. I hope what I was able to tell you helps."

"What guns did you use to fight the Dogmen?" asked Konrad. "Maybe we should get some of those."

"I don't have any of the Beowulf's at the moment," said Jason. "My stock was depleted a few months back. I do have something that might do the trick, though."

Walking over to the red Toyota, Jason reached behind the seat and brought out two nylon gun cases with the logo for Rock River Arms on the outside. Handing one to Clark and one to Konrad, he stepped back and nodded to them.

"Go ahead and open them up," he said.

Clark unzipped the bag and took out his. It was beautiful in its lethality. A modern masterpiece of form and function in steel and polymer.

"They're identical," said Jason. "Rock River Arms LAR-459 Devastator in .458 SOCOM."

"Holy shit!" said Konrad. "The gun-gods are smiling today. This thing's amazing."

"They're badass," said Jason. "That's for sure. I've got a bag full of magazines and ammo to go with them."

"What do you want for them?" asked Clark, already knowing this as a very expensive firearm.

"Call it an indefinite loan," said Jason. "I don't exactly have a lot wrapped up in them."

"They're not stolen, are they?" asked Clark.

"Shit," said Jason, "I forgot you guys were cops. My cousin says the same shit to me. No, they're not stolen. They were given to me as payment for some work I did for some people in Oklahoma. You can run the serial numbers. They come back clean. I promise."

"And you're just giving them to us?" asked Clark, cautiously.

"Giving," said Jason, "not so much."

"So, we have to give them back?" asked Konrad.

"Nope," said Jason. "I don't want them back."

"Then what's the catch?" asked Clark.

"Consider it a favor," said Jason. "I might need a favor from you sometime. If things like this continue to show up, I might need the help."

"Deal," said Clark. "If you need us, just call."

"What?" said Sanchez. "No big gun for me?"

"I'm afraid I only had the two of them," said Jason.

"I have something for you, child," said Jay.

Walking over to her, he took a leather thong from around his neck attached to a small leather pouch that was under his shirt. Placing it over her neck, he began chanting softly in his native Lakota. When he finished the song, he smiled serenely.

"This is a medicine bag," he said, patting Sanchez on the cheek. "This will bring you protection and guard you against the evil that you now face. Wear it at all times. Especially keep it with you when you sleep. You can take it off when you shower but put it right back on."

"Thank you, sir," she said. "I really appreciate it. I won't take it off."

"Jason," said Jay, "bring me my bag from the truck."

Jason did as he was asked and brought over a leather satchel bag and handed it to his grandfather. Reaching inside, Jay took out two carven figures, one of a wolf and the other of an eagle. There were symbols inscribed in the base of each figure.

"I carved these from a piece of white oak that had been struck by lightning," explained Jay. "They have been blessed by four medicine men of four different tribes. Place these in your home and it will keep the creature from entering."

"Thank you," she said and hugged the old warrior.

"You remind me of my daughter," said Jay. "You have the same spirit. Her fire. She was a warrior, much like yourself."

"Where is she now?" asked Sanchez.

"She was taken from us long ago," said Jay, "by a drunk driver."

"I'm so sorry," said Sanchez. "My parents died in a car crash, too. The other driver was drunk but was never charged because he was a judge. That's why I became a cop. To make the law apply to everyone who breaks it. Not just certain people."

"You definitely have her fire," said Jay. "If only Will could see you."

"Who's Will?" she asked.

"My grandson," said Jay. "I raised him since he was a young boy after the accident. He also became a police officer."

"Where is he now?" asked Sanchez.

93

"He found a higher calling," said Jay. "He now fights for his people."

"Thank you," said Sanchez, then reached over and hugged the old warrior.

"It is I who should thank you," said Jay. "You have shown me that my daughter's spirit still smiles down upon us. You carry the flame."

"One last thing," said Jay, turning towards the others. "You can also know the *Gugwe* by its smell."

"I've already noticed that," said Clark. "It's like a wet dog mixed with urine and rotten meat."

"That's an accurate description," said Jay. "I think it's safe to say you are dealing with a *Gugwe*."

Jason returned from the truck with a couple of large range bags, handing them to Clark. Clark was shocked by how heavy they were.

"There are a couple of dozen magazines for each gun and a few thousand rounds of .458 SOCOM in there," he said. "Some are hollow points, and some are armor piercers. Those should punch through the *Gugwe* without a problem."

"Thank you," said Clark, shaking Jason's hand.

Jason and his Jay went back to the truck. Blanchard lingered behind and approached Clark.

"Good luck hunting that thing," he said. "I'm sorry I can't be of more help. Keep me posted and I'll do what I can to help you guys."

Shaking hands, Blanchard joined the others and got into the truck. Jason fired up the engine and they headed out to the road.

"We'd better go, too," said Clark. "No sense hanging around here. I'm not ready to fight that thing, just yet."

"We will be," said Konrad.

"Yes, we will," said Clark.

"We *all* will," said Sanchez.

They headed back to their vehicles and started out of the parking lot. Little did they know that less than fifty yards away, the beast was watching them from behind a large oak tree, crouching behind the overgrown brush. It was growling low in its throat and watching them intently.

Although it could see them all, its attention was focused on Sanchez. It stayed hidden until they drove out of sight, then turned and headed deeper into the woods.

D.A. ROBERTS

Chapter Nine
Hunting the Hunters

"Every man's life ends the same way. It is only the details of how he lived and how he died that distinguish one man from another."
Ernest Hemingway

Clark turned right as he left the Joe Bald Campground, heading towards his house. Konrad followed and soon they were pulling into the driveway and stopping beside the little cabin.

"What are we doing here?" asked Sanchez.

"I thought we could divide the ammo and magazines with Konrad and not have to do it where people would wonder what the fuck we were up to."

"Ok," she said, and glanced nervously around the trees.

Clark quickly loaded two of the magazines and put one in the Devastator. Pulling the charging handle, he put a round in the chamber and checked over the weapon. Everything appeared to be in good working order.

"Wanna squeeze a few rounds off?" asked Konrad as he walked up.

"I want to feel the recoil," answered Clark, "and figure out how much ammo I can carry without killing myself."

"Yeah," said Konrad. "Those are some big rounds. Gonna be much heavier than my AR."

On the side of the house, facing deeper into the woods, Clark had built a range for himself to practice on. He had dug a trench with a backhoe and used the dirt to make a berm. The targets were all hung from heavy-gauge chains attached to a thick steel pipe. Hanging was half-sized steel targets.

Clark had loaded the mags with hollow points. He didn't want to shoot his steel targets with armor-piercing rounds. Pulling the rifle to his shoulder, he sighted in and flicked the selector switch from safe to semi.

Slowly he placed his finger on the trigger and began to take up the slack. He was roughly fifty yards from the target with no wind. Visibility was perfect except for the waves of heat that rose from the ground.

"KABOOM!" roared Devastator.

"PING!" replied the steel target, as it flipped into the air and swung around by the steel chain.

"Holy shit," said Konrad. "That's badass."

"The sights are dead-on," said Clark, flicking the safety back on.

"That thing hits like a jackhammer," said Konrad, looking at the still dancing steel plate.

"Boys and their toys," said Sanchez, smiling.

"Want to try it?" asked Clark. "The kick isn't as bad as I expected."

"Sure," she said, taking the rifle. "I'll give it a shot."

Aiming, she sighted in and started taking up the slack on the trigger. Devastator bellowed once more and there was a sharp ring as the steel plate began jumping around on the end of the chain. The echoes of the shot rolled off through the area and faded off into the distance.

"Ow," she said, handing the rifle back to Clark. "That thing has quite the punch."

"Definitely," said Clark.

"Are you going to let me show you up, Konrad?" said Sanchez, smiling.

"No," he said, with a smile.

He moved around the front of the jeep to get a clear shot. Pulling the charging handle to chamber a round, he tentatively put the stock to his shoulder and began aiming.

"Come on, Konrad," said Sanchez. "You're not scared, are you?"

"I'm justifiably cautious," said Konrad defensively.

Aiming, Konrad picked a target that wasn't swaying and squeezed the trigger. The massive report of the Devastator thundered out across the distance, but this time there wasn't a corresponding metallic ping.

"You missed," said Sanchez, giggling.

"The sights are off," complained Konrad.

"Let me see," said Clark.

Konrad traded weapons with him, and Clark took a look at the sights on the weapon.

"They look ok to me," said Clark. "Let me try it."

Stepping around the others, Clark brought the weapon to his shoulder and thumbed off the safety. Five steel targets were hanging from the pipe. Two were still swaying. Clark took a deep breath and slowly exhaled.

Five shots roared out as Devastator lived up to its name. The ring of all five steel plates sounded almost like one long ping. As Clark lowered the weapon and put it back on safe, all five targets were dancing on their chains.

"I think the sights are ok," he said, handing the rifle back to Konrad.

"Show off," said Konrad.

Sanchez just smiled at Clark. He gave her a wink and a smile, then took his rifle back from Konrad. Dropping the magazine, he cleared the weapon and locked the bolt back, inspecting the chamber to verify it was empty.

"Where'd you learn to shoot like that?" asked Konrad.

"Fort Benning, Georgia," answered Clark. "Then put that training to the test in Iraq and Afghanistan."

Konrad just nodded.

"I never joined," he said. "I sometimes wish I had. I just wanted to run around and party when I got out of high school."

"What made you decide to be a cop?" asked Sanchez.

"I was partying with a bunch of friends," said Konrad, "not too far from here. Over at Moonshine Beach. Anyway, we all had a few too many and most of us were going to sleep it off instead of trying to drive home. A buddy of mine insisted on driving home. I could have stopped him, but I thought that my bro could handle himself just fine and let him go. He killed himself and a family of four on his way home. Passed out at the wheel and hit them head-on at over seventy miles an hour. I quit drinking for a long time. I still don't drink much. I decided to go into law enforcement as a way to kinda make up for it. Maybe try to save a few lives to make up for the ones I could have saved that night."

Clark didn't say anything. Sanchez hugged Konrad and he put his head on her shoulder.

"It's not your fault," she said. "You didn't know it would happen. You can't keep blaming yourself."

"I could have stopped him," said Konrad.

"Hey," said Clark, "you can't let that shit eat you alive inside. It will. On my first tour, I lost three squadmates. All good friends of mine. I blamed myself for a long time. I kept second-guessing everything I did that day. But a lot of factors went into that event. None of which I had any control over. I realized that there was nothing I could have done differently. It was just a shit situation that nothing I did would have changed."

"But I could have stopped him," said Konrad. "He would have listened to me."

"Maybe," said Clark. "Maybe he wouldn't have. You don't know. Either way, it happened, and you can't change it. All you can do is make certain it doesn't happen again."

"And you've done a lot of good as a cop," said Sanchez. "You're making a difference."

Konrad stepped away from Sanchez and shook his head. Then he cleared his weapon and checked the empty chamber.

"Anyway," said Konrad, "let's change the subject. I don't want to think about it anymore. Let's do something else."

"Like what?" asked Sanchez.

"We need to try and locate where that thing sleeps," said Clark. "Before we go, I want to get that blood off the hood of my cruiser."

Digging out a bucket and soap from the kitchen, Clark added the soap and started filling the bucket with water from the hose. Dragging the hose over to the SUV, he soaked the bloody sections and let it set before hitting it with the soap. It took him a bit, but it finally all washed off. As he was finishing, he glanced over to the spot where he had thrown the deer head. Just as he expected, it was gone.

Putting up the supplies and reeling the hose back onto the reel, he headed inside. Konrad was sitting at his kitchen table. He was reassembling the Devastators.

"I decided to clean these things since you were busy," he said.

"Thanks, man," said Clark.

"I hope you don't mind," said Sanchez, "but I put those statues that Jay *Matoskah* gave me on the mantle above your fireplace."

"Why would I mind?" asked Clark. "But I thought he gave you those for your house."

"Well," she said, "I'm going to be staying here with you, anyway."

"True," he said, "if you still want to with this thing running around."

"I do," she said, smiling. "You can't get rid of me that easily."

"We still going looking for that thing?" asked Konrad.

"Yeah," said Clark. "We need to find it before it kills anyone else."

"Let's just take one vehicle," said Konrad. "No sense in wasting the gas. We can take my truck."

"Where should we start?" asked Sanchez.

Clark went over to an old desk and rummaged through it for a few minutes before pulling out an old folded paper map. Unfolding it, he held it up and glanced at it.

"Yep," he said. "This is a Platte map of Sloan County. I used to use it for deer hunting before the GPS on my phone replaced it. Now I have an app that tracks my best hunting spots."

"I haven't seen an actual paper map in forever," said Sanchez.

"I didn't know they still made them?" added Konrad.

"Oh, haha," said Clark. "I'm still old school, especially when it comes to maps and land navigation. I still double-check my phone with a lensatic compass when I hunt and hike."

"What's a lensatic compass?" asked Konrad.

"We learned land navigation by using a map and a special compass, called a lensatic compass," explained Clark. "It does much more than just point north. Here."

Clark tossed Konrad a black cased compass. He looked at it like it was alien technology. Taking it back, Clark opened it up.

"It's basically three parts," said Clark. "The cover, the base, and the reading lens. There's a sighting wire in the cover and you look through the lens at the wire to determine direction and course. There's a skill to it."

"Thanks," said Konrad, "but I think I'll just stick to my phone."

"Sure," said Clark, "but that only helps if you have a phone or if you are in a place where you get signal. If you lose signal or the phone breaks, you're boned."

"Well, if I lose my phone," said Konrad, "I'm screwed anyway."

Clark shook his head and put the compass on the desk. Grabbing some tape, he hung the map on the wall and grabbed a Sharpie.

"Now," he said, "the first attack was here."

He circled the area near the end of the Kimberling City Bridge where the trailer park was.

"Next," he said, "was here in the Joe Bald Campground."

Circling the area on the map, he paused.

"Then I found the body of Jacobson about here," he said, circling another area not far from the last.

"What about where that guy got snagged right in front of us?" asked Sanchez.

"That was right about here," said Clark, circling another spot.

"They look like they're heading in the same direction," said Konrad.

"I see that," said Clark, "but can we assume that? If it continues heading in the direction it's going, it will leave the lake. Thus far, it's used the lake to move around undetected. If it keeps going, it's heading into some deep timber. Then there is the fact that it was here, this morning. For some reason, it's staying close to this area."

"Maybe that was the goal all along," said Sanchez. "Maybe it was trying to get into deep woods."

"That would take it away from people," said Konrad. "Do you think it wants to avoid people?"

"My gut says no," said Clark. "Why would it go back to chasing deer and other prey animals when humans have proven to be so easy to take down and provide plenty of meat?"

"I've heard it said that once an animal tastes man," said Konrad, "like a bear or something, then they have to put it down because they won't go back to regular prey."

"Man-eaters have to be put down," said Clark. "That's the way it's always been. I can't see how it would be different with this thing."

"Alright," said Sanchez. "Where do we start looking?"

"I can't see it leaving the lake," said Clark. "The prey is too plentiful. Too many people that are easy pickings."

"What's close to the last place we saw it?" asked Konrad. "What's the most likely spot that's still close to the lake?"

"Could be any of a hundred places," said Sanchez. "I mean, there are resorts all over that area."

"Why don't we drive through that area and keep the scanner on?" said Konrad. "Then we could listen for anything weird coming over the wire."

"That's not a bad idea," said Clark. "Let's load the rifles in the truck and take extra ammo, just in case."

While Konrad loaded the guns, Clark threw his compass and basic survival gear into an OD green molle backpack. He attached a Gurkha type machete to the side. Trauma kit, a fire starter kit, a signal mirror, and a handful of protein bars. Slipping in a water bladder and a couple of survival straws, he glanced around before adding a couple of fixed blade knives. Last went a foldable tarp and a long-looped roll of 550 cord.

"That should do," he said, "for starters."

"We're not planning on invading Sloan County," said Konrad.

"I'm trying to be prepared for any occasion," said Clark. "If I have to go into the woods, I want to be ready."

"Do you want to chase that thing into the woods?" asked Sanchez.

"I don't think *want* is the right word," replied Clark. "But I will if I have to. We've got to find a way to stop it."

"Chasing that thing into the woods is practically suicide," said Konrad. "We can't hope to beat that thing in its own element."

"Let's hope it doesn't come to that," said Clark, shouldering the bag.

Heading out to Konrad's truck, Clark placed the bag and rifles in the back seat. Sanchez climbed into the back of the extended cab truck and slid the bag over. Clark got into the passenger seat while Konrad headed around to the driver's side.

Once inside, he fired up the engine and looked around the yard. Clark turned on the scanner and set it to search local channels.

"What are you looking for?" asked Sanchez.

"I don't know," said Konrad. "I thought I heard something when I came around the truck."

"What did you hear?"' asked Clark, looking concerned.

"I thought I heard something moving through the trees," said Konrad, gesturing towards the trees at the far side of the yard.

"Might be our beast," said Clark. "I know it's been here."

About that time, a large buck walked out of the trees and looked around. It had a large rack with at least ten points on its antlers. It sniffed the air and looked around the yard for threats. When it saw nothing, it began grazing in the grass. Behind it emerged four young does, who also began grazing.

"Well," said Clark, "if we needed proof it's not in the area, that's it. If that thing were anywhere near this place, they'd be off like a shot."

"Good to know," said Konrad, putting the truck in gear.

The deer ignored them and continued to graze as Konrad turned the truck around and headed down the driveway. By the time they reached the blacktop, they were seeing squirrels in the trees and birds flying around.

"It's moved out of this area," said Clark. "The game is returning. Earlier, I didn't see so much as a single squirrel. Now, they're everywhere."

"That's good," said Sanchez. "I was starting to get worried."

"I've never been a hunter," said Konrad. "I don't pay any attention to the animals and shit like that."

"It's good to know," said Clark. "You never know when it might come in handy. Besides, animal behavior teaches us a lot about human behavior. Predators are predators. There are certain signs to watch for."

As they were passing the entrance to the Joe Bald Recreation Area, there was a Missouri Department of Conservation vehicle parked at the entrance. Two agents were dragging a large logging chain across the entrance.

"Pull over," said Clark.

Konrad did as he was asked and stopped at the entrance. Clark exited the vehicle and approached the two Conservation Agents.

"What's going on?" he asked as he walked up.

"We're closing the park," said the first agent.

"Why?" asked Clark.

"It's state property," said the second agent. "We're closing it down for public safety."

"Who are you?" asked the first agent.

Producing his credentials, Clark held them up so they could see.

"Sloan County Sheriff's Office," said Clark.

"Then you should already know," said the first one. "We're closing it at the request of your sheriff."

"Is that a fact?" said Clark, not surprised.

"Public safety hazard," said the second one. "Didn't you just have one of your deputies die down here?"

"Yes, we did," said Clark, "but his death had nothing to do with the park."

"It's unsafe in there," said the first agent. "Roads are crumbling and it's overgrown. Until this place can be cleared out, we need to shut it down for public safety."

Clark just nodded and headed back to the truck. There was no point in arguing with them. For one, he wasn't even sure they worked for the Department of Conservation. Clark knew the agents that worked this area and he'd never seen either of them before.

"What's going on?" asked Sanchez when he climbed back inside.

"They're shutting off access to Joe Bald," said Clark, "supposedly at the request of Sheriff Prescott."

"That doesn't make any sense," said Konrad.

"Look at that," said Sanchez.

They all turned and back in the trees almost out of sight were two military Humvees with soldiers in full combat gear. They were gathering their equipment and scanning the trees around them.

"We'd better get out of here," said Clark. "There's something fishy going on here. With military searching that area for the beast, they're just going to force it out of the area. It's smart enough to know to avoid them."

Konrad put the truck in gear and headed up the road, accelerating swiftly out of the area. They rode in silence for a while until they were far away from the area.

"Hey," said Konrad. "I think those Conservation guys are following us."

"Pull in up here at the old Joe Bald Market," said Clark. "Let's see what they do."

Konrad pulled into the little market and came to a stop. Clark exited the vehicle and headed into the store. The Conservation Agents continued to drive by but watched him intently as they passed.

Clark went into the store and bought a few drinks and a can of chewing tobacco. Taking his time walking around the store, he looked out the window and saw the Conservation Agents parked up the road.

"They're waiting for us," thought Clark. "They're not even being subtle about it. What the hell is going on?"

Heading back out to the truck, Clark got in and handed out the sodas.

"They're following us," said Clark. "They're parked up the road waiting for us to go."

"Then they aren't Department of Conservation," said Konrad. "Who the hell are they?"

"Fuck it," said Clark. "Let's make these assholes nervous. Head over to the Kimberling City Bridge. Let's see what they do when we get close to the first crime scene. None of that is Conservation land, so they can't say shit without giving away who they really are."

As they drove past the two "Conservation Agents" Clark made sure to make eye contact with them. He wanted them to know that he knew they were following him. Sanchez smiled and waved at them. Konrad flipped them off, honking as he drove by.

"Well," said Clark, "that was subtle. Think they know we spotted them?"

"I'm gonna guess that they do," said Sanchez.

The car accelerated, not attempting to hide the fact that they were following them. When they turned towards the Kimberling City Bridge, the car stayed right with them. As they crossed the bridge and approached the trailer park where they had found the meth lab, there were several vehicles there. Black SUVs and town cars.

"Goddamn it," snapped Clark. "The feds have taken the case. Those are FBI vehicles."

"Are you sure?" asked Konrad.

"Yeah," said Clark. "I've had to hand over cases to them before when they crossed state lines. They must have pulled jurisdiction on this case."

"Do you think the two assholes behind us are Feds, too?" asked Konrad.

"I'd bet money on it," said Clark. "Why the fuck are the Feds so interested in this thing?"

"Want me to stop at the crime scene?" asked Konrad.

"No," said Clark. "Somehow the Feds have swooped in and are all over this. If we keep getting in their way, then we're going to have real trouble. It looks like Sheriff Prescott might have called them in."

"You think?" asked Sanchez.

"I'd bet on it," said Clark, "considering how hard he's worked to keep me away from the cases and the fact that he ruled Jacobson's death as natural causes despite what we all saw."

Konrad kept driving past the trailer park and the fake Conservation Agents pulled into the park and stopped. Konrad didn't slow down and continued up the hill before he began slowing down.

"Which way should we go?" asked Konrad.

"Let's go back," said Clark. "I want to see what those two are up to."

Konrad pulled into a driveway, then backed out into the road to head back the way they had just come. As he accelerated back down the hill, Clark began scanning the edge of the road for signs of the supposed Conservation Agents.

As they rounded the last corner, they saw the two "agents" speaking with the Federal Agents at the trailer park. As they drove by, the agents all turned to watch them drive by with odd looks on their faces.

"I don't think they were expecting us to come back," said Clark. "Did you see the looks they gave us?"

"They didn't look happy," said Sanchez.

"Maybe we should quit taunting them," said Sanchez. "They're Feds. They could make life suck for us for a while."

Clark turned in his seat to say something when the scanner went off.

"103 to dispatch," said a voice on the radio.

"Go ahead 102," said dispatch.

"We just got a report from a guest at the resort concerning some children who claimed someone tried to grab one of them near the marina," said 102.

"102?" said Konrad. "Isn't that Indian Point PD?"

"Yeah," said Clark. "That's not too far from here."

"Copy 102," said dispatch. "Do they have a description?"

"Negative," said 102. "All they would say was he was really big and hairy. The kids were all pretty shook up."

"Copy 102," said dispatch. "What are you requesting?"

"I need an additional unit," said 102. "I'm the only unit on duty today and would like an assist in the search."

"Copy 102," said dispatch. "Will advise when Sloan County is in route."

"Here goes the call," said Clark. "Too bad we're not on duty."

"Who's gonna get the call?" asked Sanchez. "I don't remember who's on today."

Konrad was already accelerating towards the turnoff towards Indian Point at Branson West. They were near to the outskirts of Kimberling City when the scanner kicked in again.

"Any available Sloan County Unit," began dispatch, "Indian Point PD is requesting an additional unit to assist with locating a subject who attempted to abduct a child."

"121 responding," said a voice. "I'm not far from there now."

"Copy 121," said dispatch. "Show you responding to assist Indian Point. Advise if you need additional."

"Solid copy," said 121. "Will advise. Out."

"Who's 121?" asked Konrad.

"Chuck Duvall," said Clark. "He's not going to play well with us. His nose is so far up Prescott's ass that he could tell you what he had for breakfast yesterday."

"So, we shouldn't expect a warm welcome and full cooperation," said Sanchez.

"Nope," said Clark, "however it won't be a total loss."

"Why's that?" asked Konrad.

"That's Indian Point," said Clark. "They'll tell us everything just to brag about how fucking cool they are. We've just got to catch them away from Duvall."

"I fucking hate Indian Point," said Konrad.

Konrad took the corner from Highway 138 onto Highway 76 at the stoplight in Branson West, heading towards Branson and Indian Point.

"Hey," said Sanchez. "Pull into the McDonalds."

"Why?" asked Konrad.

"Just do it," she snapped. "Quickly."

Konrad slowed down and pulled into the parking lot of the McDonalds, stopping by the door.

"Emergency pee?" he asked, grinning.

"No, moron," she said, returning the grin. "Look behind us."

As they all looked back, three black SUV's with lights and sirens but no markings shot past the McDonalds and accelerated out of town.

"Feds?" she asked, looking back at Clark.

"I would say it's a safe bet," he replied. "We're not going to be able to get anywhere near that place without being seen."

"Why are the Feds so interested in this thing?" asked Konrad. "I mean, they aren't even supposed to exist. Why would the Feds be so shit hot to find this thing?"

"Son of a bitch," said Clark. "There go two Humvees, hauling ass."

"If they take the military in there," said Sanchez, "that thing will either flee the area or go to ground. They'll never find it."

"But if they do," added Konrad, "then they'll take care of the problem for us."

"I guess we'd better stay clear and monitor the situation," said Clark. "For now."

"What worries me," said Sanchez, "is if that thing is at Indian Point, then it's right on top of Silver Dollar City and there's always a huge crowd there."

"I have a buddy that works security there," said Clark. "Greg Hanley. We went to the academy together. He's a reserve deputy with Tanner County but works full-time security for SDC."

"What good does that do us?" asked Konrad.

"I'll ask him to let me know if they see or hear anything weird," said Clark. "Especially on any of the dozens of cameras they have all over that park."

"Ahh," said Konrad. "That makes sense."

"So, what do we do now?" asked Sanchez.

"Well," said Clark. "We're at a McDonalds. Why don't we eat some lunch and listen to the scanner?"

"Sounds like a plan," said Sanchez. "Frankly, I'm starving."

"Dude let's eat some real food for a damned change," said Konrad. "I'm sick of fast food."

"Where do you want to go?" asked Sanchez.

"I want some barbeque," said Konrad. "How about Danna's place."

"Oh, hell yeah," said Clark. "I'm down like four flat tires. While we eat, I'll text my buddy at the park and see what I can find out."

Chapter Ten
O.I.S.[14]

"There are hunters and there are victims. By your discipline, you will decide if you are a hunter or a victim."
General *"Mad Dog" Mattis*

Clark pulled to a stop at a red light at the intersection of Highway 13 and Highway 138. It had been three days since there had been anything remotely resembling the creature. No missing persons, no missing pets. Nothing.

He assumed it had something to do with the presence of the Federal Agents and the military personnel. He honestly hoped that they had found and killed the creature, but he sincerely doubted it. It was laying low until they stopped searching. Either that, or it had fled the area. Although, there hadn't been any reports of similar activity anywhere that he knew of.

It was early evening, but the sun wasn't anywhere near going down. Thus far, the calls had been few and far between which was fine with him. That meant fewer reports and more time actually out on patrol, which is where he wanted to be. Staying mobile meant he could respond if the beast were seen again.

"155, traffic stop," said Sanchez's voice from the radio.

"Go ahead, 155," said dispatch.

"I have a white Chevrolet SUV, Missouri Plates Zebra Sam Five One Sam Frank," said Sanchez. "Vehicle occupied three times."

"Copy 155," said dispatch. "What's your location?"

"Show me just south of the intersection of Highway 13 and State Road DD," she replied.

"Copy 155," said dispatch. "Standby for returns."

---

[14] O.I.S. – Officer Involved Shooting

There was a brief pause before dispatch came back with the plate information.

"155," said dispatch.

"Go ahead," said Sanchez.

"Plate comes back as expired in March," said dispatch, "registered owner Samuel Adam Rayburn. Caution indicator 3, known to assault law enforcement. The subject has multiple warrant hits for felony assault, armed robbery, armed criminal action, and resisting arrest out of Springfield."

"Copy," said Sanchez. "Can you start me another unit, Code 3?"

"125," said Clark, "I'm only a few minutes from there. Show me in route."

"Copy 155, 125," said dispatch. "Additional unit in route. Use caution when dealing with this subject."

Hitting the lights and sirens, Clark pulled a U-turn in the intersection and accelerated hard. The big V-8 engine roared in response and propelled the SUV rapidly down the road. Clark knew he was less than five minutes out, but that could be an eternity if things went south.

"155, they're running," said Sanchez. "Suspect vehicle proceeding southbound towards Kimberling City."

"155," said dispatch, "be advised, Kimberling City PD is responding. Additional Sloan County Units responding, as well."

Clark pushed the accelerator to the floor and mentally willed it to go farther.

"Come on you son-of-a-bitch," he muttered, hitting the rumblers on the siren to get a car out of the way.

With the last vehicle out of the way, Clark kept accelerating until he could see a curve coming up. Letting off the gas, he never touched the brakes. Tires screamed in protest as he took a curve marked for 45 miles per hour at over 90.

"Just passing Kimberling City limits," said Sanchez. "Subject just sideswiped a minivan. They're still running."

"155," said dispatch, "Kimberling City PD is setting up spikes at the next intersection."

"Copy," said Sanchez.

Clark rounded the corner and accelerated hard. Up ahead, he could see the flashing lights of Sanchez's cruiser. He was gaining ground, but not fast enough. He knew that at any moment, the chase could turn into a gunfight when the fleeing suspect decides to turn and fight. He was confident that Sanchez could hold her own in a one on one fight, but there were three suspects.

"They took the ditch and avoided the spikes," said Sanchez. "They're back on the road but took some damage. They're slowing down."

"Goddammit," hissed Clark, striking the steering wheel.

"Shots fired!" called Sanchez. "My vehicle's hit but I'm fine."

"All units," said dispatch. "Shots fired. Repeat shots fired."

Clark was rocketing down the road over a hundred and twenty miles per hour, mentally willing himself to go faster. The fuel gauge on his vehicle was dropping almost as fast as the temperature gauge was rising. He knew that this pursuit couldn't be allowed to go much further.

"Hold it together, baby," he said to the vehicle. "We're almost there."

Up ahead, Clark saw the suspect vehicle deliberately ram a Kimberling City patrol vehicle. The officer behind the wheel overcorrected and hit the soft shoulder, then flipped the car. It flipped numerous times before coming to a stop on its top. The vehicle was smoking, but not on fire.

"125," said Clark. "Suspects rammed a Kimberling City cruiser. The cruiser flipped. Send an ambulance and rescue units. They're right in front of Table Rock Community Bank."

"Copy 125," said dispatch. "Sending rescue units now."

Clark began slowing as he got closer to the pursuit. He could see the suspect vehicle was smoking and showed obvious damage. They had slowed to close to sixty miles per hour. Sanchez was in lead on the pursuit, so Clark pulled in behind her.

"155 to 125," said Sanchez.

"Go," he said.

"You've got a push bumper," she said. "Think you can pull a PIT[15] on this guy?"

Clark knew that it was a supervisor call to make and she was technically the on-scene supervisor. However, it was usually made by a supervisor who wasn't there. If he did it, there was likely going to be hell to pay afterward. He knew that dispatch was listening and so was every other officer in the county. If they wanted to stop him, they had better speak up soon.

"On it," he said with a wicked grin. "Taking the lead."

Sanchez slowed down slightly as Clark pulled to her left and slid into the lead position. Up ahead, Clark could see another SUV coming towards them. It was Brice Meadows and K9 Rocco. Clark smiled slightly, seeing his friend entering the pursuit.

"Here goes," said Clark into the radio.

Clark slid to the left and began overtaking the suspect vehicle slowly, moving into position to shove the rear quarter panel. The plan was to cause them to spin out and end the pursuit. Just as he was getting into place, one of the suspects leaned out the window and fired into Clark's vehicle.

---

[15] PIT – Pursuit Intervention Maneuver. Used to stop fleeing suspect vehicles.

The first two rounds punched through the windshield, striking Clark in the chest and grazing his left cheek. The one in the chest had gone right behind the body armor at the right shoulder. The next rounds went into the right front tire.

Clark felt the wheel going and knew he was about to be out of the pursuit. Cutting the wheel hard, he slammed into the side of the suspect vehicle with all the force his vehicle had left, causing the suspect to spin and lose control before sliding off into the ditch and coming to a stop.

Clark's right-front tire shredded and came off the rim. The rim bit into the asphalt and the vehicle flipped end over end before bouncing to a stop on the driver's side. Glass, plastic, and loose equipment flew through the air as the vehicle settled in place.

"Motherfucker!" screamed Clark, hanging sideways from the seatbelt.

The airbags had deployed, and the windows had exploded, covering him with glass and debris from the now destroyed SUV. There was blood on his face, dripping into his eyes.

Pulling out his pocketknife, Clark cut away the airbag and then cut himself free of the seatbelt. He fell against the inside of the passenger door and almost knocked himself out. It was growing more and more difficult to draw a full breath.

With grim determination, he forced himself to his feet and put a boot to what was left of the windshield, knocking it out onto the ground. He coughed a deep rattling cough and spit bloody phlegm onto the dash.

Even though he had one bullet lodged in his body and was bleeding from numerous cuts and scrapes, he climbed out of the vehicle and looked around. He could see Meadows' vehicle was stopped sideways and Meadows was crouched behind it with his weapon drawn.

His ears were ringing, and his heartbeat thundered in his ears. He couldn't hear anything else. To his left, Sanchez was crouched behind her vehicle while it was being hit with gunfire. Anger surged through him like a dark and powerful tidal wave.

Goddammit," said Clark, drawing his Para Ordinance .45. The dark look on his face was even more terrifying from the blood that covered him and ran in large drops down his cheeks from the glass embedded in his scalp.

Moving towards the back of Sanchez's car, Clark advanced tactically. Keeping himself below the line of fire, he tried to assess the situation. There were three suspects, all shooting from behind their disabled SUV in the ditch, which was about twenty feet down an incline.

Red was beginning to tinge the edges of his vision as Clark moved up next to Sanchez. When he saw that she was bleeding from several cuts to her face and neck, then noticed the bloody spot on her left shoulder where it looked like a bullet had struck her shoulder just past the body armor. Seeing her injured, the rage in him began to boil like a pressure cooker.

He tried to smile at her but wasn't sure if he succeeded. The look she gave him was a mixture of shock and horror. He knew then that it was worse than he realized, but that wasn't going to stop him. He wasn't going to let her fight alone. He just hoped he could stay in the fight long enough to finish it.

"Oh my God," she said, looking at him with wide eyes.

Clark could barely hear her.

"You need a doctor," she said. "You're covered in blood. There's glass stuck in your face and arms."

"You could use one, too," he replied darkly. "I'm not out of this just yet. Get your rifle."

Another deep wracking cough shook him, and he spat blood with bubbles in it onto the ground. He knew from seeing the bubbles that he was hit in the lung. It was only a matter of time before he bled to death internally.

"Ok," she replied, hitting the trunk release on the key fob on her belt.

The trunk popped open and she reached in to retrieve her patrol rifle. Clark grabbed her external plate carrier and handed it to her.

"Put this on," he said, his voice gurgling slightly.

She didn't argue. Holstering her pistol, she slipped into the armor and velcroed it in place. Then she slid the strap from her patrol rifle over her head and chambered a round.

She felt the sweat on the palms of her hands and the almost sickening feeling in her stomach. Despite her time in law enforcement, this was the first time she had been shot at. She could tell from the look on Clark's face that this wasn't his first.

"Get ready to cover me," he said.

"What are you going to do?" she asked, her hands shaking a bit.

"I don't have time to explain," he answered, shaking his head. "Just cover me."

"Got it," she said, with more determination than she felt.

"Hey," he said, "we'll get through this. I promise. I've been through worse. I'll get you through this safe."

"Where?" she asked, bringing her rifle to her shoulder.

"Kandahar," he said without any further elaboration.

Somehow that didn't make her feel any better. She couldn't imagine what he had gone through that was worse than this. Clark waved his hand and got Meadow's attention. Meadows looked at him and held up his hand with three fingers, then began counting down. Meadows checked his magazine, then nodded that he was ready.

"Now!" he said, backing up a few steps.

Sanchez did as she was told and leaned around the bumper, firing at the SUV in the ditch. Meadows saw what she was doing and opened fire as well, forcing the suspects' heads down.

As soon as they started firing, Clark stepped up onto the back bumper then onto the trunk of Sanchez's car. Then he stepped onto the roof and brought his pistol into firing position.

The suspects saw him an instant too late. He was looking down almost directly onto them. His first shot struck one of the suspects in the forehead. The massive .45 caliber hollow point did its job and emptied the contents of the subject's skull onto the ground behind him.

The second subject moved to bring his pistol up and Clark shot him twice in the chest. Dead center mass shots put the subject onto his back with enough damage to the chest to pulverize the heart. He would be dead before the last bullets flew.

The third subject fired on Clark. He felt two more rounds strike him in the trauma plate and knock him back a step. Returning fire, Clark hit him once in the throat and once on the bridge of the nose, just below the left eye. A fountain of crimson gore erupted from the man's head and he fell like a puppet with the strings cut. Chunks of brain and bone hit the ground like thick raindrops.

Then there was a sudden and deafening silence. All eyes were on Clark, who stood there with his weapon still at the ready and searching for another threat. He looked around the area for additional threats, then slowly holstered his weapon.

The silence was total at that moment. No one spoke and no one moved. Clark glanced around and saw Meadows start moving towards the suspects with his weapon up and ready. He was giving commands, but Clark couldn't hear him now. The ringing had returned and the red tinge in his vision was nearly blocking out everything.

The adrenalin was fading fast and the pain was beginning to come through. He could see Sanchez reaching towards him, but he was falling. Then there was darkness. Through it, he could very distantly hear the voice of Sanchez. It too was fading away slowly.

"155, we have an officer down," she said. "We have an officer down! Request immediate rescue units. Officer Down!"

Then he heard nothing more.

Meadows ran up and helped Sanchez lower Clark down onto the ground.

"He killed them all!" said Meadows, almost hysterical. "Holy shit! Did you just fucking see that shit? He fucking killed all three of them like it was nothing!"

"I saw," answered Sanchez. "We've got to slow this bleeding, or he won't make it."

"What do you need?" asked Meadows.

"There's a trauma kit on the front of his plate carrier," she snapped, pointing towards the destroyed SUV. "Get it and get back here as fast as you can."

"On it," replied Meadows, sprinting towards the overturned SUV.

"Stay with me, baby," said Sanchez, pleadingly. Hot tears were stinging the corners of her eyes and running down her cheeks. "I love you, baby. Please hang on."

Meadows found every window in the SUV had shattered on impact. It only took him a second to find the heavy plate carrier. Attached to the front was an olive drab pouch about eight inches by four with a medical cross on the front. Yanking it free from the molle tabs on the carrier, he turned and sprinted back to Sanchez.

"Got it," he yelled as he dropped to his knees beside her.

Reaching into Clark's left front pocket, Sanchez pulled out the knife she knew he always carried and began cutting away the shirt. Meadows pulled the trauma shears out of the kit and began cutting away the shirt and the Velcro straps holding the armor in place.

Once they had Clark stripped to the waist, Sanchez began pulling the items out of the kit and laying them on the ground next to her.

122

Once they were set in place, she began her assessment. Clark was breathing in shallow, labored breaths, but he was breathing on his own. There was still a significant quantity of blood coming from the chest wound and some of the cuts.

"Ok," said Sanchez. "He's breathing. Let's get a seal in place over that chest wound, just in case it hit a lung."

"Got it," answered Meadows, taking the offered packet from Sanchez.

He quickly wiped away the blood with a piece of the shirt, then waited for Clark to exhale. Once he exhaled, Meadows placed the seal over the center of the wound.

"Done," said Meadows, glancing over at Sanchez.

"Roll him onto his side," she said. "Wound side down."

"Why?" asked Meadows.

"If he's bleeding into the lung," she explained, "then the one that isn't injured will stay clear so he can breathe."

"Gotcha," said Meadows, rolling Clark onto his right side.

"There's no exit wound on his back," said Sanchez. "We just gotta make sure he keeps breathing until an ambulance arrives. You watch his breathing while I put some gauze over the worst of these cuts."

"Holy shit," said Meadows. "How's he still alive? How the fuck is he still alive?"

"Because he's the toughest man I know," said Sanchez. "Now watch his breathing."

Chapter Eleven
The Long Road

"To know what life is worth you have to risk it once in a while."
Jean-Paul Sartre

Clark had vague recollections of what came next. There were brief flashes as he was loaded into the big blue helicopter. There was a strange sensation of flying as he faded in and out of consciousness. The pain was all-encompassing. It filled every fiber of his being, bringing clarity that only the dying find.

For an instant, his mind raced to another time in another helicopter. Only this one was a US Army Blackhawk lifting him from the battlefield in Kandahar Province. He'd lost a lot of blood then. It was also the first time he'd felt like he was dying. He didn't have another clear memory until he woke in a hospital in Germany.

This time was different. He woke up when the chopper touched down on the roof of a big hospital on the south side of Springfield. He recognized the star within a star logo on the back of the building. Glancing down, he saw the chest tube and IV tube sending blood into his arm.

Pain lanced through him as they moved him from the chopper to the awaiting gurney. Looking up, he locked eyes with someone he recognized.

"Hey, Steve," he wheezed through clenched teeth.

The nurse looked at him in confusion before recognition dawned on him.

"Daniel?" asked the nurse. "Holy shit!"

Mercifully, he blacked out again. This time, he didn't wake up for hours. He slept through the surgery to remove the bullet and to extract numerous pieces of glass embedded in his skin. He didn't regain consciousness until he was in a hospital room.

124

Opening his eyes, it took a moment for them to adjust to the light. Images were blurry and slowly began to take on form and clarity. Sitting next to him was Sanchez. She was asleep in the chair to the right of this bed, holding his hand.

There were flowers and balloons on the table at end of his bed. No curtain beside the bed showed that he was in a private room. From the window, he could tell it was dark but had no idea what time it was. The lights of what he knew had to be Springfield lit up the window like the twinkling of so many Christmas lights. Under other circumstances, he would have admired the view.

Clark performed a quick self-assessment. There were bandages on his head and arms. His chest hurt and there was a tube sticking out draining fluid. With a sigh, he closed his eyes and let sleep take him back into the dreamless darkness.

*****

The next thirteen days passed agonizingly slow. The only thing that kept him from going insane was the fact that Sanchez had barely left his side. Since they were both on administrative leave from the shooting, she didn't have to be back on duty. That was a plus.

Despite listening to the scanner, no one had seen or heard anything that might have been the creature. Clark was beginning to wonder if the beast had decided to move on or if the Feds had taken it down. No reports of missing people, no sightings, and nothing out of the usual with farm animals or pets. It was as if the thing had just vanished.

The investigation was still "ongoing" when Clark was released from the hospital. The nurse pushed him down to the main entrance in a wheelchair, despite his protests that he could walk. Sanchez was waiting for him at the entrance with her personal car, a shiny red 2015 Chevy Camaro ZL1 with black racing stripes on the hood.

"Can I drive?" he asked, smiling.

"No," she replied. "Not while you're on pain killers. Maybe when you feel better."

Clark winced as he got into the passenger side but didn't complain. The pain was manageable now and he felt better than he figured he would all things considered. The wound was healing nicely and the stitches from the cuts were all removed. It was going to leave a few interesting scars, but he was expected to make a full recovery.

Turning out of the hospital parking lot, Sanchez headed into town. The bustling streets of Springfield were much busier than either of them was used to, coming from such a rural area. Clark didn't say anything, waiting for her to explain why they weren't heading out of town.

"I thought we'd grab something to eat," she said, grinning. "I figured you're sick of hospital food."

"I could stand a good meal," he agreed, still watching her out of the corner of his eye.

After a few turns at large intersections, she turned left off Campbell street into a Springfield icon. A local place called Mexican Villa.

"What made you decide on this place?" he asked. "I'm not complaining, though. It's great."

"This is where we went on our first date," she replied, with a wink. "I thought we'd come back here to celebrate you getting out of the hospital."

"Sounds good to me," said Clark. "I'm always happy to get a burrito enchilada-style."

"That's what everyone says," she said, chuckling.

"You mean there are other things on the menu?" he replied, grinning.

As they entered the building, the hostess smiled and directed them to the back room without hesitation.

"That's odd," said Clark. "She didn't even ask how many in our party."

As they rounded the corner, Clark understood why. The room was filled with cops, nurses, and other first responders. They were friends that he had known for years. All in all, there had to be over fifty people gathered there.

Applause and cheers sounded as he entered the room. People patted him on the back and shook his hand. The entire room was decorated with blue balloons and streamers. There were chairs in the middle, waiting for him and Sanchez to join the party. On one table were a large cake and several boxes of donuts from Hurts Donuts. They were chocolate donuts with chocolate icing and a line of blue icing across them.

"Thank you, guys," said Clark as he was guided towards his seat.

"Shit," said Meadows, "it's the least we can do."

"I just did my job," said Clark. "Same as you."

"Dude," replied Meadows, "you have no idea. My department released my dashcam video. It's like something out of an action film. It still freaks me out to watch it, and I was there."

"The video has had over a million views online," said Konrad. "You're an internet star, buddy."

"For what?" asked Clark.

"It was pretty badass," said Meadows. "You came out of your crashed SUV covered in blood, charged in, and took out three armed suspects. I wouldn't have believed the story if I hadn't been there. The dashcam doesn't do it justice."

"It was a team effort," said Clark. "If you guys hadn't forced their heads down, I never could have gotten into position to take the shots."

"That's not why we're celebrating," said Sanchez. "We're celebrating because you're alive. It was a damned close call."

Several people brought him gifts. His friend Steve, the ER nurse, brought him a bottle of 15-year-old Dalmore Scotch.

"Glad you pulled through, buddy," he said, handing him the bottle. "I didn't think you'd make it when we pulled you off that chopper."

"That makes two of us," said Clark. "I had my doubts, too."

"Well," said Sanchez, "I never doubted it for a second. I knew you'd pull through."

"Don't let her fool you," said Konrad. "She didn't stop praying and crying until they said you'd pulled through the surgery."

Sanchez punched Konrad lightly in the shoulder as she laughed.

"I might have been a little worried," she admitted.

"You're damned lucky that bullet hit your rib and glanced off," said Steve. "If it had punched through and into the lung, you might not have made it to the hospital. As it was, the bullet fractured two ribs and that caused a bleed in your right lung."

"I don't feel all that lucky," said Clark, rubbing his ribcage gingerly.

"Hey buddy," said Steve, "a couple of cracked ribs will heal a hell of a lot faster than a collapsed lung or if it had hit your heart."

"Fair enough," said Clark with a grin.

****

Heading south out of town, Clark smiled over at Sanchez as she was driving. He felt content for the first time in his life, watching her and knowing that she had stayed by his side during his recovery.

"What are you staring at me for?" she asked, grinning over at him.

"Just thinking," he replied. "Nothing big."

"Did I tell you that was incredibly brave," she said. "Brave, and incredibly stupid. We had them pinned down. You didn't have to risk your life."

"I know," he said, shrugging. "I also knew that in minutes I was going to be out of the fight. I was losing a lot of blood. I had to end it before I became a liability."

"I get it," she replied. "You did what you had to. It doesn't make it any easier on me."

"Sorry, babe," he said, genuinely. "My only concern was for protecting you. I wasn't worried about me."

"Well," she said, frowning, "start worrying. I want you to stick around for a while. You know, at least until someone better comes along."

She smiled and winked at him after the last comment.

"Well," he said, "I hear Prescott's single."

"Ewww," she said, miming throwing up. "That's disgusting."

Clark just chuckled.

"Did you hear any reports that might have been that thing?" he asked. "While I was out."

"Not a word," she answered. "Maybe the government guys got it."

"Maybe," agreed Clark, "but I seriously doubt it. There haven't been any recent reports anywhere near here."

"Have you been checking?' she asked.

"I spent the last two weeks lying in a hospital bed with nothing to do," he replied. "So, I've been reading everything I can find on Bigfoot and anything like it."

"How much is out there?" she asked.

"More than you might think," he replied. "I used to think it as a big joke or a hoax, but there is just too much out there for it all to be fake. Tens of thousands of sightings all over the world."

"Eyewitnesses can be wrong," she said, frowning.

"They also have footprint casts," he added, "hair, blood, handprints, and video footage that can't be debunked by professional video experts."

"Why not any bodies or bones?" she said, glancing at him.

"You saw how smart that thing is," said Clark, wincing as he shifted his weight in the seat. "It's easily smart enough to hide or bury its dead. Besides that, I've spent half my life hunting the deep woods in North America. Do you know how many bear skeletons I've come across?"

"No idea," she said, glancing at him out of the corner of her eye.

"Not one," he replied. "And we all know for a fact that they exist. No one argues that, but most people have never seen one outside of a zoo or on TV."

"So," said Sanchez, attempting to change the subject. "Do you want to go back to your house, or do you feel like recovering for a few days at my apartment?"

"I need to go by the department and pick up all of my gear that was in my SUV," answered Clark. "After that, I don't really care."

"Your stuff is at my place," she said with a grin. "I asked Konrad to pick it up and take it to my place last week. Do you need to go in for any interviews?"

"No," he replied. "Detectives from Sloan County and Missouri State Patrol came in and interviewed me in the hospital. I just have to wait until the investigation clears before I can go back to work."

"You mean until the doctors clear you to go back to work," she corrected. "You've got a long road ahead of you to fully recover."

"I honestly feel better," he said. "Not quite ready for duty, but I'm pretty good."

"Well," said Sanchez with a smirk, "I'll just wait for the doctor to clear you before I take your word for it, thank you."

While she was driving, Clark started going through his phone to check messages he might have missed while he was in the hospital. He found a text from his friend Greg Hanley that works security for Silver Dollar City. It simply said, "call me when you get the chance. I heard something weird." It was dated the day after Clark was shot.

"Might have something here," said Clark without looking up from his phone. "I got a message from Hanley at SDC. I'm gonna call him back."

Hitting the call button, Clark put it on speaker so Sanchez could listen. After ringing four times, he heard a familiar voice pick up.

"Hey jackass," said Hanley. "How the hell are you? You still in the hospital?"

"Just got out today," said Clark. "Sorry, it took me a bit to get back to you."

"I heard about the gunfight, *brochacho*," said Hanley. "Hell of a sight. I watched the video. Still can't believe it was you."

"Me neither," said Clark. "It kinda just happened. I didn't think about it. I just did it."

"Yeah," interjected Sanchez, "he's an idiot."

"I've been saying that for years," said Hanley. "Glad you came through it, buddy. How are you holding up?"

"I'm good," said Clark. "I just read your text. What did you hear?"

"Well," said Hanley, "the night you got shot, I heard automatic weapons fire coming from across the cove below the park and to the west. It was late at night and no visitors were on park. I heard it again for the next three nights. On the last night, I heard screaming too."

"Shit," said Clark. "That's some pretty thick timber across the cove from the park."

"Yeah," agreed Hanley. "Tough to get to by vehicle. Mostly inaccessible unless you go by ATV[16], horse, or boat. Did you find out what happened?"

"That's the really weird part," said Hanley. "Indian Point denied hearing anything at all and when I called Sloan County, they said they'd send a deputy, but no one ever came."

"That is pretty damned odd," said Clark. "Anything else."

"Yeah," said Hanley. "I saw a blacked-out Blackhawk circling over the area. Never saw it land."

"Did you see it swing load[17] anything?" asked Clark.

"No," replied Hanley. "I watched it as much as I could. I never saw it pick up anything or anyone. And there's no place over there clear enough where it could land. It's been damned quiet since that night."

"If you see or hear anything else," said Clark, "let me know as quickly as you can."

"Will do," answered Hanley. "You take care of yourself, brother. When you feel up to it, I'll hook you up with a shitload of park passes. Something to keep you busy while they clear your shoot."

"Thanks, bud," said Clark, hanging up the phone.

"Well," said Sanchez. "Maybe they got the thing, after all."

"Maybe," agreed Clark. "Or they hurt it and it went to ground. If they had managed to kill it, I think they would have seen them lift the body out with the chopper."

"I hope it's gone," said Sanchez, glancing into the trees on either side of the road and the growing darkness.

"Me too," said Clark. "But I seriously doubt it."

---

[16] ATV – all terrain vehicles
[17] Swing Load – pick up from a helicopter using ropes or harness.

LAKEVIEW MAN

Chapter Twelve
Penumbra

*"It is a mistake to fancy that horror is associated inextricably
with darkness, silence, and solitude."*
H. P. Lovecraft

It was well after dark when they pulled into the parking lot of the neighborhood where Sanchez lived, just off Cottage Hill Road. It was a small, two-bedroom duplex in Kimberling City. Ironically, it was only a few blocks from where the gunfight had happened.

The greenish-yellow incandescence of the streetlights lit up the neighborhood as Clark slowly exited the passenger side of the car. Standing slowly, he winced as his ribs gave him a brief shock of pain, but it was bearable.

Slowly, he looked around the neighborhood, peering deeply into the shadows between the houses and beneath the trees. Nothing seemed out of place. Dogs barked and insects made their droning sounds, but nothing gave him any indication of trouble.

"I don't have a gun on," he said after a moment. "I feel fucking naked."

"I know," agreed Sanchez. "I do, though. They still have our duty weapons until the investigation is over."

"What are you carrying?" he asked.

"My backup," she said. "Baby Glock 26. Do you need one?"

"I've got plenty of extras," said Clark. "Is my bag in your house?"

"Uh, yeah," she said. "Konrad brought it with your other gear."

"Good," said Clark. "There is a couple of spares in there."

"A couple?" said Sanchez, shaking her head in mock disbelief.

"Yeah," said Clark. "After what happened, I think I'll make room for more. I want plenty of gear on hand."

"We can run by your place tomorrow," she said. "For tonight, I think we can survive on what we have inside."

"It'll do, I suppose," he said, grinning. "For now."

Heading inside, Clark stopped on the porch while Sanchez fumbled with her keys. The dogs had stopped barking and the insects had faded away.

"How far from the lake are we here?" he asked, glancing around.

"A block or so," she answered, unlocking the door. "Why?"

"The sounds have gone," he said, motioning her inside.

She didn't hesitate and slipped through the door, flipping on the lights as she went in. Clark didn't go in after her. He just stood there, listening and looking around.

Sanchez returned with his patrol rifle, handing it to him along with two more magazines. Slipping the mags into his back pocket, Clark held the weapon at low ready and began looking around.

"There's no way it could know we're back," she said, quietly. "Much less know where I live."

"It found *my* house, didn't it?" replied Clark, still watching warily.

"But how did it know we were back in town?" she asked, incredulously. "It's not like it has GPS locked on my car."

"Maybe I'm just being paranoid," said Clark, glancing around once more.

Before Sanchez could respond, a loud boom split the night followed by a sizzling sound. Red and green light illuminated the back of the house.

"Fireworks," said Sanchez. "There's why the dogs aren't barking."

"You're probably right," replied Clark, still not coming inside.

More fireworks lit up the night sky and echoed off into the distance. Clark could smell the burning gunpowder on the breeze and see the glowing colors in the sky above the house. With one last look around, he stepped back through the door and shut it behind him. Careful to lock both the knob and the deadbolt, he sat his patrol rifle against his pack and placed the extra mags in one pouch.

"You hungry?" asked Sanchez. "We can order a pizza if you want."

"Not really," he replied. "I'm still full from that burrito enchilada-style."

"Then how about we pick out a movie and just lay on the couch?" asked Sanchez. "I'll be more than happy to just be together."

"Sounds good to me," replied Clark. "You pick. I'll be right back."

Clark moved through the duplex checking windows and doors, making sure they were locked. When he got to the sliding glass doors that led out onto the small deck, he froze. No lock in the world would make those safe if that thing wanted inside.

Glancing around the small, privacy-fenced back yard, he made sure there was nothing there. Verifying it was locked, he dropped the wooden rod into a place that would prevent the door from opening. Then he closed the blinds for good measure.

"Relax," said Sanchez. "I don't think it knows we're here."

"You're probably right," answered Clark. "I'm just not taking any unnecessary chances. Call me paranoid."

"Fair enough," she replied. "What kind of movie are you interested in."

"Nothing crazy," replied Clark. "Maybe a comedy?"

"That works for me," said Sanchez. "I don't think I could do a cop movie. I think it might be a while before I want to watch anything with a gunfight in it."

"I imagine," said Clark. "I was that way when I got back from deployment. I didn't want to watch any military or cop movies. Not that the fight scenes bothered me, just that most of them are so unrealistic as to be laughable."

"What do you think about what you just did?" she asked. "If I hadn't seen it, I wouldn't have believed it."

"Did Meadows say that it was on the internet?" asked Clark.

"Yeah," she replied. "Do you want to see it?"

Clark thought about it a minute before answering.

"Would it bother you?" he asked. "I mean, I'd like to see it because my memory of that night is a blur. I'd like to watch it if it won't bother you."

"It will," she replied, "but it's ok. I think it would be good for you to see it. Maybe it'll get it through your thick skull just how dangerous it was."

Finding the video on the internet, Sanchez brought it up and played it on the television. Clark watched with keen interest, seeing the entire thing from the perspective of Meadows' dashcam. His vehicle had been parked at a nearly perfect angle to catch everything from the PIT maneuver until the end. Clark could tell that the video had been cut right as he was falling when he passed out.

He had to admit, it was intense. Sanchez watched his face more than she watched the video. She watched as his hand went involuntarily to the places where impacts and glass could be seen. She knew he was reliving it all, wound by painful wound. Once the video was over, he turned towards her.

"I see what you mean," he said. "That was tough to watch."

"Let's just go to bed," she said. "I think I don't feel like watching a movie."

"Fine with me," he said.

They headed upstairs to the bedroom. Clark grabbed his pack and the patrol rifle, setting them beside the bed where he was going to

137

sleep. Sanchez didn't say a word. She knew that he was just being prepared. She also knew that there was no way he was going to rest without them close to hand.

After they changed and brushed their teeth, they slipped beneath the covers together. Clark reached for her and pulled her close.

"Easy there, tiger," she said, smiling. "I don't want to hurt you."

"Then be gentle," he said, kissing her.

"I'll try, but no promises," she said, through the kisses. "Now lay back and let me do all the work."

*****

Hours later, Clark lay awake and stared at the ceiling. Sanchez was asleep on his arm. They were both exhausted, but sleep would not come for Clark. His mind would not stop racing over the things he had learned about the creatures and the things it had done.

Slipping gently out from beneath her, he crept out of the bed. Reaching into his pack, he took out a can of chewing tobacco and headed out onto the little balcony. The sliding glass door made little noise as he opened it and stepped out into the night air.

It was well after three in the morning and he was completely naked. There weren't any lights on in any of the surrounding houses, so he figured he was safe enough. Especially since the porch light wasn't on.

Breaking the seal on the can with his thumbnail, he packed his lip full and let the flavor wash over him. The nicotine entered his bloodstream and he felt the rush. It had been two weeks since his last chew and it felt amazing. It also had a soothing effect on his nerves.

Leaning against the rail, he spat the first bit of juice into the darkness of the backyard. He knew he wasn't going to hit the deck and that only grass lay beneath this balcony. He stood there, letting the cool night breeze wash over his body, easing sore muscles and sending a chilling sensation over the numerous fresh scars where the stitches had already been removed.

Taking it all in, he let the stress of the last weeks bleed away with the endorphins that the chew had released into his system. The cool night air helped him feel refreshed and he started to relax. As his tension flowed away and his mind felt refreshed, that was when he noticed things that had slipped past him before. There were no night sounds.

Looking around, he could see the lake through the trees across the way. It was a few hundred yards away, but close enough to smell the water. Something wasn't right, however. He just couldn't put his finger on it.

Letting his senses ease into the search, he closed his eyes and listened. No sounds of the usual insects, no animals, not even the sounds of traffic. It was dead quiet.

Breathing in deeply, he couldn't smell anything unusual. The breeze was blowing from his right to his left, bringing in small hints of the lake and of honeysuckle that was growing somewhere nearby.

Peering into the darkness, he searched for patterns. For shapes of anything that stood out. It was an old trick that he learned hunting deer, long ago as a boy.

Soon, he noticed something. It was stock-still, not moving in the slightest. The shape was indiscernible against all the other shapes in the trees near the lake. The more he looked, the more he became aware of something else. A shadow within the darkness.

It didn't move or do anything that would draw attention to itself. It stood as still as the large oak tree that it stood beside. It wasn't a motion or shape that drew his attention. It was the distinct feeling that it was looking back at him. He could feel its gaze upon him.

He locked his eyes on what he was certain was the creature. In the depths of the darkness, he was sure he could see the faintest glow of the creature's eyes. It was so faint as to be nearly unnoticeable, but it was there. He could even barely perceive when it would slowly blink.

In his mind, he felt a vague uneasiness and a strong desire to go towards the creature. It seemed so strong and almost lulled him into just going out there to find it. To finally see it face to face.

"What are you doing out here?" asked Sanchez, slipping up to the rail beside him. "And why are you naked?"

Clark turned to glance at her, the trance was broken. She was wearing a red silky bathrobe that was tied around her slender waist. She slipped under his arm and up against him.

"I couldn't sleep," he replied. "So, I came out here for a dip."

"You could have at least put on some underwear," she said, chuckling.

"I didn't think anyone would notice," he said, smiling.

Turning to look back into the darkness, the shadow was gone. No sign or indication that it had ever been there. Clark mentally marked the spot where it had been and decided he would go look for tracks when it was light enough to see them.

"Let's go back to bed," said Sanchez, smiling softly.

"I'll be there in a minute," he said, returning the smile. "I just want to finish my dip."

"Ok," she said, slipping out from beneath his arm. "I'm going in. It's a bit chilly out here."

"I think it feels good," he replied, with a soft chuckle.

As she headed inside, he reached down and patted her gently on the right side of her butt.

"Don't take too long," she said, disappearing inside.

Clark turned back to the trees and began scanning the tree line. Insect sounds were beginning to return and somewhere a cat squawked into the night. The creature was gone.

"Why do I have a distinct feeling that thing has been waiting for me to return?" Clark whispered to the empty darkness.

LAKEVIEW MAN

The darkness, for all its mystery, did not reply.

Chapter Thirteen
Fresh Tracks

*"Evil can be a teacher, if you look at the
wisdom of its negative power."*
Tom Brown, Jr.

Clark awoke to the smell of frying bacon. Glancing at the clock, he could see it was after nine in the morning. Slipped out of bed and put on his clothes, then headed downstairs. He arrived just as Sanchez was putting the last of the food on the table. There were scrambled eggs with cheese, bacon, sausage links, biscuits and gravy, and toast. There was a tub of butter and a jar of honey on the table, as well.

"I was wondering if I was going to have to come up there to wake you up?" she mused.

"What's the occasion?" he asked, sliding into his chair.

"The first morning out of the hospital," she said. "I wanted to make it special."

"Well, you certainly did that," he replied. "Thank you for cooking all of this."

"I don't get the urge to cook often," she said, sliding into her chair, "but when I do, I go all out."

"What else can you cook?" he asked, smiling.

"Well," she said, "I can make a lot of meals you'd recognize. And even more, you wouldn't. My paternal grandmother taught me how to cook. She grew up in a little village in Spain called *Cudillero*. They immigrated to the United States just before World War Two."

"Have you ever been there?" he asked, starting to fill his plate.

"No," she replied, "but I've always wanted to."

"Maybe we could go there together," said Clark. "Once all of this is through."

"The investigation?" she asked.

143

"Yeah," he replied, "and I'm fully recovered."

"I'd love that," she replied. "Maybe to celebrate us being back together."

"Maybe," he said, smiling.

After they ate, he helped her clear the dishes and start the dishwasher. In turn, she joined him in the shower. Despite wanting to, Sanchez limited the shower activities to merely cleanliness. Clark was favoring his ribs and didn't complain too loudly. He refused to tell her exactly how much pain he was really in and he also refused to take any more pain medication. He hated how it made him feel out of control.

After they got out of the shower, she helped him dry off gently. Drying the skin with a towel, she traced her fingers over every purple scar and wound. She kissed the biggest ones and ran her fingers along with the older scars on his back and chest. There were many scars.

Picking up the medkit, she applied antibiotic ointment to the wound and placed a fresh bandage over it. After taping all four sides of the bandage with surgical tape, she smoothed it down with her fingertips to be certain it was properly sealed.

"There," she said, softly. "Better?"

"Yes," he said. "Thank you."

Once dressed in a pair of jeans and a loose-fitting St. Louis Blues jersey, Clark took out a spare pistol from his pack and slipped the holster onto his belt. Then he added a mag pouch for three additional magazines. He checked the Glock 19 9mm to be sure it was loaded with one in the chamber before holstering the weapon and clipping his badge next to the weapon.

"Going somewhere?" asked Sanchez as she put on her jeans.

"Just thought I'd go for a walk around the neighborhood," he replied. "I think the air might do me some good."

"Want me to go with you?" she asked, reaching for her t-shirt.

"Nah," he said, nonchalantly. "I just need to get some air and to stretch my legs. I haven't gotten much exercise the last few weeks and I need to start slow."

"Ok," said Sanchez. "I'll hang here. I need to do some laundry. If you need me, send me a text and I'll come to get you."

"I'll be fine," he assured her. "It's not like I'm going for a run. Just a leisurely stroll. Nothing exciting."

"Still," she continued. "Take your cell phone with you, just in case."

"Yes, mom," he chided but did as she asked, slipping his phone into his back pocket. "I'll be back in a few."

With that, he headed out the front door. Careful to keep his baggy shirt over his pistol to avoid freaking out the neighbors, he walked slowly and surveyed the area as he walked. Taking a moment to put in a fresh dip of tobacco, he glanced around the neighborhood.

The trees didn't get close enough to her place to allow the creature to sneak up without being seen. Even during the late-night hours, there was just too much open ground for it to have to cover. He felt relatively safe in thinking it wouldn't try to get too close.

As he rounded the corner, the trees where he felt more than saw the creature's presence came into view. The undergrowth was thick enough that it didn't allow anyone to see too far into the trees, even during the day. There were a few paths that had been worn through usage that led down to the lake, but the rest was all overgrown.

Walking over to the edge of the trees, he began examining the ground closely. Moving closer to the spot where he thought the creature had been, he wanted to check the area around it before he got too close to make sure he didn't destroy any other signs.

"Something I can do for you, asshole?" asked a male voice.

Clark looked across the street and a male approximately thirty years old, wearing baggy jean shorts, a white tank-top, and carrying a baseball bat approaching him from the driveway of a house across the street.

145

"Not really," replied Clark.

"Do you fuckin' live here?" asked the man, still coming towards him with the bat brought up to his shoulder.

"Do you own this land?" asked Clark.

"No," said the man. "It don't fuckin' matter. I don't like strangers walkin' through my hood."

The man was still about thirty yards away and getting closer. Clark lifted his shirt to reveal his badge and coincidentally, the pistol.

"That's close enough," said Clark. "Since you don't own this land, then I suggest you go back home."

"I ain't afraid of no fuckin' badge," said the man, clearly not noticing the pistol.

"How about a Glock?" asked Clark. "Does that get your attention?"

"Not if I can get to you before you can draw," said the man.

"Look," said Clark. "Do you have any idea how much paperwork will be involved when I shoot you?"

"What?" asked the man, stopping in his tracks. "How about when I beat your fuckin' cop skull in for you?"

"Well, if you keep coming towards me with that bat," cautioned Clark, "you're going to find out."

"You got a goddamned warrant?" demanded the man.

"For what?" asked Clark. "Walking in the grass. How about this, you walk away and mind your own business. I'm not here looking for you or anyone in this neighborhood."

"What the fuck are you lookin' for, then?" asked the man, angrily.

Clark was beginning to lose patience with the man.

"Look," said Clark, biting back his anger, "if that was any of your goddamned business, I would have fucking told you, already. I don't want or need your fucking permission to be here. Now walk the fuck away."

The man looked like he was considering rushing him with the bat, so Clark very gently placed his hand on the grip of the pistol.

"You make me pull," said Clark, his voice ice-cold and barely above a whisper, "I'll put one between your eyes. Walk away, now!"

The man just stared defiantly at him before slowly backing away. He kept his eyes on Clark as he backed towards his driveway.

"I'll be watchin' you, asshole," said the man.

"Sounds like a grand time," said Clark. "Why don't you avoid the Christmas rush and go ahead and fuck off right now."

The man looked slightly confused, like he wanted to make a snappy comeback but couldn't think of one.

"If you're looking for something smart to say," said Clark sarcastically, "I don't have all day. I know it might take you a while. If you like, you can go home and write it down when you finally think of one. You can give it to me later."

"Fuck you, asshole," snarled the man.

"He said instead of a witty response," said Clark, mockingly. "Is that really the best you can do?"

The man looked like he was about to have a stroke. His face was turning multiple shades of red and there was spit on his lips.

"You have a nice day, now," said Clark, smiling and waving at the man, dismissively.

Turning around, the man stormed into a house. Clark took note of the address and filed it away. He made a mental note to ask Meadows if he knew the asshole and find out if he had any warrants.

Clark waited for a few minutes to make sure the man wasn't going to come back out with a gun before going back to inspect the ground. Keeping half an eye on the house, Clark looked for tracks or signs of disturbance in the undergrowth. Since it had been weeks since the last rain, the ground was hard-packed, and nothing looked out of place. If there had been any trace of that rancid smell, it was already gone.

Following the trail down to the edge of the lake, he looked around the damp ground at the edge of the water. A few yards away, he found what he was looking for. Two massive prints leading into the water. One was partially filled with water. Like the times before, it had used the lake to make its getaway.

He winced in pain as he knelt next to the tracks. Ignoring the pain, he took out his cellphone and brought up the camera. After snapping a few pictures, he backtracked to the tree where he knew it had been. There he began searching for hair or scat. Finding neither, he did manage to find two impressions in the ground clutter. Although the leaves and sticks were too thick for him to find a discernable print, he could see where it had to have stood.

Looking over the bark, he looked up and down the tree. About seven feet up, he found a tuft of dark hair stuck in the bark. Fishing through his pockets, he managed to find a folded piece of paper in his wallet. Collecting the hair with the paper so he didn't contaminate it, he folded the paper and slipped it into his wallet. Then he went back to checking the ground.

He looked up when he heard a vehicle approaching. Glancing up, he saw a familiar-looking Kimberling City Police K9 SUV approaching him. It was Meadows. Pulling to a stop, Meadows got out when he saw Clark.

"Let me guess," said Clark, stepping out of the trees, "some asshole called 911 about someone claiming to be a cop?"

"Something like that," said Meadows. "He also claimed you were waving a pistol around and threatening him."

"I never drew it," said Clark, "but I did put my hand on it when he kept coming towards me with a baseball bat."

"He failed to mention that part," said Meadows.

Just then, the man emerged from his house and started angrily walking towards them.

"Well, shit," said Clark. "Speak of the devil. Here comes fuckface."

"I know that asshole," said Meadows. "That's Morris Avery. He's got a rap sheet as long as my Johnson."

"So, no charge history then?" asked Clark with a wicked grin. "Must be a really short list."

"Smartass," said Meadows. "He's got an extensive history. Mostly drugs and drug-related. One attempted robbery that he got reduced. Pled down to probation."

"So, a real winner then," said Clark.

"Basically," replied Meadows.

Avery continued to advance towards them with an angry look on his face.

"I want this asshole arrested," snarled Avery.

"Morris Avery," said Meadows, "meet Deputy Clark. You might have heard of him. He was the deputy involved in the shootout a few blocks from here a couple of weeks back."

Avery froze in his tracks.

"That was you?" he asked, looking at Clark with an odd expression.

Clark only smiled at him.

"Mr. Avery," began Meadows, "are you aware that filing a false report and abusing 911 are both crimes?"

"What?" said Avery, clearly confused.

"I've known Deputy Clark for years and I doubt seriously he was waving his gun around," said Meadows. "In fact, if he had pulled his weapon, it was likely he would have shot you. If you'd come at me with a bat, I would have."

149

"W…W…What?" stammered Avery.

"No harm done," said Clark. "I think he's learned his lesson."

"Is that true, Mister Avery?" asked Meadows.

"Uh," said Avery, "I didn't know he was really a cop."

"Well, I can assure you that he is," replied Meadows.

Avery looked confused and looked back and forth between Clark and Meadows.

"So, why is he in my fuckin' hood?" demanded Avery.

"Well," began Clark, "since this is still America, I don't need a reason. Also, this isn't exactly the 'hood' as you called it. Nor does it belong to you."

Avery looked angrily at him but said nothing.

"So, why don't you go back to fucking off, now?" said Clark. "For one, you don't need to know why I do a goddamned thing. For another, you need to stay the fuck away from me before I decide to run you for warrants. Understand that, dumbass?"

Avery looked like he wanted to say something but thought better of it. Turning around, he headed back to his house at a brisk pace.

"Yep," said Clark. "He's got warrants."

"You have such a wonderful way with people," said Meadows. "I can truly see why people just adore you."

"It's my winning smile," said Clark, with a grin.

"Asshole," said Meadows, grinning. "I think you made a friend, there."

"Me too," said Clark. "Might get a Christmas card from him this year."

"I sincerely doubt it," said Meadows. "For one thing, I doubt he can spell, much less fill out an entire card. Can you stay out of trouble if I leave or are you gonna end up shooting him?"

"Well, it's early," said Clark. "Honestly, it's really up to him."

"Might not look good," said Meadows. "You shooting someone while on administrative leave."

"Speaking of administrative leave," said Clark. "How are you back to work already?"

"Prosecutors cleared me, already," said Meadows. "Ballistics came back, and my weapon never hit any of the subjects."

"What about Sanchez, then?" asked Clark.

"Not yet," said Meadows, "but I'm sure it's coming. Since it was her call originally, they'll probably keep her included until they clear you, too. From what my FOP[18] lawyer was saying, it might take them a while. There are a lot of people looking at this incident. Did you know the families of those shitbags are trying to sue?"

"Doesn't surprise me," said Clark. "Always happens. Never mind the fact that they fired on an officer first and tried to kill the three of us. Hell, they put one of your guys in the hospital. How is McNamara, by the way?"

"Mac's a tough kid," said Meadows. "He's got a broken collarbone and left arm. He'll be out of action for a while, but he'll be back."

"Good," said Clark. "Let him know I asked about him. I don't know him that well, but he seems like a good kid."

"He's gonna be a damned good officer," said Meadows, "once he tones down the blue flame a bit."

"Well, he's young," said Clark. "Give him a bit to knock off the academy edges."

"Yeah," said Meadows. "He's got good instincts. I think he's gonna do well."

---

[18] FOP – Fraternal Order of Police – like a union for police officers.

"Sweet," said Clark. "Maybe this incident will be an eye-opener for him. See that this shit isn't all kicking in doors and high-speed pursuits. Sometimes we get hurt, too."

"Why don't you jump in," said Meadows. "I'll give you a lift back to Sanchez's place."

"Sounds good to me," agreed Clark. "I'm done here, anyway."

Hopping in the passenger side of the SUV, Clark immediately got licked in the face by K9 Rocco when he stuck his head through the little window into the back. Scratching his ears, Clark ruffled Rocco's fur and hugged his head.

"Hey there, Rocco," said Clark, said in a goofy tone. "Who's a good boy?"

Rocco whined excitedly and continued to lick Clark's face.

"You two need a room?" asked Meadows as he got in the truck.

"Jealous?" asked Clark as he continued to pet Rocco.

"Nah," said Meadows. "Rocco knows who has the treats."

Upon saying the word "treat", Rocco's ears perked up and he turned towards Meadows.

"Oh, I see how it works," said Clark, laughing.

"He who controls the treats," said Meadows, handing a snack to the dog, "controls the doggo."

Glancing towards the house, Clark saw Avery flipping him off as they began driving away. Clark just smiled and waved back, like he was saying farewell to an old friend.

"Asshole," said Meadows, chuckling.

Chapter Fourteen
A Bigger Gun

*"If trouble comes when you least expect it then maybe
the thing to do is to always expect it."*
Cormac McCarthy

Waving to Meadows as he walked back into the house, Meadows chirped the siren and headed down the street. Clark watched until he rounded the corner, then shut the door. Sanchez was sitting on the couch, folding laundry.

"Back already?" she asked as he walked into the living room. "Was that a siren?"

"Yeah," he said. "I ran into Meadows. He dropped me back at the house."

"He's already back at work?" she asked, turning towards him.

"He is," replied Clark. "The P.A.[19] already cleared him since he didn't hit anyone."

"Are they going to clear me?" she asked, laying a pair of neatly folded black-lace panties on a pile.

"Meadows says his FOP lawyer thinks they'll wait to clear you until the end," he replied, "since it was your call."

"You're probably right," she agreed.

"It might take a bit," said Clark, "since the families of the three douchebags are threatening to sue."

"They shot at us first!" said Sanchez, angrily.

"It won't get anywhere," said Clark. "Your dashcam footage will clear us. They fled a traffic stop, then started shooting at pursuing officers. It's fairly open and shut."

"Good," said Sanchez. "I've never been through an OIS investigation before."

---

[19] P.A. – prosecuting attorney

"This is my third," said Clark. "The other two were minor, though. No one was killed and they were both ruled justified because they both shot at me first. I think we'll be fine. Besides, that's not my biggest worry right now."

"What is?" she asked, dreading the answer.

Clark thought about it for a moment before speaking. Then, he decided to tell her everything. He covered what he noticed last night and included finding the hair sample and the tracks at the edge of the lake. He left out the part with Avery.

"So, it's back," she said, a note of fear in her voice.

"Looks like," said Clark. "I knew the feds didn't get it. I could just feel it in my gut."

"What's next, then?" she asked.

"Well," he began, "one thing's for certain. This puny 9mm isn't going to stop it. I've got the Devastator .458 SOCOM for a rifle, but I need a pistol with more stopping power. Let's go to the gun store in Springfield."

"Ok," she said. "Let me put these away and I'll grab my purse."

Fifteen minutes later, they were backing out of the driveway. Clark was driving the Camaro and Sanchez was picking music for the drive. Once they cleared the neighborhood and turned onto the highway, Clark began accelerating. The Camaro ZL1 had the 580 horsepower, 6.2-liter V-8 with a six-speed manual transmission.

"Don't hotrod my car too much," she admonished. "This is my baby."

"This beast was made to run fast," said Clark. "You drive it like you're going to church."

"No," she argued, "I drive it like someone who doesn't want speeding tickets."

"Then why did you buy such a powerful car?" he asked. "The Camaro comes in a V-6 version that doesn't have near this much power."

"My dad gave me this car when I graduated from the police academy," she said. "I didn't pick it out."

"Well, I'm going to knock the cobwebs out of it," said Clark, accelerating quickly and running the gears.

Sanchez put on her sunglasses and leaned back, enjoying the ride. Clark pushed the engine until he hit sixth gear, then began backing off slightly.

"Be careful," said Sanchez.

"There is hardly any traffic," he replied. "I'll slow down in a sec."

He held it for a few more seconds, then backed off on the throttle. The highway speed limit in the area was sixty miles per hour. Clark backed it off to just below seventy and held it there. He enjoyed driving the high-performance car and let himself relax as they listened to a playlist of classic rock.

They were blasting Bob Seger's "Her Strut" when they entered the town of Nixa. Slowing down to just above the speed limit, Clark accelerated again once they cleared the other side. Then it was a straight shot into Springfield.

It was just after noon when they pulled into the parking lot of Cherokee Firearms on North National Avenue in Springfield. With his police credentials, the paperwork was expedited, and he was able to purchase the pistol he came to see.

He bought a Guncrafter Industries .50 GI complete Glock conversion pistol with Trijicon night sights already installed and a TLR-1HL tactical light. Retooled and rechambered by Guncrafter Industries, they had taken the basic Glock design and created an entirely new caliber. The fifty caliber G.I. packed more power than almost any automatic pistol available.

He also bought a dozen extra magazines and more than a thousand rounds of ammo for the new pistol. He grabbed a Blackhawk Serpa

155

holster for it and two magazine pouches for good measure. Plus, a Crossbreed molded Kydex holster for concealed carry.

"Think that thing is big enough to get the job done?" asked Sanchez as they got back into the car.

"God, I hope so," replied Clark. "If this big bastard won't knock it down, I don't know what will."

"I don't see how you can afford that," she said, shaking her head.

"Well," explained Clark. "Well, I just maxed out a credit card. At least I don't have a house payment, but I'll still be paying it off for a while. It's worth it, though. I needed something with more knockdown power. It's just a matter of time before I run into this thing again."

"Let's get something to eat while we're in town," she said. "I'm starving and I don't want to wait until we get back to Kimberling City."

"Where do you want to eat?" he asked.

"What's the name of that Italian buffet place you took me to when we were first dating?" she asked.

"The Hill," replied Clark. "You want to go there?"

"Definitely," she said. "Their food is amazing."

"The Hill, it is," he replied, pulling out of the parking lot.

After they finished eating, they hit the highway back towards Kimberling City. Sanchez drove this time, so Clark could load magazines and get the pistol ready. Taking off the Glock 19 and the mag pouch, he slipped them into the glove box. Putting the new holster and both mag pouches in place on his belt, he racked the slide on the GI 50 and dropped the magazine. Holstering the pistol, he loaded another round in the magazine, then replaced it in the pistol.

The mag pouches each held two magazines, so he filled both. That left him another eight loaded magazines in his bag. He'd filled all of them with .275 grain jacketed hollow points. In trials, that round had penetrated forty inches of ballistic gel and had been used to take big game of all types. That included Grizzly Bear. Clark knew that it would definitely get the attention of the creature he was preparing for.

The sun was still high in the sky when they entered the city limits of Kimberling City. The return trip had taken a bit longer since Sanchez rarely drove over the speed limit.

"Back to my place?" she asked.

"Let's go to mine," he said. "I haven't been there in weeks. I need to check on it and make sure no one has broken in and stolen everything."

"Are you sure?" she asked. "If it's back, then won't it be waiting for us to come back there?"

"Probably," he replied, "but it seems to prefer the darkness."

"Jacobson was hit during the day," she said, shaking her head.

"That's true," he said, "but he was alone and usually oblivious. I hate to speak ill of the dead, but he was one of the least observant people I know. He was a terrible cop."

"You think it will be there?" she asked, sounding more than a bit nervous.

"If he is," said Clark, "I'll get to try out the new pistol sooner than expected. Besides, the Devastator is there. If this thing shows up, I want that big rifle with me. The pistol is good for only close range. I want to hit it before it gets that close if I can."

"Can't say that I blame you," she replied.

"Besides," he said, "I don't like being in town. I prefer my place. If I want to walk outside butt naked, there's no one there to complain. It's all my land around the house. Over a hundred acres of it."

"I would ask who walks outside naked," she said, shaking her head, "but you've already demonstrated you're more than willing to do it."

"I didn't hear any complaints last night," he said, chuckling.

"Thank God no one was awake," she replied. "I'm sure we would have had KCPD knocking on the door."

"Probably," agreed Clark. "See. I'm not fit for city living. I'm ruined to the good country life."

"Alright then," she said. "If we're going to stay out there, then let's swing by my place and grab all of your gear. We just might need it."

"Not a bad idea," he agreed.

A few minutes later, they pulled into her driveway. She helped him load everything into the trunk, except for the rifle and several magazines. Those went into the seat next to him. If there was any chance at all running into the creature, he wanted to have something capable of hitting a target at a distance.

The 300-blackout round might not have the punch of the .458 SOCOM, but it was still a potent round. It might not be a match for the SOCOM in a round for round contest, but a full magazine would ruin the day of anything he was shooting at.

The sun was still high in the sky when they pulled into the driveway leading up to Clark's cabin. Nothing looked out of place and they could hear birds calling back and forth in the trees.

When the house appeared out of the trees, they could see two large ravens perched on the porch. They were cawing back and forth while they were eating on the head of a deer. This wasn't the same one as before. This time it was a doe.

"Looks like it's been here," said Clark. "From the look of that doe, it's been a few days. It's already starting to rot."

"That thing is going to stink," said Sanchez. "Can you get rid of it."

"You cover me with the rifle," he replied, handing it to her. "I'll grab some gloves out of the jeep and get it out of here."

Pulling in where the patrol SUV normally set, she shut off the engine and climbed out. Bringing the rifle to her shoulder, she glanced around the yard looking for any sign of movement. Clark went to the jeep and returned moments later putting on a pair of leather work gloves. Reaching for the head, the two ravens cawed furiously and flapped up to perch on the edge of the porch.

"It's ok, fellas," he said. "I'm just moving it. You can have it back."

Picking it up by the lower jaw, he started carrying it towards the edge of the woods at the far side of the yard. There were maggots already wriggling in the poor thing's mouth, eyes, and the ragged stump of the neck where it had been torn from the rest of the body.

Tossing it into the trees, he turned and headed back towards the house. The two ravens circled over him once, then flapped to the ground beside the gruesome buffet that they had been dining on. Soon they were back to eating the rotting corpse. Clark took that as a good sign, indicating no large predators were in the area, at the moment.

Rejoining Sanchez, he took off the work gloves and tossed them onto the porch.

"I don't think it's been here for a while," he said. "That head is several days old and there are no recent tracks. Plus, the birds are still singing. Those two old ravens over there would be long gone if there was a big predator around."

"So, what do we do now?" she asked.

"You can wait here or go with me," he said. "I'm going to walk around the house to see if it looks like anyone has broken in. Then I'm going through the front door and clearing the house, just in case."

"Do you think that thing broke in?" she asked.

"I doubt it," he replied. "As big as it is, it would have a tough time fitting through the door. It would have to rip it apart to get inside. Even then, it couldn't stand up. The ceiling is only seven feet."

"Ok," she said. "Let's check the perimeter then clear it."

She kept the rifle at low ready and followed Clark around the outside of the house. Clark drew the GI 50 and kept it up and against his chest, the barrel pointing to his left and down.

None of the windows were broken and both the front and back doors were still closed. That seemed like a good sign. Once they reached the front of the house, Clark checked the doorknob. It was still locked. Cautiously, he re-holstered his pistol and unlocked the door. After putting the keys back in his pocket, he drew the pistol and brought it up.

"Ready?" he whispered.

"Ready," she whispered back.

In a flash, Clark threw open the door and made a rapid entry, sweeping the room as he moved. Sanchez entered behind him and swept the other side of the room. The cabin wasn't overly large, and they searched it in minutes. Once they were satisfied that no one was inside, they both put their weapons away and sat down in the living room.

"Now what?" she asked.

"The really scary part," he replied.

"Oh, crap," she said, wide-eyed. "What's that?"

"Clearing out my refrigerator," he said with a mock scowl. "I'm sure almost everything has gone bad."

"Well, I certainly wouldn't trust the milk, eggs, and anything that had already been cooked," she said, chuckling.

Clark grabbed an empty trash bag and opened the door. After a few minutes, he had cleared out everything bad and questionable, then took them out to the trash can. The birds were still singing as he went back inside.

As he preparing to shut the door, he had a distinct feeling that he was being watched. The birds were still singing, but he couldn't shake the feeling. Slowly, he panned back and forth through the trees, straining to look deep into the shadows of the forest. Nothing stood out or made any sudden movements. After a moment, he shook his head and shut the door.

"Everything ok?" asked Sanchez.

"Yeah," he replied after a short pause. "I think so. I just had a feeling that I was being watched, but I couldn't see anything. It's odd, but the bird sounds were still going on and I could see squirrels."

"Maybe it was just your imagination," she said, frowning. "I mean with everything you've been through the last few weeks; I'd think you might be justifiably jumpy."

"Maybe," he said, taking a seat on the couch next to her.

"Want to watch a movie?" she asked. "Maybe take your mind off it for a while."

"I don't have cable," he replied. "I have an old VCR with a bunch of tapes."

"Oh my God," she said, "I didn't know anyone still had a VCR. I haven't seen one in years!"

"I don't even have satellite TV," he said. "It's always been just me here. I don't watch much TV. I'm usually outside doing something."

"Like what?" she asked, leaning against the arm of the couch to face him.

"Well," he began, "I cut, split, and stack wood for the fireplace."

"It's still summer out there," she said. "Why do you need the fireplace now?"

"It's not for now," he explained with a smile. "I primarily heat the house in the winter with wood. I stack it for the winter. Let it season a bit before I burn it."

"Sounds exciting," she said without much enthusiasm. "What else?"

"Well," he said, "I'm sure my garden is dead since I haven't been here to water it."

"Not true," she said. "I forgot to tell you, Tiffany from dispatch and her husband have been coming out to take care of your garden while you were in the hospital."

"Really?" said Clark, genuinely surprised. "I guess she wanted to make sure my garden survived so I can make homemade salsa again this year."

"Hey, don't knock that salsa," said Sanchez. "It's damned good, especially since you grow all the ingredients."

"Well, I'm happy to know my garden isn't dead," he replied with a chuckle.

"What else do you do outside?" she asked.

"There's always work to do around here," he said. "I have to occasionally mow the yard. I was planning on building a chicken coop and need to clear a spot for it. If I have chickens, they'll help keep down the tick and insect population. They'll eat any bug in the yard."

"Plus, the eggs," she added.

"Oh yeah," he said, smiling. "Definitely the eggs."

"What else?" she asked.

"Well, I like to shoot," he said. "That's why I put in my own range."

"Do you think the sound of gunfire would keep that thing away or attract it?" she asked, frowning.

"I would be afraid it would attract it," he said, "but having said that, I would like to try out this GI 50. I want to get a feel for the kick."

"Can I shoot it?" she asked, smiling.

"Absolutely," he replied. "Let's grab the mags and ammo and head out to the range."

162

Picking up the range bag with the GI 50 ammo in it, they headed out the back door to the small range. Clark had placed stakes in the ground at different range intervals so he would know the distance from the target. They moved out to the fifteen-yard line and set the bag down.

"This should do," said Clark. "Not too far, not too close."

The five steel targets were still hanging in place, swaying gently in the soft evening breeze. Clark drew the GI 50 and dropped the magazine, then switched it out with one loaded with ball ammo. After he cleared the chamber of the one remaining hollow point, he handed it to Sanchez. She took it gingerly and looked it over, careful to not put her finger on the trigger.

"You get the very first shot," said Clark.

"Thanks," she said, "I think. Look at the size of the barrel on this thing. It's massive. How many rounds does it hold?"

"It has five in the magazine and one in the chamber," said Clark. "The mags hold six, but I already chambered a round for you. Careful, they're 275 grains."

"What's that mean?" she asked.

"It means it's roughly twice the size of the bullet in your nine-millimeter," he explained. "A hell of a lot more gunpowder, too. It's going to have a bit of a kick."

"How much?" she asked, cautiously.

"I don't know," he replied honestly. "I've never fired one before, either."

"Well," she said, turning towards the targets and bringing up the pistol, "here goes nothing."

"Hang on a sec," he said, placing hearing protectors over her ears and putting on a set of his own.

Putting his hand on her elbow, he looked her in the face and said loud enough to hear over the hearing protectors.

163

"Keep your elbows locked and your wrists stiff," he said, touching her elbow and wrist for emphasis. "It will probably have more barrel climb then actual recoil, but it might surprise you."

She nodded her understanding and brought the pistol up in the ready position. Giving her a thumbs up, he took a step back to give her room to shoot. She focused on the front sight, then her finger slipped onto the trigger. Controlling her breathing, he exhaled and took up the slack.

"BOOM!" roared the pistol.

"PING!" roared the target, which was now flopping on the end of its chain.

Taking her finger off the trigger, she glanced over at Clark and mouthed the words "Oh my God!"

Turning back to the targets, she repeated the process and fired at the targets, taking her time and emptying the magazine. She only had one miss, but four of the five of the targets were dancing on their chains.

When the slide was locked back, she dropped the magazine and checked the chamber to verify it was empty. Showing it to Clark so he too could verify, she then handed the confirmed empty weapon to him while keeping the barrel pointed downrange.

"Thank you," said Clark, accepting the pistol and still maintaining a downrange direction.

While Sanchez recovered the empty magazine, Clark did a quick inspection of the weapon. He double-checked that the polymer frame was holding up under the power of the massive .50 GI round. When he failed to find any sign of damage, he took a magazine from his mag pouch and slapped it into the weapon.

Verifying that Sanchez was out of the line of fire, Clark released the slide to chamber a round.

"Going hot," he said, as he released the slide and put the weapon into battery.

Clark didn't wait for the targets to stop moving. He sighted in on one and took up the slack on the trigger. He was prepared for the massive report and didn't flinch. What he was unsure of was the kick. He had observed that Sanchez was able to handle it without problems. He was pleased to note that it wasn't as bad as he was expecting. It only caused a slight twinge of pain in his ribs.

Immediately following the report, there was a shrill ring of steel as the target began jumping on the end of the chain, again. Aiming, he fired a second time, and the ring of steel on steel reverberated through the air, leaving another target dancing on its chain.

Pausing a moment, he exhaled slowly and in rapid succession emptied the remaining four rounds in the magazine, ringing steel each time. Rapidly, he dropped the magazine and held the pistol up in front of his face without taking his eyes off the targets while he inserted a fresh magazine. Bringing the pistol back on target, he released the slide and chambered another round.

Instantly, he began firing again until the slide locked back. Six rounds in just under five seconds and rang steel all six times. Bringing the pistol back against his chest, he scanned his surroundings for additional threats before dropping the magazine and reloading. Then he returned the pistol to its holster.

Turning around to face Sanchez, he found she was looking at him with an odd expression on her face.

"Were you born with a pistol in your hand?" she asked. "That was unreal. How long did it take you to learn to shoot like that?"

"I've been shooting since I was a little kid," he explained. "When I was old enough to hold a gun, my grandpa was teaching me about gun safety and how to shoot. I got my first deer at eight."

"That's unbelievable," she said. "That reload took you just a couple of seconds. It was like a machine."

"It takes a lot of practice," he said. "You start slow, then drill a lot. There's an old expression that says slow is smooth and smooth is fast. The military hammers that into you. You practice slowly until it becomes second nature, then you gradually begin to increase speed. Before you know it, you're blazing through without even thinking about it. You build muscle memory."

"We did drills in the academy," said Sanchez, "but that's amazing. We never learned anything close to that."

"I can teach you," he said. "It just takes time and practice. In the winter when it's too cold to be outside, I sit on the couch and do dry fire and reload drills."

Opening the bag, Clark refilled the empty spots on his mag pouches with full magazines.

"Want to shoot it again?" he asked.

"Not right now," she said. "My wrists are sore. I would hate to spend all day shooting that thing."

"It would take a toll on your wrists and ears," he said, chuckling. "I think I'm going to run a couple more mags. I want to try it with one hand and with my off-hand."

"I'll just watch," she said, stepping back.

Clark smiled at her and turned back to the targets. Drawing the pistol, he said "Going hot!"

Working the slide, he put a round in the chamber and put the pistol in low ready using his right hand only. Keeping his left hand tight up against his body, he brought the pistol up and began sighting in. After a moment, he eased into his breathing and steadied himself.

Six shots rang out and six hits were registered, but they were a bit slower than the last run. It was harder to keep the pistol on target using one hand. Also, the recoil was more difficult to control with only one hand.

Changing the magazine, he released the slide and chambered another round. Switching to his off-hand, he brought his right arm up against his body. After sighting in, he began shooting. Had he not been the type of person who trains with his off-hand, he might have had more trouble.

He emptied the magazine in about the same amount of time it took him to empty it with his dominant hand. Steel rang six times, but he noted that two of the shots only caught the edge of the plate. He managed to keep it off his face but running that many rounds through it had caused his ribs to ache a lot.

"Nice shooting," said Sanchez as he dropped the empty magazine and slid a full one into the butt of the pistol.

Releasing the slide, he returned the pistol to his holster. Ejecting the magazine, he added a round to the magazine and replaced it in the pistol. After recovering the empty magazines, he spent a few minutes picking up the expended brass. Sanchez helped and it went quickly. They tossed the expended brass in a five-gallon bucket that Clark kept next to the bench he had built at the fifty-yard line.

The area was completely silent now, but it usually was when he finished shooting. Clark picked up the range bag and they headed back inside. Sanchez went on inside and Clark turned to scan the trees before going in, as well.

At first, he didn't see anything. The shadows were beginning to deepen beneath the trees as the sun sank lower in the sky. Just as he was about to turn around, he saw it. It was not attempting to hide. It was standing in plain sight, approximately forty yards from the back of the house and just outside the edge of the trees.

It was easily ten feet tall and covered in black fur or hair that had shoots of grey in the shoulders and on the chest. The beast had a slightly elongated snout that made it look more like a mandrill than an ape but there was no other color in the muzzle. Just black and a few streaks of grey. The eyes looked dark and devoid of anything but malice. It stared at him with hatred in its dark eyes with its large canine teeth revealed as the lips pulled back in a silent snarl.

167

The beast was truly massive. The shoulders looked to be over four feet across with rippling muscle. The hands hung down to the knees and the tips of the enormous fingers ended with dark claws. Clark could see the barrel-like chest heaving as the beast breathed in and out deeply. It just stood there, glaring hatred and death at him, plain for all to see.

Clark locked eyes with it, matching its intensity. He wanted it to know he wanted it dead as much as it wanted him. He also refused to show it any sign of fear. It met his gaze and then took two gigantic steps towards him. Clark did nothing, refusing to react. Two more steps and he began to twitch the fingers on his right hand. Two more gigantic strides and it had closed almost half the distance. It was now only about 20 yards away.

It began making short grunts and swaying side to side. Slamming its gigantic fists into the ground, he roared a horrendous deep bellow that Clark felt in his chest and his bones. It tore up the ground and threw clumps of grass into the air, beating its fists against the dirt and making a thumping sound that Clark could feel shaking the ground through his boots.

"What the hell was that?" screamed Sanchez.

"Stay inside," yelled Clark. "Get the Devastator and extra magazines!"

The beast looked like it was about to charge when Clark decided he had enough.

"Come on, motherfucker!" he screamed and rapidly drew the .50 GI in one fluid motion.

The creature saw the movement and started to move forward until it saw the gun pointed at it. Clark could see the realization in its eyes. It understood what a gun was. Like lightning, the beast spun and headed for the trees, swaying as it ran.

Clark began squeezing off rounds as fast as he could, but the creature was faster. He saw one send fur and blood flying from its left shoulder just as it entered the trees. It looked like he'd only caught flesh, not hitting thick enough meat to cause any real damage.

The slide locked back, and he could hear the beast screaming and tearing off through the trees with inhuman speed. Clark never took his eyes from the direction the sounds were coming from as he changed magazines and brought the pistol back to the ready position. As the sounds faded into the distance, Sanchez ran out onto the back porch holding the Devastator and six magazines.

"Did you see it?" she asked, her voice nearly frantic.

"Yeah," said Clark. "It almost charged me."

"Did you hit it?" she asked, looking at him with fear in her eyes.

"Once," he said. "Looked like I grazed its shoulder. No real damage. I don't think it was ready for me to fight back. A monster like that is used to everything running from it when it threatens to charge. There's one problem with that. This is my goddamned home and I won't run off my land by man nor beast. I did learn one thing, though. That fucking thing is fast."

"Why does it keep coming back here?" she asked.

"The only thing I can figure is that it either somehow has fixated on me," he said, "or it's fixated on you. Either way, I'll die before I let it take us."

"Maybe we should stay at my place for a while," said Sanchez, sounding scared.

"One problem in that," he said. "It knows where you live, too. If it shows up there, I can't start shooting at it without having to worry about where the civilians are. Too much chance for a bystander picking up a stray round."

"If we stay here," she said, "it will be back."

"Next time it comes here," said Clark, picking up the Devastator, "I won't be using a pistol."

"Can it get in the house?" she asked.

169

"From the size of that thing and the muscle on it," said Clark, "I think that thing could rip its way inside anything short of a bank vault."

"I was afraid you were going to say that," she said, her voice quivering slightly.

LAKEVIEW MAN

Chapter Fifteen
Thief in the Night

"He was a silent fury who no torment could tame."
Jack London

Clark spent the next hour reloading all his empty magazines and cleaning guns. He wanted everything he had to be ready if the beast returned. Although he knew it could easily smash its way into the house, he would make sure it paid a heavy price to do so. Now that the beast knew he wasn't afraid to shoot, it might be a bit more cautious in trying to approach.

The sun was almost down, and Sanchez was pacing nervously, making sure to stay well away from the doors and windows. She was holding Clark's patrol rifle and had slipped two magazines into the back pockets on her jean shorts.

Clark retrieved a military loadbearing vest from his closet and began buckling it into place. Then he filled all four mag pouches with two mags each, giving him a total of eight mags for the Devastator, plus the one in the gun. Between the four mags on his belt and the four extra pouches on the vest that accommodated the Glock mags, he had eight mags on him and one in the gun.

"Are we going to be alright?" she asked, her voice full of fear.

"I won't let that thing take you," he assured her. "Come hell or high water. It'll have to kill me first."

"Aren't you going to wear your plate carrier?" she asked.

"No point," replied Clark. "It's just added weight. That thing isn't going to be shooting at us. I need to be able to move quickly."

"Do you have another one of those vests?" she asked.

"Yeah, I think so," he said, motioning for her to follow him into the bedroom.

Rummaging through the footlocker, he was tossing items onto the bed while searching.

"Looks like a Tactical Yard Sale," she said, chuckling.

"Now that's funny," he said, glancing at the bed behind him.

"I try," she said with a mock bow.

After a moment, Clark pulled out another vest and helped her into it. Adjusting the straps to fit, he buckled it into place for her.

"There," he said. "Now you can carry up to eight extra mags for the rifle."

"Your rifle is a larger caliber than my patrol rifle," she said, looking at one of the rounds.

"It's a .300 Blackout instead of the traditional 5.56mm NATO round," he explained. "It doesn't go as far as the 5.56mm, but it hits a hell of a lot harder. It's a much larger bullet. The plus note is that the mags still hold thirty rounds. My SOCOM mags only hold ten."

"What if it tries to get in?" she asked.

"Then empty the magazine into the son of a bitch," he said. "Then reload and do it again. Eventually, that big bastard will drop or get the hint it's not welcome."

"Should I aim for center mass?" she asked, glancing at the window and the growing darkness.

"If you have time to pick a target," he said, "then aim for big arteries. Hit the inside upper thigh, the inside upper arm, and the neck. If you don't have time, then hit it wherever the hell you can. Just hit it as many times as you can. Worst case scenario, shoot it in the dick. Pelvic girdle shots bleed like a bastard."

"It might also cool any amorous intentions he might have towards me," she said, chuckling softly. "Joe *Matoskah* said they have been known to carry off women as mates."

"That should do the trick," said Clark, with a smile. "Nothing says I'm playing hard to get quite like getting shot in the penis."

173

"I can't imagine anything still being in the mood for love after taking a bullet to the *juevos*," said Sanchez, chuckling.

Clark smiled and shook his head.

"You know what we need?" she asked.

"What's that?" he said.

"Dogs," she replied. "They'd sense whenever that thing was around."

"You're not wrong," he said. "Alright, if we get through this, I'm buying two of the biggest bastards I can find. We'll teach them to protect both us and this place."

"What kind of dogs are you thinking?" she asked, smiling. "I love dogs."

"German shepherds, at the very least," he said. "Maybe something bigger like some kind of Mastiff. Maybe an African Mastiff. Boerboel, I think they're called. They were bred to defend people and livestock from large predators like lions."

"How big are they?" she asked.

"Well," he said, thinking, "they get to around 200 pounds, I think. Then there's the Caucasian Ovcharka or Caucasian Shepherd. They get to around 200, also. They were bred in Russia to protect livestock from large predators, mostly bears."

Sanchez got out her phone and started Googling both breeds. After several minutes, she held up the phone with a picture of it. It was an Ovcharka.

"I want these," she said. "They're adorable and according to the AKC, they're bold, fearless, self-confident and fierce when a threat is present, but he is soft, devoted, kind and endearing to his family, including other family pets. Let's get two of them."

"Sounds good to me," said Clark. "Find a breeder and we'll see how much they are and if we can find any available."

174

"Wow," she said. "They're not cheap. Like two grand a puppy."

"That might be a bit out of my budget," said Clark.

"When I move in with you," she said, smiling, "our budget doubles. Neither of us will have a house payment. I can buy two out of my savings, instead of paying interest on a credit card. When this is over, I'm buying two. How can we train them?"

"I'm pretty sure that Meadows can help with that," said Clark. "Rocco would love the company and training them to law enforcement standard would make them smart and obedient as well as fearless."

"I can't wait," she said, smiling. "I'm gonna start picking out names!"

Clark smiled and was about to say something when they heard the beast roar off in the distance. It was loud enough to hear inside the house as clear as if it were across the room. The color drained out of Sanchez's face and Clark reached for the Devastator.

"Oh God," said Sanchez. "It's coming back."

Clark went to the back door and looked out. He didn't see anything, so he opened the door and stepped out onto the back porch. Sanchez followed behind him but stopped at the door.

"Are you crazy?" she whispered. "Why are you coming out here with it?"

"That roar was quite a way off," explained Clark. "Maybe half a mile. It'll take a bit for it to cover that much ground."

Off in the distance, it roared again. This time, it was much closer.

"That thing covers a lot of ground quickly," said Clark. "That's maybe a quarter-mile off."

"Let's get inside," said Sanchez.

"In a sec," said Clark, pulling the charging handle on the Devastator. "I want to see if it's dumb enough to come out into the open again."

175

"I don't think it's going to happen twice," she answered. "We already know it's smart."

Bringing the rifle up into low ready, Clark watched the trees for any sign of movement. It roared once more, this time only a few hundred yards away towards the lake. Then everything went silent. The night sounds were all gone.

"It's coming," said Clark. "You'd best get inside."

"What about you?" she asked. "You're still hurt."

"I can shoot," he said. "I want to see how close it will get before it starts getting cautious."

Sanchez took a step back but stayed where she could see him. Pulling the charging handle on her rifle, she brought it up to her shoulder and kept it at low ready.

Seconds crept by like hours as they waited for the beast to show itself. There was no sound to break the silence other than the gentle whisper of the breeze through the trees. The woods were bathed in impenetrable darkness, leaving the entire area in stygian gloom.

"Shut off the interior lights," said Clark in a whisper.

"Why?" she asked.

"It already knows we're here," he said. "The light only helps it see us. It also kills our night vision."

"Got it," she said, moving around and flipping switches off, plunging the house into sudden darkness.

Returning to the back door, she whispered, "See anything."

"Not yet," he whispered back.

They waited there in the darkness, ears straining for any sound. The quiet was intense and weighed heavily upon them, as thick as an enveloping mist. Slowly, their eyes began to adjust, and they could make out the dark shape of the trees, a deeper shadow against the deep darkness of the night. Only the starlight above them gave any inkling of light. There was no moon.

Clark stared into the darkness, waiting for any sign of movement or of the feeling he had the night before when he could feel it staring back at him. Nothing stirred and he felt nothing. The silence was as oppressive as the thick humidity of the hot August night. The waiting was excruciating.

Neither of them dared to break the silence, even breathing as quiet as they could. They didn't want even the slightest noise obscuring any sign that might give away the beast's location. It was quiet enough that they could hear their hearts beating.

"WHAM!"

Something struck the side of the cabin with enough force to knock pictures off the wall.

"It's to your right!" screamed Sanchez.

Clark spun to his right and brought the rifle up to fire. A shadow in the darkness was streaking rapidly for the tree line, heading right past where the range was set up. Clark brought Devastator to his shoulder and began firing at the retreating shadow. The massive reports of the .458 SOCOM echoed off into the night. Six times he fired, but he didn't hear the beast roar or grunt in pain. He had to assume that he had missed it.

"Goddamn that thing moves fast," he hissed, pain lancing through his ribs.

"Get inside!" she pleaded. "It was nearly on top of us before we even knew it was there!"

Clark stepped back and into the kitchen, shutting the door behind him and locking it with both the knob and deadbolt. Moving over to the table, he could barely make out where everything was in the scant light of the stars filtering in through the windows. By memory, he reloaded the Devastator with a fresh magazine.

Laying the partial mag on the table, he reached into the duffel bag and pulled out a box of ammo. After verifying that it was the correct ammo, he refilled the magazine and replaced the empty spot in the pouch on his LBV[20].

"Did you hit it?" she whispered.

"I don't think so," he replied, keeping his voice low. "If I did, it didn't make a sound. All I can say is, that bastard is quick."

"How are you supposed to hit it if it moves that fast?" she asked.

"I've got to lead it more," he said, "or wait till it stops. If I can get a dead bead on it, I'll put enough lead in it to drop a goddamned rhino."

"Do you think it will come back?" she asked, dreading the answer.

"I'd say it won't stop coming back until the sun comes up," he said. "Maybe not even then, if it thinks it has us trapped."

"Maybe we should call someone," she said. "If someone else shows up, maybe it will leave."

"Unlikely that it'll leave at all," said Clark. "If someone shows up tonight, it'll probably attack them."

"Maybe we should've gone to my place when we had the chance," she said, softly.

"Maybe," said Clark, "but we'd only be putting off the inevitable. I've got to deal with this thing, eventually."

"Here's hoping that it doesn't deal with us, instead," she said, shaking her head.

"When the sun comes up," he whispered, "I'll call Konrad. He's got the other Devastator. If I don't get it tonight, maybe we can track it in the morning."

"You're going to go after it in the woods?" she said in disbelief.

---

[20] LBV – Load Bearing Vest

"Might be the only way to find it and finish it off," he said. "Believe me, nothing would make me happier than just finishing this damned thing off tonight and be done with it."

Off in the distance they heard cracking and splintering wood, then the rushing sound of a tree falling.

"What the hell was that?" she asked.

"Sounds like a tree dropped somewhere down towards the road," said Clark.

"Does that happen very often?" she asked.

"Only when I cut one down," he said. "I've cleared all the deadwood out down that way. That wasn't a deadfall tree. I could hear the leaves rushing through the air."

The silence returned and they looked back and forth at each other for a long moment. They knew that it was out there, waiting for an opening to attack them.

"WHAM!"

Something heavy hit the side of the cabin, again. Only this time, on the opposite side. Clark could hear something crash to the floor in his bedroom. He started to head for the back door when Sanchez grabbed him by the left arm.

"Don't go," she hissed. "I think it's a trap. It's trying to draw you out of the house."

Clark started to say something but reconsidered. She might be right. So far, the thing has shown remarkable intelligence and cunning. It very well could be trying to set a trap. The back door was solid wood with no window. Clark went over to it and rattled the doorknob like he was trying to open it.

"SLAM!"

Something heavy hit the door, almost knocking it inward. Only the heavy oak door and frame, plus a deadbolt prevented it from bursting inward.

179

"Holy shit," hissed Clark. "That goddamned thing was waiting for me to come out."

When the door didn't fly open, the beast snarled and smashed what sounded like one of his rocking chairs against the wall. Then it threw the barbeque grill out into the yard, undoubtedly destroying it from the sound it made when it hit. Roaring in frustration and anger, it stormed off the porch and headed towards the shed.

"What the hell is that thing doing, now?" asked Clark.

"I don't know," said Sanchez, "but it ain't happy."

Clark moved over to the kitchen window above the sink. It faced the shed. He could see the dark shape heading towards the front of the large wooden shed where he stored his tools and lawnmower.

Raising the window as silently as he could, Clark aimed at the creature. When it heard the window, it froze and started to turn around.

"BOOM!" roared Devastator.

It seemed even louder in the confines of the house. Clark's ears were ringing, but he could still hear the roar of pain and surprise from the beast. It was a solid hit. He saw blood and hair fly from the beast's left shoulder.

Grunting in pain and anger, the beast raced off into the darkness of the surrounding forest, crashing through the underbrush like a freight train. Clark listened until it faded in the distance.

"I got you, motherfucker," he said, smiling with satisfaction.

"What now?" she asked.

"I'm sure it's gone for the night," he said. "I hurt it. I don't know how bad, but it's hurt. I'll know more in the morning when I can get out there and examine the ground by the shed. If there's a blood trail, then Konrad and I can track it. If we can find its lair, we can finish this."

"I heard it grunt in pain," she said, "I think you got it pretty good."

"I hope the bastard bleeds out," said Clark. "For all our sakes."

D.A. ROBERTS

Chapter Sixteen
Blood Trail

"He was sounding the deeps of his nature, and of the parts of his nature that were deeper than he, going back into the womb of time."
Jack London

Clark let her sleep on the couch, far away from the windows. He stood watch over her for the rest of the night. Sleep was not with him. Despite knowing that he had wounded the beast, he was worried that it might come back. He wouldn't risk it getting inside and hurting her. Or worse, taking her off into the night.

Shortly before daylight, he sent Konrad a text. He knew Konrad had worked the night before and was likely asleep. Hopefully, he would see the text before he slept too much of the day away to make tracking viable.

The text said, "You awake?"

Wincing in pain as he stretched, he felt the grating of the ribs. He'd fractured two of them when he'd been shot. Although not fully broken, they were painful as hell if he moved just right. It wouldn't take much of a blow to that side to break them completely.

The doctors had told him to take it easy for the next few weeks while they healed. They didn't consider a killer Bigfoot terrorizing them. Taking it easy might not be on the menu for a bit.

To his surprise, Konrad texted him back almost immediately. It simply said, "What's up?"

"Come to my place once the sun is up," he texted back. "It's back and I need your help."

"I'll come right now," said the reply.

"No!" said Clark. "Wait till the sun's up. It might still be in the area."

"Copy that," said Konrad. "See you in an hour."

183

Clark could see the reddish glow on the horizon indicating the sun was about to come up. Most days, he would take a cup of coffee outside and sit on the porch to watch the sun come up. He didn't think that was such a good idea, under the circumstances. That was going to have to wait until they were sure that it was gone or dead.

Sanchez was sleeping soundly. Clark considered making her breakfast but remembered that he'd thrown out most of the contents of his refrigerator the day before.

"Well, so much for that idea," he whispered.

He considered texting Konrad to bring something but thought better of it. It would be a good excuse to get Sanchez to leave. Send her away and tell her not to come back to his place until he called her. The more he thought about that, the more he knew he would be wasting his time.

She was stubborn and would refuse to leave them, much less let them track it without her coming along. As much as he loved that about her, he needed her to be safe. He knew that the creature had been watching her and didn't want to take the chance of it grabbing her. That thought sent anger surging through him like a wave. He would not let that happen.

Just after seven, the sun was fully up, and he could hear Konrad's truck coming up the driveway. It stopped about halfway and didn't come any closer. Then he heard the door of the truck open and then shut.

Clark picked up his Devastator and went out onto the front porch. The smell of the beast still lingered in the air, permeating the entire area. He watched the driveway, keeping the rifle at high ready. He could hear boots crunching on the gravel and soon saw Konrad emerge from the trees. He had the Devastator at low ready and was wearing a large backpack.

"Morning!" he said as he walked across the grass. "Did you know you've got a big fucking tree down across your driveway?"

"No," said Clark. "It wasn't there yesterday. I think that thing didn't want us to leave. I heard a tree fall last night. That goddamned thing's smarter than we thought. Last night, it set a fucking trap for me. I damned near walked right into it, too. If Sanchez hadn't warned me in time, I would have."

"By the way," said Konrad, "What's that nasty smell?"

"Guess," said Clark.

"That thing really stinks," replied Konrad. "You'd think it would smell better as much time as it spends in the damned lake."

Konrad joined him on the porch and handed him his rifle. Clark took it and looked quizzically at him. Konrad just held up one finger and smiled. Taking off the backpack, he unzipped one of the large compartments and took out two large McDonalds' bags. Instantly, the smell of the food hit him, and his mouth began to water.

"Breakfast is served," said Konrad, grinning like a school kid.

Sanchez began to stir on the couch.

"Do I smell McDonalds breakfast?" she asked, sitting up.

"Damned straight," said Konrad. "I take care of my people. You just remember who brought you breakfast. If you ever wise up and leave this asshole."

Clark just chuckled and motioned him inside.

"Fat chance," said Sanchez. "You don't have a beautiful cabin in the woods for me to live in."

"I don't have a big fucking hairy monster chasing me, either," he answered, laughing.

"Touché," said Clark. "If we're lucky, neither will I after today."

"Think you have a lead on where it lives?" asked Konrad.

"No," replied Clark. "I shot the goddamned thing and I think there'll be enough of a blood trail that we can track the bastard."

"Nice," said Konrad. "Let's eat and then go monster hunting. I get to be Van Helsing. You're the jackass priest."

"Please," said Sanchez. "Neither of you are half as sexy as Hugh Jackman."

"You'd leave me for Hugh Jackman?" asked Clark, with a smile.

"I'd leave the Catholic Church for Hugh Jackman," she answered with a smile.

"That hurts," said Konrad. "I was hoping you'd be Kate Beckinsale. She's hot."

"Would you leave me for Kate Beckinsale?" asked Sanchez, looking at Clark.

"No," said Clark without hesitation. "I'm not really into older women. She's almost twenty years older than me."

"Still," said Konrad. "She was fucking hot in Van Helsing. Hell, the Underworld movies too. I'd still hit that."

"How romantic," said Sanchez, laughing and snagging one of the bags of food. "What did you bring us?"

"I wasn't sure what you'd want," said Konrad, "and dickhead here eats like a horse, so I just brought a shitload of stuff."

"Good," said Sanchez. "I'm starving."

After they had all eaten their fill, Clark picked up the trash and tossed it in the trashcan by the refrigerator. Sanchez put the leftovers in the fridge and sat back on the couch.

"Thanks," she said, smiling at Konrad.

"My pleasure," he said. "Now, what's the plan?"

"We get our gear together and track that thing," said Clark. "Hopefully, we find it and kill it."

"I'm going with you," said Sanchez.

"I wish you'd go somewhere safe while we find it and deal with it," said Clark. "It seems like it has a crush on you and wants to take you to the monster prom."

"Better rent a limo," said Konrad. "Picking a chick up in a limo is a done deal. Guaranteed those panties are coming off."

"You're an asshole," said Sanchez, laughing.

"You didn't deny it," said Konrad with a wink. "That's practically an admission."

"Well," said Sanchez, "it would have to be a nice limo with a privacy screen. I don't want no creepy limo driver watching me and the big guy getting busy in the back."

Clark just shook his head.

"I'm glad you two can laugh about that," he said. "The thought of it getting you scares me to death."

"Me too," said Sanchez. "But I'm not going to go hide and wait for someone else to solve the problem for me. I'm going to put on my big girl panties and deal with it. If I was the type of person who ran and hid when things got tough, then I wouldn't be much of a cop, now would I?"

"I suppose not," said Clark. "I was hoping I could just get you out of harm's way while I went after this thing."

"No can do, *Kemosabe*," she said, shaking her head. "We're together and that means we handle our problems together. I'm just as terrified of losing you as you are of losing me. Remember that. I already came too close to losing you. I don't want to go through that ever again."

"You're right," admitted Clark. "I guess I didn't think of it that way."

"That's right," said Sanchez. "You're primitive macho Cro-Magnon brain wants to protect me from the bad guys. But you seem to forget that your macho Cro-Magnon brain also almost got you killed last night if I hadn't stopped you. Baby, you need me."

187

"I probably do," said Clark, smiling at her.

"Awww," said Konrad. "You guys are so sweet. Will you adopt me and be my mommy and daddy? You two sound like Ward and June fucking Cleaver."

"Fuck off, asshole," said Clark, smiling and flipping him off.

"Don't look at me," said Sanchez. "I'm not wearing a frumpy dress and apron. I'm more likely to wear just the apron."

"Now that's a mental image," said Konrad.

"What do mean mental?" asked Clark. "Next time I go to town, I'm buying an apron."

"You two," said Sanchez, smiling and shaking her head.

"Speaking of naked, are you two ever going to tell me about the Shaving Thing?" asked Konrad, hopefully.

Clark and Sanchez both laughed but didn't reply.

"I hate you both," said Konrad. "I hope you know that."

Then they all laughed.

"Let's get our gear together," said Clark, after a moment. "I want to start tracking that thing before the trail gets too cold."

Sanchez emerged from the bedroom, having changed into khaki tactical pants and boots instead of the short shorts she'd been wearing. Both Clark and Konrad were already wearing BDU[21] pants and tactical boots. Clark was already wearing his LBV and Konrad was wearing his plate carrier vest.

Everyone began gathering their gear and checking the loads on their weapons. Clark added a D.A.R.K. medical kit to his LBV and put another larger kit in his bag. Loading up extra ammo into his large pack that already had the Gurkha machete strapped to the side, he

---

[21] BDU – military Battle Dress Uniform

shouldered the bag and adjusted the weight, then secured the waist strap. The weight caused his ribs to hurt, but it was bearable.

With the .50 GI on his hip and the Devastator hanging around his neck from the single point strap, he was as ready as he ever would be. He only hoped that it went the way he planned instead of them merely walking into another trap. If they did, he was planning on them finding his body in a pile of expended brass.

Once the others were ready, they headed out the front door and locked it behind them. Clark went around to the back door and checked for damage. He found what he had expected. One of the rocking chairs he'd bought at Silver Dollar City had been smashed against the back wall of the house, reducing it to so much kindling. The barbeque grill was smashed to pieces and lay strewn across the back lawn.

"Well fuck," said Clark. "I guess they're both easily replaced, but I loved that rocking chair."

The back door had a big chunk of wood taken out of it. Laying on the deck by the door was a large rock, about a foot in diameter. Clark attempted to lift it, but it was heavier than he thought. He was able to roll it off the porch and into the grass next to the steps.

"If that had hit you," said Sanchez, "it would have killed you instantly."

"I'm really glad you stopped me from opening that door," said Clark.

"Now maybe you'll listen to me," she chided, smiling.

"Probably not," said Konrad. "He's kind of an idiot."

"No arguments there," she said, smiling at Clark.

Shaking his head and smiling, Clark headed towards the shed. About ten feet from the door, he saw blood on the grass. There was quite a bit of it.

"Holy shit," said Konrad. "That's a lot of blood. You got him good."

"Maybe," said Clark. "A beast that size has way more blood than you or I. That would be enough to put one of us in the hospital or maybe the morgue depending on where I hit it. While I doubt it's just a flesh wound, it might not be as hurt badly as you think. No sense taking any chances and assuming it won't still be able to fight back."

"Good point," said Konrad. "Alright, dude. You're the hunter. Let's see if you can track this big bastard."

Clark began studying the ground closely. Following the indentations in the grass, he could easily make out the direction of travel. The real question would be, would there be a blood trail. About twenty feet away, he found the answer to his question. A large blood drop about the size of a quarter, sitting pristinely on a leaf.

"Bingo," said Clark. "We have a blood trail."

Moving into the trees, he glanced back to see if they were following. They were both holding their rifles at low ready and were watching both sides of them and continuously glancing around them, even looking into the canopy of the trees, just in case.

Clark nodded acknowledgment at them and went back to studying the trail. Every ten to fifteen feet, he found another drop of blood. The blood spatter left trails that indicated the direction of travel. Either the creature wasn't used to being tracked, or it didn't care in its haste to get away.

Even without the blood trail, he could see where the beast had smashed through brush and broken small saplings in its wild crash through the trees last night. Clark remembered the sound of it making its escape and knew that there was no way it could make that much noise and not damage the undergrowth.

There were a few places where he had to take out his machete and cut some brush out of the way that the beast had simply stepped on or over as it went through. It wasn't difficult to pick the trail up again on the other side.

It wasn't long before they found a muddy spot where a small spring emerged from the ground. They were nearly a quarter of a mile away from his cabin, now. Far enough that the sounds of crashing would have been fading away. There in the mud were deep finger gouges where it had pulled up handfuls of thick, dark mud.

"What do you think it was doing here?" asked Konrad.

"Packing the wound with mud," answered Clark. "While not ideal, it will stop the bleeding. They teach that in military survival courses. It's a great way to get an infection, but if you must stop a bleed and that's all you have then you use it. Better to fight infection later than bleed out right now."

"So, no more blood trail?" asked Sanchez, looking around warily.

"Probably not," answered Clark. "But we're close to the lake. We're also getting close to some houses. We're running out of places where it could go."

Picking up the trail again, Clark no longer saw blood drops. Instead, he found a clear trail of crushed down bushes and broken saplings. It had still been moving rapidly, trying to get out of the area.

To his left, he could see glimpses of houses through the trees. They were far enough away that he doubted they could see them. Besides, it was still very early in the morning. Hopefully, they were all still asleep.

The trail veered to the right and headed down a slight incline. Clark continued to follow the trail until it emerged on an empty section of rocky beach along the edge of Table Rock Lake. Although there were no tracks to be found in the rocks, Clark assumed he knew where it had been heading.

Proceeding to the edge of the water, Clark found two massive prints in the soft sand at the water's edge. They were side by side. It had stood here for a while before moving into the water. There was a third print just inside the edge of the water. Although already being eroded by the constant lapping of the water, the track had been deep

191

enough for it to still be discernable as a large footprint. There was no indication that it had come back out of the water in this area.

"Son of a bitch," said Clark. "It went into the lake."

"So much for tracking it to its den," said Konrad.

"It can't be far from here," said Clark. "Every incident has been within a mile or so from this point. There's got to be a cave."

"Then how do we find it?" asked Sanchez.

"Anyone feel like taking a boat out on the lake?" asked Clark.

"I packed my bikini," said Sanchez. "It's in my bag at your place."

"You had me at bikini," said Konrad, lecherously.

"Pervert," said Sanchez with a smile.

Taking a piece of red ribbon out of his pack, Clark tied it to the branch of a tree just at the edge of the tree line.

"What's that for?" asked Konrad.

"I want to see exactly where we came out," said Clark. "This will be how we recognize the spot from out on the boat."

"Good plan," said Sanchez.

Once the ribbon was secured to the tree, Clark took his phone out and marked the spot with a GPS tag. Putting away the phone, he turned to the others and nodded.

"Let's head back to my place," said Clark. "Looks like we're going out on a boat."

Chapter Seventeen
On the Water

"From even the greatest of horrors irony is seldom absent."
H.P. Lovecraft

After backtracking through the woods, they loaded all their gear into range bags and put them into Konrad's truck. While Sanchez was getting ready, Clark and Konrad began discussing the best way to get the tree out of the driveway without spending hours cutting it up

"I could cut it up for firewood," said Clark. "But it'll take hours to cut it up and get it all dragged up here to the splitter."

"Do you have a better solution?" asked Konrad.

"I've got some big log chains in the shed," said Clark. "We can hook up to it and drag it out of the road if you think your truck can handle it."

"It's worth a shot," replied Konrad. "If it can't handle it, maybe we can drag it with the truck and push with your jeep."

"Maybe," said Clark. "Let's see if we can drag it, first."

Heading for the wooden shed, he stopped when he smelled a familiar rank smell coming from the interior. Admittedly, it had been weeks since he had been in the shed, he was certain that it hadn't smelled like that the last time he had been inside.

Turning, he mimed for Konrad to grab the rifles and get over to him. Konrad looked confused but did as instructed. Clark drew the .50 GI and watched the door, waiting for Konrad to arrive with the Devastators.

Although he didn't hear anything moving inside, the smell was warning him something was very wrong. He knew that smell. He'd caught glimpses of that smell each time he'd been near the creature. It was that same rancid smell, equal parts rotten meat, wet dog, urine, and feces. If it wasn't inside, then it had been recently.

Konrad came over holding the two Devastators. Clark was still wearing his LBV and had plenty of extra ammo. Clark took his rifle from Konrad and slipped the single point sling over his head and shoulder. Bringing it around to the low ready position, he nodded at Konrad. At the same time, they pulled their charging handles and racked a round into the chamber. Then they both thumbed off the safeties with an audible click.

"Ready?" mouthed Clark.

Konrad nodded assent and focused his attention on the door to the shed. With one quick motion, Clark yanked the door open and flung it wide. The smell instantly flooded over them and almost caused them both to retch. It was nearly overpowering and took all their willpower to stay on task. Daylight flooded into the interior of the shed, but most of it was still dark shadows. Nothing moved inside.

Cautiously, Clark advanced and let go of the Devastator with his forward hand. Struggling to breathe through his mouth and not his nose, he fought down the urge to vomit. Keeping the rifle tight against his shoulder, his finger stayed next to the trigger. Slowly, he reached inside the doorway and hit the light switch. Instantly, the shed was filled with light. Both Clark and Konrad brought their rifles up into position and their fingers were on the triggers.

Nothing moved inside. The darkness had been chased away, but nothing had rushed towards them. There were still places where things could hide, mostly behind the large zero-turn radius lawnmower and the tool benches.

Motioning for Konrad to follow, Clark began moving into the interior, clearing it as he went. Sweeping the entire shed, they found nothing living inside. What they did find was quite shocking.

In the back-right corner of the shed behind a workbench, was a large nest made from branches and leaves interwoven together. The bottom was covered with thick layers of moss and leaves.

"That looks like a gorilla's nest," said Konrad. "I've seen that shit on Animal Planet. I love animal documentaries."

194

"It's been living in my goddamned shed the entire time," said Clark, shaking his head. "How long has it been in here?"

"When was the last time you were in here?" asked Konrad.

"Maybe more than a month," said Clark. "I haven't needed to mow because it hasn't rained, and the heat has all but killed the grass."

"Well," said Konrad, "it might have been here almost that long."

Moving closer to the nest, Clark lit it up with the tac light he'd installed on the Devastator. Numerous small bones were littering the inside of the nest. Some of them were deer and other small animals. Those didn't bother Clark as much as the pieces of the tiny human skull that were sitting at the back of the nest.

"Goddamn it," hissed Clark.

"We've got to get rid of this shit," said Konrad. "There's no way you can explain why that kid's skull is in your goddamned shed. We need to bury it or throw it in the lake or something. Prescott would crucify you with this."

"Fuck!" hissed Clark.

"It's gone for now," said Konrad. "Do you think it will come back here?"

"Well, it might," said Clark. "Remember what Jay *Matoskah* said? The deer heads might be a territorial marker. I didn't think too much of that, at the time. Now, I'm not so sure."

"Well, if that's the case," said Konrad, "then let's get the bones out of here, and then you can piss all over that nest. I read that's how large predators mark their territory."

"That would do it," agreed Clark, "but you can bet your ass it'll piss it off."

"I would say so, yeah," said Konrad. "So, what do you propose?"

"Let's get rid of the bones first," said Clark. "Then I'm gonna piss all over that goddamned thing."

195

"My man," said Konrad, grabbing an empty plastic five-gallon bucket.

It only took them a few minutes to pick up all the bones and place them in the bucket. Once that was done, Clark made good on his threat and urinated on as much of the nest as he could. If anything, it made the smell inside even worse.

"When this is all over," said Clark, "I'm going to pour an entire fifty-five-gallon drum of Febreze in here."

"Probably won't be enough," said Konrad, making a disgusted face. "Maybe you should just burn it down and rebuild."

"That might be a better option," agreed Clark.

"We still planning on going out on the lake?" asked Konrad.

"Why?" asked Clark.

He could see that Konrad was staring towards the house. He turned around and saw Sanchez standing on the porch in a string bikini that left very little to the imagination. Clark noticed that she was still wearing the small medicine pouch that had been given to her by Jay *Matoskah*.

"You like?" she asked, smiling.

"I want to take pictures," said Konrad.

"Yes, I like," said Clark. "You might give some folks a heart attack, though."

"Well, that was the effect I was going for," she said, chuckling. "When are you two going to get ready?"

"Let us move that tree and we'll change," answered Clark.

"Ok," she replied, turning and heading back into the house and revealing that the bikini was a thong. "Call me when you're done."

Clark glanced over and Konrad's mouth was hanging open.

"Holy shit," he said.

"Easy there," said Clark, chuckling. "Don't sprain something."

Konrad just turned and looked at Clark and shook his head.

"You lucky bastard," said Konrad. "I think I know what the shaving thing was now."

Clark just smiled and him serenely and said nothing.

"I hate you," said Konrad. "Let's get that goddamned tree out of the road so we can go to the lake. I gotta do something to distract me before one of you shoots me."

"Probably her," said Clark. "She can take care of herself."

"No wonder Bigfoot has the hots for her," said Konrad, heading back into the shed.

It took them another thirty minutes to pull the tree out of the driveway. After they put away the log chain, they shut the door to the shed and headed inside.

"Are you going to tell her about the thing living in your shed?" asked Konrad.

"Absolutely," replied Clark. "But she might want to burn it down after I tell her."

"I don't suppose I would blame her," said Konrad.

As they walked inside the cabin, they found Sanchez sitting on the couch reading a book. Konrad just looked at her and smiled, then headed into the bathroom to wash up and change.

"What's the matter with him?" she asked, smiling.

"I think he's going to be in there for a few minutes," said Clark. "I think that bikini might have been too much for the poor boy. By the way, he's under the impression that bikini has something to do with the Shaving Thing."

"Oh my God," she said, laughing. "I take it you didn't say anything to change his mind."

"Not a word," he replied, grinning.

197

"That's too funny," she said. "I'll let him squirm for a while before we let him know that's not it."

"You're evil," he said, chuckling. "Come into the bedroom with me while I change."

She followed him into the bedroom and lay across the bed on her stomach, kicking her feet into the air while he searched for his swimming trunks. The thong made it impossible for him to give searching for his trunks his undivided attention.

After rummaging around for a few minutes, Clark emerged from the bathroom wearing a pair of black and grey swim trunks and a grey tank top.

"When this is all over," said Sanchez with a smile, "I'm taking you shopping. I can't let you go through life with every piece of clothing you own is black or grey."

"Hey," said Clark, "I have a couple of pairs of khakis, too."

"Yeah," said Sanchez. "But they're uniform style cargo pants."

"I have blue jeans, too," he added.

"That I rarely see you wear," she replied with a grin. "Seriously, I'm going to have to start dressing you in something that doesn't look like a uniform accessory."

They emerged from the bedroom, still chuckling. Konrad was sitting on the couch, flipping through channels.

"Why the hell do you only get like three channels?" he asked, glaring at Clark.

"Because I don't have cable or satellite," he replied. "I have an antenna so I can catch the local news once in a while."

"Holy crap," said Konrad. "How can you live like this. What is this Little House on the Prairie shit you have going on out here? You need to get with the 21st Century."

"I have a cell phone," said Clark. "If I need to look something up, I use it."

"Do you even have a computer?" asked Konrad. "Other than the MDT for your patrol vehicle?"

"Well," said Clark, "if you don't count that, then no. I never needed one."

"And you want to live with this guy?" said Konrad, looking at Sanchez. "What are you, Amish?"

"Let's get our gear and head for the lake," said Clark. "We're burning daylight."

"Do you still think it's got a lair somewhere else?" asked Konrad.

"What do you mean 'somewhere else'?" asked Sanchez.

"Oh, shit," said Konrad. "You haven't told her, yet. Sorry, man."

"Told me what?" asked Sanchez.

"We found a nest in the shed," explained Clark. "It looks like that thing has been living right here for a while. Maybe since the beginning."

"When were you planning on telling me that little detail?" asked Sanchez, angrily.

"I was going to tell you," said Clark. "I was just waiting for the right time. It's not like that would be something that I would just casually bring up."

"Do you think it will be back?" asked Sanchez, glancing around nervously.

"Probably," said Clark. "I would assume it would be back at some point. However, after having shot it and chased it through the woods, it might decide to move on. That's why I want to still check the lake. Just in case it's got another den. If we find it, maybe I can finish the job."

"I already loaded all the gear into the back of the truck," said Konrad. "I even loaded the gear bags of guns."

"Good," said Clark. "Let's get to the marina and see if we can rent a pontoon boat."

"Why rent one?" asked Konrad. "We can take my dad's boat out. It's at the marina in Kimberling City. He has a private boat slip there."

"Will he mind if we take it out?" asked Sanchez.

"Nah," said Konrad. "I'll send him a text and let him know we're taking it. He doesn't care so long as I fill the tanks with gas when I'm done. I take that thing out all the time."

"And we're just learning this now," said Sanchez with a smile. "Once this is over, I know how we're going to be spending the summer."

"I'll take you out anytime you like," said Konrad. "You can sunbathe or swim or whatever. I like to fish."

"And I like to sunbathe," said Sanchez with a smile and a gesture at the bikini. "But I hate tan lines."

"Me too," agreed Konrad, waggling his eyebrows.

"Let's go," said Clark, "before Konrad has to go use the bathroom again."

Heading out to the truck, Clark glanced around the area. There was no indication that the beast had returned. Squirrels were playing in the trees and running through the grass. Several rabbits were munching on clover near the back deck. He could even hear birds singing in the trees.

Satisfied, he climbed into the truck with the others. Soon they were heading down the driveway and off to the lake. When they passed the Joe Bald Recreation Area, a thick chain was blocking the entrance with a sign that read "Closed by order of the Army Corps of Engineers."

"Well, that's new," said Konrad.

"I honestly doubt that the Corps of Engineers had anything to do with it," said Clark.

"Me too," agreed Sanchez.

Fifteen minutes later, they were carrying their equipment out onto a pontoon boat. Once they had carried everything out, Konrad began casting off lines and started the engines. Idling back out of the slip, he began a wide turn once clear of the end of the dock.

Throttling up, he headed out of the small inlet and out onto open water. Rounding the end of the peninsula, he moved out towards the center of the lake and angled to pass beneath the Kimberling City bridge. After a quick check at the depth finder, he looked over at Clark.

"Hey," said Konrad. "We're in some deep water here. Grab that green bucket of bones and dump them over the side."

"Good plan," said Clark.

He dumped the contents of the bucket into the water and watched as they vanished from sight, taking the last contents of the nest to the bottom of Table Rock Lake.

"What was that?" asked Sanchez.

"All of the bones we took out of the thing's nest," said Clark. "There were some human bones in the mix. We thought it best to get rid of them because it would be tough to explain how they got on my property."

Sanchez thought about it for a moment before nodding.

"You're probably right," she said. "There's no logical way you could explain them being there. If the sheriff or the feds found them, then they could use it to blame you for the deaths. It would be an easy way for them to shut you up if you tried to go public with what you know."

"I'm not even going to try," said Clark. "Nothing good would come from it. Most people wouldn't believe it unless I dragged the body into the center of town. Even then, there would probably be an attempt to cover it up and discredit witnesses."

"After they said that Jacobson died of natural causes," said Konrad, "I think we can safely assume they have no intention of going public with anything they know. The sheriff probably called the feds in to help him keep this quiet."

"Even if you manage to kill this thing," said Sanchez, "I doubt it would be very smart to try to take it public. I'd bet they would go after you and do everything they could to destroy your credibility."

"Likely end your law enforcement career," added Konrad.

"All of us," said Sanchez. "I don't think they'd let the two of us off the hook. Besides, I wouldn't let you face them alone."

"Thanks," said Clark. "But let's just avoid the entire possibility. I have no desire to try and make this public. I just want it stopped."

"Good plan," said Konrad. "I had an uncle who claimed he saw Bigfoot back in the seventies. People made fun of him for years. Hell, I thought he was crazy until this shit started."

"And now?" asked Clark, grinning.

"Hell, I think *I'm* crazy," said Konrad, shaking his head. "This has got to be some kinda crazy-assed dream. If I hadn't seen it with my own eyes, I never would have believed it."

"Same here," said Sanchez.

"I don't care if anyone believes it or not," said Clark. "I just want that goddamned thing dead before it gets one or all of us."

"Alright then," said Konrad. "Where do you want to start searching?"

"Since we're right at the big bridge," said Clark, "head over past the bluff where I chased it the first night."

"Gotcha," said Konrad, angling the boat to head across the lake.

"Do you think it'll be there?" asked Sanchez.

"I have no idea," said Clark, "but it's a place to start."

Once they cleared the bridge, they followed the shoreline as it curved around to the southwest. Clark moved to the front of the boat and sat on one of the bench seats. Sanchez unfolded a towel and placed it on the deck, then lay down to catch some sun.

"Enjoying yourself?" asked Clark, smiling at her.

"If you see anything, I'll grab a gun and help," she said, beginning to put suntan lotion on herself. "Until then, I'm going to enjoy the warmth of the sun and work on my tan."

"Yeah," said Konrad, smiling. "Leave her be."

"Watch the water, not her ass," said Clark, smiling. "I don't want you to run us aground."

Sanchez just smiled and rolled her eyes. The banter with Konrad was always funny to her. Even if she wasn't with Clark, Konrad was more of a kid brother than a serious prospect for dating. Besides, she was ten years older than him. He was still a kid to her.

As they rounded the last turn of the coastline, the bluff came into view. At its height, it was close to forty feet to the water.

"Where did it jump from?" asked Konrad.

"Hard to give you an exact spot," said Clark. "Not much to use as a landmark. It had to be right about where that big oak is leaning out."

"I see it," said Konrad, throttling back the engine.

"What exactly are we looking for?" asked Sanchez. "It hasn't been here for weeks, as far as we know."

"I'm looking for signs of it being here," explained Clark, "or, more importantly, signs of a cave or some other place where it could hide. How deep do you think the water is here?"

"This is a pretty deep area," said Konrad. "Probably sixty feet or more. Could be closer to eighty. Why?"

"Because when it hit the water," said Clark, "I never saw it come back up."

"I bet the damned thing can hold its breath a long time," said Konrad. "I mean, as big as it is, you'd think it would have a pretty massive set of lungs."

"I would imagine it can," said Sanchez. "It probably swam away underwater so you couldn't find it."

"Makes sense," said Konrad. "I wonder how far it can swim without coming up?"

"God knows," said Clark. "Unless there's a cave in that bluff that it swam back into."

"It's possible," said Konrad. "There are caves all over the place. Missouri's riddled with them."

"Even if there is a cave," said Sanchez, "you wouldn't be able to find it without diving equipment."

"You're probably right," said Clark. "Let's check the shoreline over near Joe Bald. That puts it pretty damned close to my house, too. If it's going in and out of the water there, we'll be able to see a sign."

"Heading that way," said Konrad, throttling up the engines and heading across the lake.

It only took a few minutes to cross the lake and round the peninsula where both the Joe Bald Recreation Area and Clark's land were located. As soon as they started to get close to the area, Konrad took them in as close to the shore as he could without risking hitting submerged rocks.

"Yell if you see any tracks or anything," said Konrad. "I need to watch for submerged rocks. I've gotta keep my eye on the lake."

"I'll yell if I see anything," said Clark.

They cruised along for almost half an hour with Clark scanning the shoreline for anything that looked out of place. They paused as they passed the spot where they had tracked it earlier in the day. They could see where Clark had left the red ribbon tied to the trees, indicating the exact spot that they had emerged. They could see the tracks leading into the water, but nothing returning.

"That's where we came out," said Clark.

He took his phone out and verified the GPS, just to be sure the flag hadn't been moved.

"I only see our tracks," said Sanchez, using the binoculars. "The monster's tracks go into the water, but don't come back out. Ours go back into the trees."

"Good," said Clark. "That means no one else has discovered the tracks."

"Ok," said Konrad, "it went in here. We haven't seen where it came back out. Let's keep watching the shore."

Sanchez continued to sweep the shoreline with the binos while Clark watched the trees for movement. As they rounded the bend of the shore, they emerged on the edge of the Joe Bald Recreation Area. They could see the boat landing as they cleared the end of the peninsula.

To their astonishment, there were about a dozen military vehicles parked near the boat ramp and six boats patrolling the area. As they came into sight, one of the boats broke off from the others and headed their way.

"Do you have any fishing gear?" asked Clark.

"Yeah," said Konrad. "In the gear box. Why?"

"Because we're about to have a boatload of Federal Agents wanting to know what the hell we're doing in the area."

Quickly, they broke out the gear and set it up along the side of the boat. Clark checked to make sure that there were lures on the ends of the lines, then cast two of them into the water. He grunted and winced in pain when he cast the second one.

"Be careful," admonished Sanchez. "Those ribs are gonna be sore for a while."

Clark just gave her a half-smile and finished getting the fishing poles set. Once they were cast, he handed one to Sanchez. Taking the other one, he sat back in one of the chairs and began slowly reeling in the lure.

Just as predicted, the boat approached them quickly and pulled alongside their pontoon boat. Clark noted that they were wearing the uniforms of the State Water Patrol, he didn't recognize any of them. Clark had worked closely with the Water Patrol many times on drowning cases and missing persons in or near the water. He knew every Water Patrol Officer assigned to Table Rock Lake. The men in the boat were strangers.

"Morning, folks," said one of the men.

He was wearing a name badge that said, Harrington. Clark knew Water Patrol Officer Mike Harrington, and this certainly wasn't him.

"Morning," replied Clark. "Something we can help you all with?"

"What brings you folks out to this part of the lake today?" asked Harrington.

Clark noticed that he didn't act like a Water Patrol Officer, either. Generally, the first thing they would ask was if everyone on board that was fishing had the proper license and if there were enough life preservers on board for everyone. Clark decided to wait and see if he asked any of those questions at all.

"Doing a bit of fishing," replied Clark, gesturing with his pole.

"Me, too," said Sanchez, smiling and showing him her fishing pole.

The man seemed more interested in her bikini than in the fishing pole.

"I'm afraid you folks can't be in this area," said Harrington.

"Why is that?" asked Clark.

"This entire area is closed by order of the Missouri State Water Patrol," explained Harrington. "There was a high level of mercury sulfide detected in the water in this area. The Army Corps of Engineers is attempting to clean up. It's not safe to eat the fish in this area."

"Oh god," said Sanchez, acting ditzy. "Won't that contaminate the entire lake?"

"Not to worry," Harrington replied. "It's contained in this area. We'll have it cleaned up in a few days. Until then, we need you folks to please leave the area."

"No problem," said Konrad. "What about the other side of the lake over by Evans Bluff? Is it safe over there?"

Harrington glanced over and gauged the distance before answering. He glanced back at the others, then again at Sanchez.

"Please," said Sanchez, smiling her best smile at him. "We have good luck in this area. We always catch our limit."

Turning to pull her line out of the water, she leaned down and made sure to show off the thong to Harrington.

"I, uh, I think that will be fine," said Harrington. "Just stick to the far side of the channel and you should be fine."

"Thank you!" squealed Sanchez, playing up the part.

"No problem," said Harrington. "You guys have a nice day, now."

Getting back onto his boat, they remained in the area until Konrad fired up the engines on the pontoon boat and headed across the channel to the far side of the lake. Once they cleared the halfway mark, Harrington's boat turned and headed back to the others near the boat ramp access at Joe Bald.

"Lying prick," said Konrad, "there isn't any mercury sulfide in the water here. For one thing, it's not even water-soluble."

"How do you know that?" asked Sanchez.

"I told you," said Konrad, smiling. "I watch way too many documentaries. I love History, Discovery, and Science channels. That's all I watch."

"So, bullshit cover story," said Clark, "and they're still keeping everyone away from Joe Bald. I wonder if they think it's lair is in there somewhere?"

"That's all I can think of," said Sanchez. "Unless they think it will be back, for whatever reason."

"What reason would make them think it would be back?" asked Clark, rhetorically.

Konrad was still idling the boat towards the far side of the channel but had brought his binos up to scan the boat launch area of Joe Bald.

"What the fuck?" he said. "You guys might want to take a look over there."

Clark picked up the other set of binos and began scanning the area.

"What am I looking for?" asked Clark without lowering his binos.

"Look to the left of the last Humvee," said Konrad. "Between the two large trucks."

"Those are called Deuce and a Half's," said Clark, panning the binos around. "What the fuck?!"

"I see you found it," said Konrad.

"Found what?" asked Sanchez. "Clark took my binoculars."

Handing her the binos, Clark looked at Konrad with a dark look on his face.

"They caught its kid," said Clark.

"Hey," said Sanchez, "they have a smaller one in a big steel cage over by the two trucks. It looks like it can't be much more than a few years old, compared to the size of the big one."

"If they caught that one," said Konrad, "then they had to have found it right after Jacobson was killed. That means that it's probably been living in your shed since then."

"That also means they're trying to use the kid as bait to lure the big one in," said Clark. "That means they've got to have the firepower to put that thing down."

"Wait," said Sanchez. "It was living in your shed since then!"

"We don't know for sure," said Clark. "From the smell, it had to be for a while. We found pieces of the skull from the missing girl. I can't explain how that got there if it was living in Joe Bald then."

"Maybe it has more than one lair," suggested Konrad.

"Maybe there's more than one creature," said Sanchez. "I mean, the little one had to have come from somewhere and the one that attacked the house last night was a male."

"I didn't notice," said Clark. "I wasn't checking."

"It was a male," she reiterated. "I saw it clearly."

"Well," said Konrad, "if that's daddy then where's mommy?"

"Or aunts and uncles," added Sanchez. "Or possibly siblings."

"That may be the most terrifying thing I've heard in a long time," said Clark, shaking his head. "God help us if there's more than one. If there's an entire clan, then we're in a lot of trouble."

D.A. ROBERTS

Chapter Eighteen
Gugwe

"For the female of the species is more deadly than the male."
Rudyard Kipling

It was mid-afternoon when they arrived back at Clark's cabin. They were greeted with a terrifying sight. The shed that the creature had been living in had been reduced to splinters. His zero-turn lawn mower had been thrown across the yard and lay broken into pieces near where he used to park his patrol SUV. His toolbox had been smashed apart and tools were scattered across the yard.

There were impact marks on the side of the cabin, and it looked like one window had been broken out. The front door was still closed but they couldn't see the back door from where they were. The porch swing on the front porch had been ripped from its chains and smashed to pieces in the front yard. Clark's jeep had been rolled over onto its top and the windshield had been ripped off it.

"What the fuck!" yelled Konrad as soon as he saw the carnage.

"Goddamn it!" snapped Clark, leaping out of the truck before it came to a complete stop.

Clark pulled the duffel bag out of the back of the truck, then started attaching the holster for the .50 GI on his belt, plus ammo pouches. Wincing in pain from his tender ribs, he fought back the pain and shook his head to clear it. He then slid into his plate carrier, adding magazines for the Devastator to the pouches. Slinging the Devastator's strap over his head, he pulled the charging handle and loaded a round into the chamber.

"Konrad," he said, "stay here and protect her. I'm going to check the back of the house."

"How are we supposed to know if you need help?" asked Sanchez.

"Trust me," said Clark. "If you hear all Hell break loose, come running with guns."

"What do you want me to do?" asked Konrad.

"Turn the truck around and get your rifle ready," said Clark. "Get this pointed towards the highway, just in case we have to get out of here fast."

"What about me?" asked Sanchez.

"Get the other rifle and be ready," he said. "I might need you guys to cover me while I run for the truck."

"I meant; do you want me to come with you?" she said, a note of anger in her voice.

"I need you to stay here," he replied, pleadingly. "Please."

She thought about it for a moment before nodding.

"I will," she agreed, "this time. But we're both in this fight."

"I know," he said, turning and heading off towards the house with the rifle tight against his shoulder.

As he approached the house, he could see that the window that he'd shot from when he hit the creature had been smashed with something heavy. He made a mental note that it would have to be boarded up before nightfall and headed around the back of the house.

At the back, the other rocking chair had been smashed to kindling and one of the porch rails had been ripped off the porch and thrown across the back yard. There were numerous gouges in the back door, but it was still closed. He was starting to move up onto the porch to check the door when he heard a woman's scream followed by gunshots.

Turning, he sprinted around the house. Pain thundered through his ribs and chest, but he kept running. As he rounded the corner of the house, he saw two of the creatures were at the truck, tearing the doors off and shattering the glass. A third creature was beside the bed, rocking the truck back and forth to flip it over. All three of the creatures were at least eight feet tall and had to weigh close to seven-hundred and fifty pounds.

212

Konrad was firing with his Devastator but couldn't get a clear shot because of the movement of the truck. Clark brought his rifle up and aimed, firing as he ran. He fired five rounds at the creature trying to get to Sanchez but missed it cleanly with two rounds and only scored minor hits with three. None of them were enough to prevent it from reaching her.

Seconds later, the beast pulled her from the vehicle, screaming as she was thrown over the beast's shoulder. Clark stopped to steady his aim but couldn't risk hitting Sanchez. Instead, he targeted the one shaking the truck and fired twice. This time, his rounds found their mark, striking the creature in the side of the head.

The creature spun to its right and faced Clark, a wild look of pain on its face. It took two steps towards him before crumpling to the ground in a heap. Blood was pouring from the creature's ears. It was clear that it was dead.

In a flash, the third beast grabbed Konrad and yanked him free of the vehicle. Konrad managed to fire three rounds point-blank into the beast's chest before it tore his head completely from his shoulders, then threw it at Clark while blood fountained from the ragged stump of his neck.

"Goddamn it!" screamed Clark, as he sighted in on the beast that had killed his friend.

The head struck him in the legs with enough force to make him fall to the ground. His shot went wide and missed the creature completely. He hit the ground hard and felt his left hip dig into the rocks on the ground. He felt something crunch in his pocket. Despite the pain, he forced himself to get quickly back to his feet.

The beast tossed Konrad's lifeless body aside and turned to charge at Clark. The creature stumbled as it began running towards him but kept coming and gaining speed. He could tell this one was a female because of its large breasts that bounced as the she-beast ran towards him.

Clark could see the large holes in its chest and abdomen from the hits that Konrad made before it killed him. The she-beast was still eating up the ground between them, despite the wounds. Clark took a moment to orient himself and steady the rifle.

The she-creature had closed the distance to less than twenty yards. Clark exhaled and took up the slack on the trigger. The round struck the beast in the left eye and exploded from the back of its skull. It still took three more steps before it crumpled to the ground less than six feet away from him.

Ignoring the dead fiend, Clark turned to look for the one that was carrying Sanchez. Just at the edge of the trees, he saw Sanchez raise her head and look at him with absolute terror on her face. The beast was moving fast, trying to escape with her before Clark could stop it.

He knew he couldn't shoot it without risking hitting her. He considered shooting it in the legs but knew it was moving too fast for a clear shot. Just as it was about to vanish into the trees, Sanchez lifted the leather bag from around her neck and shoved it into the beast's mouth.

There as a loud snap that sounded like electricity and the creature went rigid, then collapsed to the ground. Sanchez leaped away from it and sprinted towards Clark. Her bikini top had been torn off in the struggle and she was having difficulty running barefoot through the gravel on the ground.

Behind her, the creature began to stir. It was shaking its head and screaming in pain. Clark could feel the force of the beast's scream in his chest. The sound hit him like a wave.

"MOVE!" screamed Clark as he brought his rifle up to sight in on the monster.

Sanchez dove to the side and out of the line of fire. Clark fired two times and the beast's scream silenced into a gurgle as its head came apart from the impact of the massive slugs.

Running to her, Clark helped her to her feet then grabbed the fallen Devastator that was still clutched in the hands of Konrad's lifeless body. He noticed that the bolt was locked back, indicating that the weapon was empty. Clark grabbed the duffel bag that had the extra ammunition and gear in it, then slung it over his shoulder.

"Get to the house!" he screamed, turning towards Sanchez.

She got to her feet and headed for the front door as fast as she could go. Clark followed her by running backward to cover her and watch for more of the creatures emerging from the trees. When they reached the porch, Clark threw her the keys and she unlocked the front door.

Clark was backing through the door when he saw four more of the creatures emerge from the trees. One was larger than the others and its left arm hung limply at its side. It was glaring at Clark. He knew it had to be the big one he'd hit in the shoulder from the kitchen window. He considered firing at the creatures, but he knew he needed to change magazines in both rifles.

The other three creatures quickly picked up their fallen brothers and sister, then headed back into the woods. The big one continued to stare death into Clark's eyes as it picked up Konrad's body and disappeared back into the trees, then vanished from sight.

Slamming the door shut, Clark locked the deadbolt and collapsed to the ground. His breath was coming in ragged gasps as the pain from his ribs shot white-hot needles into his chest cavity.

"It...fuckin'.... killed .... Konrad," he wheezed. "It tore ... his fuckin' ... head off!"

He fought to get his breath, but it wouldn't come. Sanchez took Konrad's Devastator and checked the magazine. Dropping the empty to the floor, she took a loaded mag from Clark's LBV and reloaded the Devastator. Then she did the same with Clark's.

"Breathe, baby," she said, "calm down and breathe. You're hyperventilating."

Rolling over onto his back, Clark forced himself to take deep lungsful of air and fought to control his pain. Slowly, it began to subside, and his breathing began to improve. Sanchez sat on the floor and laid his head in her lap, stroking his hair.

Her long black hair fell around her shoulders and breasts, sticking to her skin from the sweat that covered her. There were cuts and scratches on her skin both from the beast's claws and the glass from the windows of the truck. Tears streamed down her face as she continued to stroke his hair. While her right hand stroked his hair, her left still clutched the medicine pouch tightly. The bottoms of her feet were bloody from the sharp rocks she had sprinted through to get to the house.

"There were too many of them," she said, sobbing. "They killed him. They tried to take me."

"We killed three of the goddamned things," said Clark, grimly, his breath still heaving.

Outside, they heard a horrendous scream that they both felt in their chests. It was followed by a creaking sound of splintering wood and the rush of leaves from a tree falling. There was a massive impact and they both heard the crunching of metal and breaking of glass.

Clark got slowly to his feet and looked out the window. The creatures had shoved a large walnut tree over, dropping it on the broken remains of Konrad's truck and blocking the driveway completely. Although Sanchez's Camaro was still parked beside the well-house and hadn't been touched, there was no escape by vehicle for them. Another tree crashed to the ground farther down the driveway. They weren't going anywhere unless it was on foot.

"Should we call for help?" asked Sanchez, still sitting on the floor.

Clark took out his cell phone and checked it.

"It's smashed," he said.

"Do you have a landline?" she asked.

"No," he said. "I let it go a long time ago. I never needed it. Where's your cell phone?"

"In the truck," she said, "in my bag that had my pistol and extra ammo."

"We're fine for guns," explained Clark. "I've got more than enough. The ammo supply is good, too. We can last a good long while."

"What about food?" she asked.

"I have enough food and bottled water to last for weeks," he said.

"What if they cut the power?" she asked.

"Good luck with that," said Clark. "After having my power taken out by two different ice storms, I had the lines all buried. All my lines are underground. Unless they're smart enough to go take out the poles along the road, we're fine."

"What about Konrad?" she asked, tears flowing freely now.

"They took his body," said Clark. "We can at least bury his head."

Another scream shook the windowpanes and made them both jump. It was much closer than the last time. It sounded like it had come from just outside.

Clark pulled aside the curtain and looked into the front yard. Standing less than twenty feet away in plain view was another of the creatures. This one was massive, closer to nine feet tall. It was also clearly female. From the grey in the beast's hair, it had to be the Alpha female and likely the mate of the big one that Clark had wounded the night before.

"There's a big female outside screaming at us," said Clark. "I think it wants something."

It was staring at him as if to challenge him to come outside. It snarled, showing massive canine teeth, and screamed again. The sheer volume almost shattered the glass in the windows. It screamed again and beat massive fists on the ground with enough force that Clark could feel the vibration in his feet.

"It wants revenge," said Sanchez, still not getting up from the floor. "You killed three of her children."

When Clark didn't exit the house, the beast reached down and picked up Konrad's head. The eyes were wide open and frozen in terror. His mouth was open in a silent scream.

"What the fuck are you doing?" said Clark, striking the window frame with his fist.

The beast turned and began walking away towards the trees, not in any hurry. It was eating Konrad's head, crunching into the face and skull, like you would an apple.

"Goddamn it," hissed Clark. "I'm going to kill every one of those goddamned things!"

"Not if they get us first," said Sanchez, still sobbing.

Clark turned and gently picked her up like you would a small child. Carrying her to the bedroom, he lay her gently on the bed. Going into the bathroom, he gathered first aid supplies and a damp cloth.

Returning, he cleaned and disinfected her wounds and made sure that none of them had any glass or pieces of rock in them. After cleaning away the worst of the dirt, he applied antibiotic ointment to them and began wrapping her feet in gauze. When he was done, he went into the kitchen and returned with a bottle of Bushmills Black Bush Irish Whiskey. Pouring a small amount into a glass, he handed it to her.

"Drink this," he said, gently. "It'll help your nerves."

She did as he requested and drank it in one gulp. He took the empty glass from her and sat it with the bottle on the bedside table. Covering her with the blanket, he tucked her in and kissed her on the cheek. Picking up the glass, he poured himself a generous measure and took a sip.

"You're safe in here," he said. "Get some rest. I'll watch over you."

"I hope when I wake up that this was all a bad dream," she said, closing her eyes.

"Me too," he whispered. "Get some rest, while you can. It'll be dark soon."

Chapter Nineteen
Death Comes at Night

*"There is no hunting like the hunting of man, and those who
have hunted armed men long enough and liked it,
never care for anything else thereafter."*
Ernest Hemingway

Clark went out the back door cautiously and picked up several boards, then slipped back inside quickly. Getting a hammer and nails out of the big drawer in the kitchen, he nailed the boards over the broken window and then tacked plastic over that to keep out the wind. When he finished, he crept in and checked on Sanchez. The noise hadn't bothered her in the slightest. She was still fast asleep.

With that complete, he sat down at the kitchen table and broke down one of the Devastators and thoroughly cleaned it. Once it was clean, he reassembled and reloaded it. With that complete, he repeated the process on the second Devastator.

Once they were both cleaned and loaded, he took apart the .50 GI and inspected the frame before cleaning it and putting it back together. Loading it with the massive hollow points, he made sure that there was one in the chamber and then topped off the magazine.

When he was satisfied with that, he started checking the load on all his firearms. He had an extensive firearm collection. He placed rifles and pistols in strategic places around the house in case he had to grab one quickly. Despite some of them being smaller caliber than the others, he proceeded on the logic that any gun was better than no gun.

With that accomplished, he sat on the sofa and slowly sipped his glass of Irish Whiskey. It wasn't enough to get him intoxicated but might knock the edge off the pain and the nerves.

He knew he had to hold it together for Sanchez. She'd been through hell, nearly being abducted and watching those things kill Konrad. His mind raced over the possibilities, including the very real possibility that once this was over, she would get as far away from him and this place as humanly possible. Hell, he wouldn't blame her.

"How many more of those goddamned things could there be?" he wondered. "I know of at least five, and that's assuming I saw all of them. There could have been more hiding in the trees."

The sun was creeping low on the horizon and he knew that he didn't have long before the sun went down completely, and they would come for them. He could only hope that whatever protection Jay *Matoskah* had put into those two carvings would hold. If they breached the house, there was nothing left to stop them.

Knocking back the remainder of the glass, he set on the coffee table and got up. Heading over to where his gear was laid out, he put on his LBV and buckled it into place, then added full magazines to the pouches. Slipping the single point sling around his neck and chambering a round, he flipped the selector to safe.

He was turning to go wake up Sanchez when he heard the shower start. Smiling, he prepped her gear for her. Moving over to the front door, he peered out the small window. The sun was getting low in the sky and the shadows were growing longer. There was nothing in the yard and he couldn't see anything moving. Despite that, he knew that they were there, waiting for darkness to come before they began their attack.

They had tried their attack in broad daylight and lost three of their own. They wouldn't make that mistake again. They would come under the cover of darkness and from different angles. The creatures were smart enough to know that there were only two of them in the house. They could only cover so many directions at one time.

Clark was lost in thought, considering angles of approach and directions of fire when he felt Sanchez slip her arms around him from behind. She nestled her cheek up against his back and held him tight enough that he felt his ribs twinge in pain, although he refused to let her know. He didn't want the embrace to end.

"We're not going to make it through this, are we?" she asked after a moment.

"Don't give up on us, just yet," he replied softly. "They're going to be cautious. We hurt them, last time. None of them will be willing to rush into the range of my rifle. What I wouldn't give for a box of claymores[22], right now."

"There are only two of us," she said, "and they can come at us from any direction."

"Not as much as you might think," he replied. "Those things are too damned big to come through any of my windows. Grandpa build this place solid and didn't believe in big windows. The only way they're getting inside is through a door, and even that's gonna be a tight squeeze. If they come through a door, I'll choke them to death in the doorway. I've got enough ammo to hold them for a long time."

"How many of them do you think are left?" she asked, clearly dreading the answer.

"We saw five, for sure," he replied. "From the sources I read, researchers speculate that groups can be as large as twenty. I seriously doubt that there are that many. For one, a group that large would need a massive amount of food to keep them going. I seriously doubt that they have all that many more than we already saw unless they're small like the one we saw in the cage."

"How many do you think is likely?" she asked.

"I would bet there's likely to be a couple more than what we saw," he replied. "Maybe a total of eight adults. I also think that they're smart enough to know when revenge is too expensive for the clan. We take out three to five more and I bet they fade away into the darkness and don't return."

"You really think that'll happen?" she asked, sounding hopeful.

"Yeah, I do," he said. "Right now, they're pissed because we took out three of them. They'll hit us in the dark when they think they have the advantage. If we can drop a few more, they'll see that the dark isn't

---

[22] Claymores – a type of landmine used by the US Military.

that big of an advantage. I don't think they'll remain in the area after that. We just have to hurt them bad enough to make us a target they can't afford to take."

"Then it'll be over?" she said, sounding hopeful.

"I think so, yeah," he replied. "I mean, they've proven that they're intelligent. I don't think they'd risk wiping out their entire family group when it gets too expensive to keep attacking us."

"If they move out of the area," she said hesitantly, "won't they just become someone else's problem?"

"Yeah," said Clark, "but even if we got them all, I know that this group isn't all of them in the world. There are more of them out there, probably in the deep woods."

"Then let's give these things a reason to leave," she said, sounding determined. "This is our home. They won't run us out of here."

"That's the plan," he agreed. "I think if we kill enough of them, they'll go back to the deep woods. I believe that the reason we've never heard of attacks like this before is partially that the government covers it up and partially that they only hit people in remote areas. This was a big push into a well-populated area. If we bloody their nose bad enough, I think they'll go back to the deep woods and get clear of this area."

"Good," she said, "I want them gone."

Before he could say anything else, they heard a resounding whack of wood against wood from somewhere close by. Then they heard it again from the back of the house, also close by. It was repeated on both sides of the house.

"They're signaling that they're in place," said Clark. "They'll make their move once it's completely dark."

"Then I'd better get ready," said Sanchez.

Walking over, she picked up her LBV and buckled it into place, then filled the magazine pouches with magazines for the Devastator. Then she loaded up on extra magazines for her Glock 9mm, securing them to the vest. Checking the load on her Glock 19, she then slid it into the holster on her hip.

"I'm ready as I ever will be, I suppose," she said, slipping the single point strap over her neck and shoulder, then adjusted the sling to fit her.

Clark went over to her and stood beside her. Slipping his arms around her, he kissed her gently on the forehead. She melted into his arms and he held her there for a long moment, taking it all in. This could be the last time he held her, so he was going to make it memorable.

"I love you," she said, softly.

"I heard you the first time," he said, leaning his cheek against her still-damp hair.

"What do you mean?" she asked, confused.

"I heard you," he said, "when I was bleeding on the ground behind your squad car. The day of the shooting. I heard you then."

"Really?" she asked tears in her eyes.

"Really," he said. "It's what gave me the strength to keep fighting. It's why I refused to let go."

"I thought you were going to die," she said, sobbing.

"I nearly did," he replied. "But I knew when I heard you say it that I wasn't going to die. I wasn't going to let that be the first and last time I heard you say it."

"Then don't let this be the last time, either," she said, crying.

"It won't be," he said. "Because I love you, too. I won't let this be the last time you hear it, either."

"Then let's show these things that we won't let them win," she said, her voice full of resolve.

"Sounds good to me," he replied. "Let's knock these fuckers off the top of the food chain."

Outside the house, first one of the creatures let out a blood-curdling scream that they felt in their bones. One by one, the others took up the cry. Soon, it seemed like a cacophony of inhuman screams were bombarding the cabin from every direction.

"They can probably hear that in town!" yelled Sanchez, trying to be heard over the screaming.

"I hope so," screamed Clark.

"Why?" she asked, clearly confused.

"Because the military and those feds are still at Joe Bald and that's only about a mile from here. They should be able to hear them!"

"Let's hope it brings them running," said Sanchez.

Clark released his hold on her, and they slipped apart. Clark went over to a large wooden cabinet that sat against the back wall and started pushing it over in front of the back door. Sanchez helped him and soon the cabinet completely blocked the back door, hiding it from view.

"That should slow them down," said Clark. "It means that we'll hear them coming long before they get through that door."

"Then we only have to watch the front door," she agreed.

"They might break the windows and reach through," said Clark, "but I seriously doubt that they'll be able to get through one of them."

The screaming abruptly stopped and was replaced by large stones hitting the roof and walls of the cabin. A few times, they heard the shattering of glass from the bedrooms and the kitchen. A large rock about the size of a bowling ball smashed through the living room window and destroyed the television set, sending glass and sparks flying across the floor.

Clark backed up to a point in the center of the room and faced the front door. Sanchez stood beside him and looked at the kitchen window and glanced towards the bedroom door. They could hear the creatures making hooting and whooping noises as they closed in towards the cabin from the darkness of the surrounding woods.

225

"Here they come," said Clark. "Watch for targets. Hit them whenever and wherever you can. If they stick an arm in through a window, put a bullet hole in it."

"Got it," she replied.

A massive hair covered arm came through the front window and started reaching around for anything it could grab. Clark brought his rifle up and fired three quick rounds, striking the beast in the upper arm and shoulder. The snarls and screams of the beast as it sped away from the cabin indicating that the beast had been hurt. There was a large puddle of blood on the floor beneath the window and the windowsill.

"Take that," said Clark, "you bastard."

Three more shots rang out as Sanchez put high-velocity hollow points into the arm of another beast that had reached in through the bedroom window. It too fled off into the night, screaming in pain. Then everything went quiet.

"What are they doing?" she whispered.

"Changing tactics," whispered Clark. "They won't try anything so direct again. They were testing us. Maybe trying to force us to run out the doors."

"Steel shutters," she said.

"What?" he asked.

"When this is all over," she said, "I want to put lockable steel shutters over the windows. It will be tougher for them to get through."

"Sounds good to me," replied Clark, "but honestly I'm hoping there won't be a next time."

"I think I'd rather be prepared," she answered, "just in case."

"Fair enough," said Clark.

Dropping the magazine, he quickly put three rounds back into it from the boxes he'd prepared on the kitchen table. Sanchez did the same thing. Placing the refilled magazines back into their weapons, they went back to watching the doors and windows.

"What are they doing, now?" whispered Sanchez.

"Stay here," he whispered, "and watch for anything."

Crouching low, Clark crept until he was behind the couch. Laying the Devastator on the arm of the couch, he began looking through the sights, searching the darkness beyond the window for any sign of movement. Slowing his breathing to prevent the weapon from moving, he watched and waited patiently. His patience was soon rewarded when he saw movement near the wreckage of Konrad's truck.

It was a smaller male, about six feet tall. It was sneaking towards the house, unaware that it was being watched. There was enough light left in the sky that lit up the outside of the house more than the inside. He could see it, but it couldn't see him.

Flicking the selector switch from safe to semi, he slipped his finger onto the trigger and began taking up the slack. Just as he was about to take the shot, a massive roar shook the house. The young male *Gugwe* stood up and looked towards the trees to its left. In responding to the call of what had to be the Alpha, it lined up perfectly for Clark's shot.

BOOM!!

Devastator roared like its namesake and sent high-speed death streaking to its target. The beast, alerted by the sound, turned towards him with a look of shock on its face. It didn't seem to realize until it was too late what that noise had been.

Clark could see the look of utter shock on the beast's face as the hollow point struck it in the middle of the forehead. Even in the growing darkness, Clark could see bits of skull, blood, and brain erupt from the back of the beast's head and it collapsed like its bones had just turned to jelly.

The beast hadn't even hit the ground when a roar of rage and anguish split the night. Large rocks began to rain down onto the roof and smash into the sides of the cabin. Clark didn't let the tactic distract him. He waited patiently until he saw one of the creatures attempting to spider walk up to the fallen creature. It was walking on its hands and feet, crouched low to keep its profile down and unnoticeable.

"Come on, you son-of-a-bitch," whispered Clark.

When the creature got close to its fallen brother, Clark fired twice in rapid succession. The rounds struck the beast in the neck and just below the collarbone on its left side. The beast collapsed to the ground, screaming out a gurgling howl as it bled through its throat and into its lungs. Clark knew it was dying but might take a few minutes to bleed out completely. In the meantime, it was going to serve as a gruesome reminder of what was waiting for the others.

"That should get their attention," said Clark, glancing over at Sanchez.

She was watching him with a smile on her face. She had taken her attention off the other windows. Clark could see movement behind her as one of the smaller ones was creeping towards her. Somehow it had managed to get through the window.

"Down!" he screamed.

Sanchez didn't hesitate and went straight to the floor. The creature turned its attention from her to Clark and it raced towards him. He tried to spin with the Devastator, but the beast bore him to the ground with nearly bone-crushing force.

Clark felt the breath knocked from his lungs as the beast landed right on top of him. The Devastator was knocked from his grip and fell to the floor next to him. Although still tethered to him by the single point sling, there wasn't enough room between the two for him to bring the weapon to bear.

The beast dug its long claws into his shoulders and pinned him to the ground. Slowly, it opened its massive jaws revealing three-inch-long canine teeth. The beast's breath was fetid with the stench of dead animals and rotten flesh. The sheer heat of its breath and the smell made Clark feel nauseous and he thought he might pass out.

228

Inch by painful inch, it lowered its fangs towards his face to live up to the name *Gugwe*. It flashed through his mind that Jay *Matoskah* had said it meant "face eater." Clark was afraid he was about to find out why they called them that.

Struggling against the creature was futile as it was many times stronger than him. For some insane reason, he felt like there was no reason to resist. Almost like it was telling him in his brain to just relax and let it happen. It was nearly overwhelming, and he felt himself starting to let go and stop struggling when he heard Sanchez screaming.

That sound snapped him out of his trance, and he forced his right arm to react and drew the .50 GI Guncrafter Industries Glock Conversion pistol from his holster and shoved it into the beast's armpit, then emptied the magazine.

Screaming in pain, the beast let go of him and fell to its side, to his left. There was a massive amount of blood pouring from the fist-sized hole in its ribcage. It was gasping for air and a look of panic was on its face. It was dying and didn't understand how it had gone from predator to prey in the blink of an eye.

Clark ignored the dying beast, reloading as he stood. He saw Sanchez backing away from two more of the creatures. The beasts saw him stand but didn't understand the danger they were in and failed to notice their dying comrade.

Clark leveled the .50 GI and put three rounds into each of their heads in rapid succession. Both creatures stumbled back and collapsed to the floor with massive cranial trauma. Clark started to reload when he saw Sanchez roll onto her stomach and point her Devastator in his direction.

"Move!" she screamed, and Clark dove to his left, landing on the corpse of the one that had taken him to the ground.

The massive roar of the Devastator bellowed three times. Clark rolled over to see one of the larger creatures slumping dead, halfway through the window. Sanchez had blown the top half of the beast's skull completely off leaving part of the brain and brain stem visible.

Spinning around, she fired twice more into the bedroom. A grunt of pain then a roar of fury sounded as he heard one of the creatures crashing away from the house and into the woods at a high rate of speed.

"Goddamn it," snapped Clark. "How many more of those bastards are there?!"

"Too many!" she replied, her chest heaving. "How long will they keep up the attack?"

"I would have thought that they would have called it off already," said Clark, looking around at the dead creatures in the room.

"You also thought they couldn't get in through the windows," Sanchez pointed out.

"I guess those wooden figures that Jay gave us didn't keep them out," said Clark, glancing at the mantle of the fireplace.

"Well," said Sanchez. "He did say nothing would stop them if they wanted to attack us. The medicine bag and the figures were to ward them off, but I guess even that wasn't enough."

"Apparently the Devastator can," said Clark, reloading his rifle, then reloading the pistol.

"Do you hear that?" asked Sanchez.

"Hear what?" asked Clark, glancing around.

"Exactly," she said. "It's dead quiet out there, now."

"What the hell are they planning now?" asked Clark.

"Look," said Sanchez, pointing out the front window.

Clark turned and saw lights approaching the front of the cabin. He could tell by the way they moved; they were coming in a tactical formation. All the screaming and gunshots had attracted attention. Whether they liked them or hated them, the feds and the military were coming in.

"It's the people from Joe Bald," explained Clark. "Here comes the military."

"Let's hope they're actually on our side," said Sanchez.

Chapter Twenty
The Cavalry Arrives

*"The game of life is good, though all of life may be hurt,
and though all lives lose the game in the end."*
Jack London

"Deputy Clark," said a man in a camouflaged uniform. "I'm Major Levi Saunders."

The man extended his hand and Clark shook it. They were standing on the front porch of Clark's cabin. There was at least a platoon of soldiers that had taken up defensive positions around the cabin. He could hear vehicles coming up the driveway. They had to have dragged trees out of their way before driving through.

"Major," said Clark, releasing his hand. "How do you know who I am?"

"We have a dossier on you, Deputy Konrad and Corporal Sanchez," said Saunders. "Where's Deputy Konrad and Corporal Sanchez?"

"They got Konrad," said Clark. "Tore his head off and dragged off the pieces. Sanchez is inside. Bathroom, I think."

"I'm sorry," said Saunders. "I wish we had known you needed us sooner."

"We couldn't call for help," said Clark. "My cell was crushed when we were fighting them, and Sanchez's cell was in the truck."

Clark gestured at what was left of Konrad's pickup.

"I see," said Saunders. "How many of these things do you think you killed?"

"Total?" asked Clark. "Or just in *this* fight?"

"How many times have you fought them?" asked Saunders.

"Three or four," said Clark. "I'm pretty sure we've killed at least eight and wounded a couple of others."

"Eight?" asked Saunders, incredulously. "Holy shit! That's impressive. Have you noticed that they carry off their dead?"

"For the most part," said Clark. "There's one still hanging out the window right here in the front and two more dead inside."

"We'll be taking custody of the bodies," said Saunders. "I'm afraid we're going to have to ask you folks to never speak of this. We can't release this to the general public."

"Don't worry about that," said Clark. "I held a Top-Secret Clearance in the military. I understand the compartmentalization of information. Besides, I don't want people to think I'm crazy. I would like to continue being a cop."

"That's probably for the best," said Saunders. "I appreciate your cooperation on this. Believe it or not, some people fight us on that. They say the public deserves to know. The fact is, if the public knew everything, there would be a goddamned panic."

"It would certainly keep a lot of people out of the woods," said Clark.

"And get even more killed," said Saunders, "when they decided they wanted to go hunt these things. Frankly, I'm amazed that you did so well against them. I've heard of entire Special Forces Units wiped out, going after these things in Alaska."

"Well," said Clark, "we aren't exactly using standard-issue 5.56mm M-4's. We both are using the Rock River Arms LAR-459 Devastator in .458 SOCOM. Hollowpoint ammunition, too."

"Shit," said Saunders. "That ought to do the trick."

"It'll put them down," said Sanchez, exiting the door, "but sometimes it takes more than one shot."

"That's good to know," said Saunders. "We might have to rethink the weapons issued to our teams."

233

"Teams?" asked Sanchez. "You mean there are teams of you that do this?"

"Yes, ma'am," said Saunders. "Several, actually. Although it will never be admitted to the general public."

"How often do you have to deal with things like this?" asked Clark.

"More often than you'd think," answered Saunders. "I can't give you any details, but this isn't that uncommon. Although I will say that it's usually in an area far less populated than this."

"Remote places in Alaska?" asked Sanchez.

"Yeah," said Saunders, "and Montana, Wyoming, Oregon, Washington, and Idaho."

"What about Canada?" asked Clark.

"While it's not our problem," said Saunders, "I'm given to understand that they have teams like ours. Once in a blue moon, one of ours gets called to assist them. Usually up near the Alaskan and Canadian border."

"So, why all the secrecy?" asked Clark. "I mean, we got the cold shoulder from two guys who claimed to be Conservation Agents then another guy who claimed to be Water Patrol. Hell, even our sheriff did his best to keep it quiet."

"Between you and me," said Saunders, "I hate dealing with the Federal Agents. They're all assholes. They have operational control, though, so we play nice. However, your sheriff is a fucking idiot. He pretty much just rolled over and let the Agents do whatever they want."

"I noticed that too," said Clark. "Both the idiot part and the rolling over. In case you hadn't noticed, I'm no fan of our sheriff."

"He's not smart enough to realize that he has jurisdiction," said Saunders. "He's an elected Law Enforcement Official. He could order them, and thereby us, out of here and there wouldn't be anything we could do or say about it. He just wanted these things stopped and for it to all go away. Well, be careful what you wish for."

"Exactly," said Clark. "Well, thank you for being honest."

"It's the least I can do," said Saunders, "one old soldier to another. Tell me something?"

"What's that?" asked Clark.

"Why'd you leave the military?" he asked. "With your record, you could have gone a long way."

"After Kandahar," said Clark, shaking his head, "I just didn't have it in me. I needed a change."

"And look where it got you," said Saunders. "This fight here had to rank right up there with some of the shit you were in over there. This looked like fucking World War Three when we rolled in."

"It did," said Clark, frowning. "But it's different, this time."

"How so?" asked Saunders. "If you don't mind me asking."

"This is my home," said Clark. "It's different when you're defending your own home."

"I suppose you're right," said Saunders. "Well, we better cut this short. They have the road cleared and the Agents will be here in a moment to speak with you."

"Thank you," said Clark, shaking Saunders' hand again.

"My pleasure," answered Saunders, heading back to his men.

"We're going to be debriefed by the feds," said Clark. "Just agree with keeping this quiet. No need to let them resort to threatening us. If we tried to come forward, they would just ruin our careers and lives. I know they can do that, too."

"Alright," agreed Sanchez. "I'll just tell them I have no intention of ever telling anyone about this."

"That's my girl," said Clark, kissing her on the cheek.

"Do you think the creatures are gone?" she asked.

235

"Maybe," said Clark. "They certainly won't come around while they're here. I hope we did enough damage that we won't see them again."

"Oh, I hope you're right," she replied, grinning.

*****

Three hours later, they had been cleared by Agents who wouldn't identify which agency they were with. Clark and Sanchez watched as they loaded up the bodies into two Deuce and a Half's and took them away. Sometime during their debriefing, Sheriff Prescott had arrived. He was waiting for Clark and Sanchez when they finished.

"Danny," said Prescott.

Clark could see Sanchez wince. She knew how much he hated being called that.

"Yes, *sir*," Clark said, somehow able to not sound like he wanted to punch him.

He even managed to force a smile.

"I'm glad you're both ok," he said. "I was told about everything by the Agents."

"Sir?" asked Clark, not sure what he meant by "Everything."

"I know what happened to Konrad," said Prescott. "We'll list him as killed in a terrible accident. No one will question why there will be a closed casket. That's how it'll have to be since we'll likely never recover the body."

Clark fought down the urge to scream at Prescott. He didn't ever want to hear him so diminish the sacrifice by his friend. It made him want to choke the life out of the smug bastard. He knew it was going to be listed as something innocuous like an auto accident and that thought enraged him to think that Konrad wouldn't be remembered as a hero.

236

"Thank you, sir," said Sanchez, stepping in between them. "I'm sure his family will understand. Are you making the notifications and arrangements?"

"I'll take care of all of that," said Prescott. "By the way, the Agents told me that you played ball. You're both cleared to return to duty as soon as you're ready. I know Clark still hasn't been released by his doctor. From the looks of you both, you might want to see a doctor now."

"I think we'll be ok," said Clark, regaining his composure.

"Suit yourselves," said Prescott. "I've got to go. I need to start making arrangements."

As the sheriff walked away, Clark turned to see Saunders and four of his men rolling his jeep back onto its wheels with a Humvee. There was another crew removing all the blood, leaving no sign of the creatures for anyone to find. No DNA, no hair, no bodies, no evidence whatsoever.

"Did you hear that?" asked Clark. "They were holding up clearing us on the shooting until the Feds decided we weren't going to blow the whistle on any of this."

"Does that surprise you?" she asked.

"Not really," he replied.

"What do you think they're doing here?" she asked.

"Well," said Clark, "it looks like they're sterilizing the area. Leaving nothing that we could use to corroborate our stories if we wanted to say something."

"Yeah," said Sanchez, smiling enigmatically, "it sure looks like it, doesn't it?"

"What did you do?" asked Clark, quietly.

"I'll tell you later," she assured him, with a wink. "For now, we might not want to be talking about this."

"You're probably right," he agreed.

Clark was surprised when Saunders' men cleaned up the debris in his yard and did a thorough sweep of the surrounding trees. Once they were certain that the creatures were out of the area, they began loading up and preparing to leave. Saunders came over to Clark and shook his hand, again.

"I had my men clear the area as much as we could," said Saunders. "We didn't find any sign of them in the area. They've left, for now. I doubt they'll be back considering how much damage has been done to the clan."

"Thank you for all you've done," said Clark. "If you guys hadn't shown up when you did, I don't think we would have lasted much longer."

"Don't sell yourself short," said Saunders. "You guys racked up an impressive body count, all by yourselves. I've had teams not do as well with a full platoon of soldiers."

"Desperate times," said Clark, with a shrug.

"If you ever decide you want back in the game," said Saunders, handing Clark a card, "you call me. I'll get you activated and assigned to my team. Probably with a nice promotion."

"I'll keep it in mind," said Clark, taking the card and glancing at it.

"That's my personal cell number," said Saunders. "Call me anytime."

"Thanks again," said Clark.

Saunders nodded then saluted Clark, slowly and respectfully. Clark returned it with equal respect. Once completed, Saunders smiled and did an about-face. He headed across the yard and joined his men, climbing into the front passenger seat of a Humvee.

"Why did he salute you?" asked Sanchez. "I thought you were an enlisted man."

"I was," replied Clark. "I was an E-6 Staff Sergeant when I got out."

"I thought that enlisted men saluted officers first," said Sanchez.

"They do," said Clark, "under most circumstances."

Sanchez wondered what he meant by that, but didn't press the issue. She was sure he'd tell her eventually, but this wasn't the time to press him about it. She'd learned that he was very reluctant to talk about his time in the military. Something very bad happened in Kandahar and she wasn't sure if it was a good thing to pick at that scar. She'd let him tell her when he was ready.

Chapter Twenty-One
Final Gift

"Kill or be killed, eat or be eaten, was the law;
and this mandate, down out of the depths of Time."
Jack London

Once everyone was gone, Clark sat on the steps of his porch. He still had the .50 GI on his belt and the Devastator in easy reach. He looked around the yard, seeing that all signs of destruction had already been removed.

The sheriff had Konrad's truck towed to add credence to the terrible accident cover story. The truck did indeed look like it had been in an accident. Even his destroyed lawnmower had been picked up and sat in an orderly pile near where the shed once stood. He wasn't sure it could be fixed, but at least all the pieces were together.

With a sigh, he reached into his pocket and took out his can of tobacco. Putting a large pinch into his lip, he sat there for a moment before leaning back, relaxing only a fraction. The carnage might have been cleared, but it was still firmly fixed in his mind. He saw it all as clearly as when it happened. It was his curse. He could never forget the carnage, no matter how much time passed.

"Here," said Sanchez, handing him a glass with about four fingers worth of Bushmills in it.

"Thank you," Clark said, accepting the drink.

"Want to talk about it?" she asked.

"Why?" he asked. "You were here. You saw the same things I saw."

"That's not what I meant," she said. "I know that more than that is bothering you."

"I might," he said, "one day."

"But not today?" she said, not really asking.

"No," he replied.

"You know what I find ironic?" she said, changing the subject.

"What's that?" he asked, glancing at her.

"Through all of this," she said, "they never touched my car. The Camaro is just sitting there pristinely."

"They probably didn't see the need," said Clark, "especially after they blocked the driveway."

"Think maybe we should go stay at my place?" she asked.

"Probably," said Clark. "I think they broke out every piece of glass in the cabin."

"Yeah," she said. "I think they did."

"I'll need to cover them with plastic," he said. "Just in case it rains."

"You're not worried someone will get in and steal your stuff?" she asked.

"Not really," he said. "No one even knows this place is back here. You can't see it from the road. But you've got a point. I might want to keep animals out. I'll get some plywood and nail it over the windows until I can get them replaced."

Clark looked up when he heard trucks approaching. It was clear that it was more than one. Standing up, he put his hand on the .50 GI and waited. Sanchez casually picked up her Devastator and kept it out of sight. After a moment, three military trucks rolled in and parked in the driveway.

A man in military fatigues wearing the rank of an E-5 Sergeant got out of the lead truck and headed right towards them. He stopped short of the porch and nodded at them both.

"Staff Sergeant Clark?" he asked.

"Former," corrected Clark.

"Regardless," said the sergeant. "I'm Sergeant David Ramsey. Army Corps of Engineers. Major Saunders requested we come here and fix the damage done by our training exercise."

"Training exercise," repeated Clark.

"Yes, sir," said Ramsey. "I was told that Major Saunders' unit was training near here in the old Joe Bald Rec Area and they wandered onto your land by mistake. The Army apologizes for the damage done to your property. We're here to replace all the broken windows and rebuild your shed."

"Tell Major Saunders that it's very much appreciated," said Clark. "You and your men can go ahead and do whatever they need to do."

"We're upgrading to the tempered glass thermal windows," said Ramsey, "to make up for the damage."

Another truck rolled into the yard. It was a large flatbed truck carrying a premanufactured wooden shed, much larger than the one that had been destroyed. It backed up and stopped almost exactly where the old shed had been. Within minutes, they were rolling the shed off and anchoring it to the concrete slab where the old shed had stood.

The other crew began the process of removing the wooden window frames and measuring for replacements. After measurements were taken, Ramsey got on the phone and gave the dimensions to another crew who would pick up the windows and deliver them.

By evening when the trucks were leaving, they had replaced every window in the cabin with tempered glass thermal windows and even hooked up the new shed to electricity. The last thing they did was bring in a new mower and boxes of tools.

"I don't understand why they did all this," said Sanchez.

"Maybe it's their way of making sure we keep our mouths shut," said Clark. "By giving us all this and fixing the damage, it's as if it never happened. I didn't even think to take pictures of the damage after it happened."

242

"Maybe," said Sanchez. "It would certainly be tough to claim that something terrible happened here when it has already been fixed. Actually, improved over what it was before."

"Exactly," he said. "Every trace of evidence is gone now."

"Not every trace," she said, smiling.

Clark turned to face her and cocked his head to the side.

"What did you do?" he asked.

"I didn't want to say until they were all gone," she said. "When they first got here, I knew that something like this was going to happen. They were going to take the bodies, clean up the blood, and erase the evidence. I wanted to make sure we had something to hold onto, just in case."

Clark just waited for her to explain.

"While you were talking to Saunders when he first got here," she said, "when I was supposed to be in the bathroom."

Clark smiled and waited for her to continue.

"Well, I took video and pictures of the dead ones inside," she explained. "I took blood samples and sealed them in plastic bags."

"They can discredit all of that," said Clark. "They've done it before. It's only good as supporting evidence."

"I know that, too," she replied, smiling. "You know, I'm a cop too, right?"

"Ok," said Clark, returning the smile. "What else did you do?"

"Well, when I went into the bedroom," she said, still smiling, "I looked by the window. Remember the one I shot at while you were getting up?"

"Yeah," he confirmed.

"Well," she said, "I did more than just hit him in the shoulder. The arm was severed at the shoulder. There's no way that thing survived for very long."

243

"What did you do with the arm?" he asked.

"I wrapped it in plastic and put it in the deep freeze," she said. "I figured they'd check there, so I buried it under all of those packages of venison you have. They never checked there. I just checked a few minutes ago. It's still there."

"We have an arm?" he said, clearly surprised.

"And photos, blood and hair samples," she added. "Plus, video."

"You are amazing," he said, pulling her into his arms and kissing her on the neck.

"I know," she said, giggling, "but it's great to hear you say it."

He held her in his arms and kissed her on the lips, a long and lingering kiss.

"I think I want to spend the night at my place tonight," she said. "No offense, but I want to get a good night's sleep. I may not want to be here for a few days, at least until we're sure they're gone."

"Ok," said Clark. "We'll grab our gear and head out. I want to take the guns, just in case."

"That's fine," she said. "I wouldn't feel safe if we left them here, anyway."

Clark went inside and gathered the gear, placing bags on the front porch. Sanchez started getting her things together and packing them in a backpack. While she was doing that, Clark pulled the Camaro into the yard and started putting bags in the trunk.

While he was placing one of the range bags in the trunk, he stopped and listened without standing up. Something was tugging at the primitive part of his brain, sending him a warning. There was a change in the air. Albeit subtle, something had changed.

Cocking his head to the side to listen, he made no sudden movements to indicate he had been alerted to the danger. It took him a moment to realize that the sounds of birds and small animals had vanished like smoke in the breeze. It was absolutely silent.

Standing quickly, his hand went for the .50 GI on his belt. Too late he realized, the big creature was standing right behind him, looming over him with malice in its eyes. Before his hand reached the gun, the massive beast backhanded him and sent him flying twenty feet across the yard. The beast had struck him in the chest, and he felt the cracked ribs break completely, along with a few others.

Clark had just managed to draw the pistol when the beast struck him. He had no idea where it had landed. Right now, his world was filled with white-hot agony as every breath he took sent waves of extreme pain through his body. He screamed out in anguish, knowing that with no weapon he was now easy prey for the massive beast. He only hoped it was alone.

The creature bellowed a ferocious roar of fury and the promise of death. Clark knew it meant to kill him the way they had killed Konrad. Through tears of agony, he saw the beast advancing on him. The beast's left arm still hung limply at its side. Clark could see maggots in the wound on the shoulder. This was the big male that he'd shot from the kitchen window. It towered over him, well over ten feet tall.

A scream brought it up short. It froze and turned towards the cabin. It was Sanchez screaming at the beast, a mixture of anguish and fear in her voice.

"Don't kill him!" she pleaded. "Please! Take me! Don't kill him!"

It turned towards her, cocking its head to the side as if it comprehended what she had just said, and it was considering it. It started walking towards her and Clark forced himself to his feet. The beast's focus was completely on her and it didn't notice Clark get up.

It was less than six feet from Sanchez and reaching out towards her with its good hand. Clark rushed forward and drove his shoulder into the beast's forearm. He couldn't reach the shoulder, so he hit something attached to it. The results were nearly the same.

245

The beast roared in pain and fury, its good hand going involuntarily to its wounded shoulder. This close, Clark could smell the rot that had set in. The wound was turning septic and the beast likely wouldn't survive it. It was here to kill him before it died. A last act of revenge before it fell. It was likely another Alpha had already been chosen for the clan.

Turning towards him, it swatted him with a crushing blow from a huge right hand. The long claws on the ends of its fingers tore through flesh and muscle, revealing the bones on his ribcage and sternum. The force of the blow threw Clark through the air, bouncing off the passenger side rear fender of the Camaro before landing in a heap behind the car. There was a large dent in the fender.

Agony filled Clark's world. Every nerve in his body screamed out in pain and he fought to not lose consciousness. He knew that if he blacked out, he would die, and the beast would carry Sanchez off. There wouldn't be anyone left to stop it. She would never be heard from again, likely to die a slow lingering death at the hands of the clan. He wasn't going to let that happen, even if it killed him.

Reaching over the bumper of the Camaro, he fumbled for anything that he could use as a weapon. He could see through the fog that was starting to cloud his vision that the beast was slowly advancing on him, preparing to finish what it had started. Clark's fingers clasped a familiar handle. It was his Gurkha machete that was strapped to the side of his pack. Pulling it free, he fell back onto his back and tried to breathe.

The beast moved over him and leaned low, its mouth opening impossibly far. It was open far enough to take his entire head in its mouth. The breath was noxious and reeked of death. Clark was afraid that it was going to be the last thing he remembered before dying.

Clark knew that whatever he was going to do, it had to be now. He was close to losing consciousness and that meant he would never wake up again. In desperation, he grabbed the beast by the side of the head and jammed his thumb into its eye. Roaring in pain, it leaned its head back and started to stand. Clark held fast and waited for it to drag him to his feet.

Before it could stand completely up, Clark swung the Gurkha with all the strength he had left, slicing deep into the beast's throat. Blood fountained out and sprayed all over him, covering him crimson. He could no longer tell which was his blood and which was the beasts.

Swinging its massive arm, it knocked Clark away from him leaving the Gurkha embedded in its throat. It glared death at him as it reached up and pulled the blade free. It snarled a gurgling, ragged sound that still conveyed enough force to feel in his chest. It was determined to finish him before it died.

Stumbling over towards him, its remaining eye was locked on his. Its lips curled back in a snarl of pure hatred as it made its way towards him. Clark tried to push away from it, but his legs didn't have enough strength left to move him. He was mere inches away from death. The glistening claws reached for him and began digging into his throat.

BOOM! BOOM! BOOM!

Three massive reports broke the moment and the beast lurched to the side. Clark felt fresh blood running down his neck where it had begun to cut into his skin.

BOOM! BOOM! BOOM!

Three more shots rang out and the beast fell to the ground, laying on its side, facing him. He rolled his head to the side and once more their eyes locked. There was recognition there as it stared at him. Weakly, it was still reaching out towards him. Even dying, it still wanted to finish him off. Then the light faded from its eyes and its arm dropped to the ground. The beast was finally dead. Clark could see six ragged bullet holes in its chest, abdomen, and throat.

Rolling his head to the side, he could see Sanchez advancing tactically as she reloaded the .50 GI without taking her eyes off the target.

"That's my girl," he managed to say before he blacked out.

D.A. ROBERTS

Epilogue

Sanchez sat on the observation deck, looking out over the ocean. There were scars on her tanned skin that peeked out from beneath the flowery sundress she wore. A gentle breeze blew in from the Atlantic, ruffling her long black hair.

The old-world look of the small village was both amazing and relaxing for her. She took in the smell of the salty air and then settled into a small table of an outdoor café.

"Welcome to the *Restaurante La Paloma, señora*," said the waiter, in heavily accented English. "My name is *Mateo*. Is this your first time in *Cudillero?*"

"Yes," she replied, in English. "My grandmother was born here, but this is my first visit."

"May I start you with a glass of wine?" he asked. "There is a local vintage that I think you would very much enjoy. A wonderful red."

"I'll have that," she said, wistfully.

She was still taking in the scene around her. She never thought she would find herself here. The horrors she had undergone at the hands of the *Gugwe*, seemed so far away. Like a distant and painful memory. In a flash of memory, she saw Clark laying there on the ground, covered in blood and unmoving. She winced at the memory but said nothing.

"And for you, *señor?*" he said, turning towards Clark.

"I'll have the same," he said, smiling.

Clark wore a white long-sleeved cotton shirt that she had bought him at the market. It fit well, but it hung loosely from his chest and shoulders, revealing a network of jagged scars across his shoulders and upper chest.

Moments later, *Mateo* returned with two wine glasses then filled them from a bottle with a label written in Spanish. The wine was deep red with an aroma that filled the air. It smelled like red fruit and faintly of vanilla. Clark took his glass and brought it to his nose to inhale the fragrance.

"This smells amazing," he said, smiling.

"Thank you, *señor*," said *Mateo*. "The vintage is excellent. I think you will both be pleased. Have you decided on something to eat?"

"What do you recommend?" asked Clark.

"*Cudillero* is famous for its seafood," said *Mateo*. "Perhaps you would like to share an assortment of flavors. The large platter allows you to sample nearly a dozen of our best dishes and provides enough food to satisfy your hunger."

"Let's do that," said Clark.

"Excellent, *señor*," said *Mateo*.

As he walked away, Clark turned back to Sanchez.

"Are you ok?" he asked, taking her hand.

"I'm fine," she said, smiling. "Just lost in my thoughts. I can't believe we're finally here."

"Me either, baby," he said, taking her hand and kissing it.

"Thank you for bringing me here," she said, smiling.

"I know we've been through hell the last few months," he said. "With everything that happened since the night we got back together."

"We've both came close to dying," she said. "More than once, I might add."

"And we came through it," he said, smiling. "You saved my life. I thought I was trying to protect you and you wound up saving me."

"I know," she said, smiling. "Ironic, isn't it?"

"Very," he replied. "That's why I wanted to bring you here. I wanted to bring you to the one place you've always wanted to see. I wanted to show you how much you mean to me."

"I love you," she said. "I think if we survived those monsters, then we can survive anything."

"That's kind of what I thought," he said. "That's why I brought you this."

She turned as he was bringing it out of his pocket. It was a tiny ring box, worn but still beautiful.

"What is that?" she asked, her voice growing thick with emotion. "What are you doing?"

"I'm asking you to marry me," he said, getting down on one knee. "If you'll have me."

He opened the box and revealed a beautifully crafted ring, wrought in gold, and bound with more than a dozen small diamonds that surrounded a much larger one in the center. It was flawless and beautiful.

"Oh my god," she said. "Yes!"

Clark smiled and took the ring out of the box, then slipped it on her finger. It fit perfectly.

"It's beautiful," she said, holding it up to the light. "How could you afford this?"

"It belonged to my grandmother," he said. "My grandfather bought it when he was in Europe fighting in World War Two at a little shop in Barcelona, just after the war ended."

"It's beautiful," she said. "I love it."

"It pales next to you," he said.

"I can't wear this," she said, "it must be worth a fortune."

"When I had it resized to fit you," he said, "the jeweler in Springfield offered me a quarter of a million for it. I turned him down because giving it to you means more to me than money. It was like it was meant for you. You trace your family to Spain, and this is where my grandfather bought it. I've thought that since we first started dating."

"You know I can't wear this on-duty," she said, tears in her eyes.

"I know," he said. "We'll figure that out, later."

She leaned towards him and they kissed over the table. She kissed him several times and held his face in her hands.

"I can't believe we're here," she said. "This has to be a dream."

"Nope," he said, "pretty sure I'm awake."

She laughed and sat back in her chair. Clark took a sip of the wine and leaned back in his chair.

"There's just one other thing I want to talk to you about," he said, sliding a card across the table. "We've got two options when we get back. I won't make a decision this big on my own, especially since you said yes."

"What decisions?" she asked, glancing down at the small card.

"You know we can't go back to the way things were," he explained. "We'll be looking over our shoulders waiting for Prescott to shove us aside or fire us. He covered up the deaths of two officers and lied to the public. I can't let that go. If we quit, he'll do his best to ruin our reputations."

"So, what do we do?" she asked, dreading the answer.

"Well," said Clark, hesitating, "I figure we have exactly two options. We either meet him head-on or we go somewhere he can't touch us."

"What do you mean?" she asked, sipping her wine.

"Either I run for sheriff and get him out of office," said Clark, "or I call the number on that card and go to work for Saunders."

"Which do you prefer?" she asked, studying him closely.

"I already spoke to Saunders to see what he had to offer," explained Clark. "I go back active as an officer, promotion to captain and I take over as Executive Officer with Saunders' team. That's a lot of money.

Way more than I'd make as the sheriff of tiny little Sloan County. Plus, I'd travel to a lot of different places hunting those things."

"Where does that leave us?" she asked, frowning.

"I'd still live at the cabin," he said, "I would only deploy when they had a call-out for the team."

"Then what do I do?" she asked.

"You run against Prescott," he said. "You fix that department and become sheriff."

"Sheriff Sanchez," she said, musing, "that does have a nice ring to it."

"Not bad," he replied, smiling, "but aren't you forgetting something?"

"Oh yeah," she said, glancing at the ring. "So, whatever we decide, the next sheriff of Sloan County will be named Clark."

"That's how I see it," replied Clark.

"Amanda Clark," she said, smiling. "I like the sound of that even better."

"How about Sheriff Amanda Clark?" asked Clark.

She smiled at him before making her decision.

"How long will you be gone?" she asked, smiling at him.

Teaser Sample

Coming Soon from D.A. Roberts

and J. Ellington Ashton Press.

Apex Predator: Blood Moon

D.A. ROBERTS

PRELUDE
DARKNESS RETURNS

The gentle early spring breeze brought with it the smell of budding flowers as Deputy Frank Bonner rolled down the windows of his white Karol County patrol SUV. He chose a remote section of the county to park and eat his lunch. He worked the graveyard shift and thankfully the calls had been few and far between tonight.

Parking next to a cemetery might creep most people out, but Bonner felt it to be peaceful there. Especially late at night when there weren't any cars on this stretch of Arkansas Highway 62. He wasn't far outside of Eureka Springs and decided to take a few moments to eat before things got busy.

He had no sooner unwrapped his sandwich when he heard a familiar whine from the backseat. He took a breath and blew it out slowly while shaking his head.

"I haven't forgotten you, Bosco," he said, reaching back and ruffling the fur of his partner, a three-year-old Belgian Malinois. "God forbid I get the first bite. Greedy *Mali-gator[23]*."

Chuckling, he broke off a chunk of the cold sub sandwich he'd bought hours ago at a convenience store in Eureka Springs. He didn't like giving Bosco bread, but a few bites wouldn't hurt him. Bosco took the offered morsel with eager anticipation, leaving a sufficient quantity of slobber on Bonner's now empty hand.

"Eww, gross," he said, laughing. "Thanks a lot, buddy."

Bosco ignored him and happily scarfed down his food with the eagerness that only a hungry dog can show. Flicking the worst of the slobber out the window to not get it on his seats, Bonner wiped the rest on a towel he kept by the MDT[24] for the occasional slobber-based emergency.

---

[23] Mali-gator – nickname given by some law enforcement agencies to Belgian Malinois for their high energy and proclivity for biting.
[24] MDT – Mobile Data Terminal – the multifunction laptop in most police

"Great," he mused. "Another sandwich with the distinct aftertaste of dog-slobber."

Bosco looked back through the little pass-through window in eager anticipation of another bite.

"Good lord, boy," said Bonner, chuckling. "Can I get a bite first?"

Just as he was starting to take a bite, the radio picked up and a call came across.

"Any available unit," said dispatch. "Report of possible domestic violence in progress in a vehicle parked off highway 21 near Urbanette."

"226 responding," said a voice from the radio.

"Thatta boy," said Bonner. "I'm twenty minutes away from there."

"229 responding," said another voice.

"Even better," said Bonner. "Now I won't get called as a backup."

"Copy 226 and 229," said dispatch. "Showing you both in route."

With that, the radio returned to silence. Bonner started again to take a bite when Bosco growled. At first, he thought Bosco was growling at him for eating the sandwich but dismissed that thought when he realized Bosco wasn't looking at him. He was staring out the back passenger window and his hackles were up.

"Calm down, buddy," he said. "It's probably a damned skunk, anyway. I'm not letting you out so you can come back to the car smelling like skunk spray."

Bonner took a bite and looked out the window while he chewed. He didn't see anything moving. He cocked his head to the side and didn't hear anything. It took him a moment to realize that he didn't hear anything at all. No night sounds of spring, no frogs, no bugs, no anything at all. It was dead silent.

vehicles

Setting the sandwich down on the console well out of Bosco's reach, he chewed slowly as he flicked on the LED spotlight mounted by the driver's window. He began panning the light across the trees, searching for anything out of place. He paused at a section of trees at the back of the graveyard where he saw eyeshine.

Not that eyeshine is out of the ordinary in the woods, it just surprised him to see four of them. That coupled with the fact that they were all yellow and at least eight feet off the ground was rather disconcerting. Bosco continued to growl low in his throat.

"It's probably just owls," he said, not sure if he was reassuring the dog or himself.

One by one, they blinked out and vanished completely. He frowned and panned the light back and forth across the trees but couldn't find them again.

"Where are you?" he muttered to himself. "And more importantly, what are you?"

Bosco growled again, but this time he was on the opposite side of the SUV.

"What's up, buddy?" he asked, turning that direction.

There wasn't anything he could see, but he was beginning to get a really bad feeling that something was out there. Something that was hunting him and that thought made him very nervous. He started to reach for the gear shift but stopped himself just before shifting into drive to leave.

"Easy there," he said. "I'm supposed to be the guy who goes looking for the scary stuff. I can't be running from some damned animal."

Stepping out of the vehicle, he took out the flashlight he kept on his belt and clicked it on. The light of the powerful Surefire XM-L U2 lit up the area with its 1200 lumen beam. Placing his hand on his duty pistol, a Gen 4 Glock 17, he began shining the light around the area.

Behind him, Bosco's growling had ceased and he was starting to whine. Bosco usually whined whenever Bonner got out of the vehicle, but this time it was different. It wasn't an eager sound. It sounded afraid and that bothered Bonner even more.

Suddenly, Bosco went completely silent. Turning around, Bonner looked into the window and saw him down in the floorboard as far down as he could go. Bonner looked around the vehicle but didn't see anything. Glancing inside, he didn't see anything wrong but something stuck out to him. His sandwich was gone.

"Bosco," he said, sternly, "did you steal my sandwich?"

Behind him, he heard the soft crunch of gravel as something stepped onto the white chat driveway near the back of the SUV. Turning quickly as he drew his pistol, his flashlight lit up the hair-covered chest of something enormous. He froze, midway through raising his pistol. Standing before him was something out of a nightmare.

Slowly panning the light upwards, he saw the outline of a gigantic wolf, only it was towering over him on two legs. It brought one massive arm up to protect its eyes from the intense beam of the flashlight. It suddenly occurred to him how much of a mistake he'd made by not leaving when he'd had the chance.

Bonner started to regain enough composure to bring the weapon up the rest of the way when he felt the hot breath of something behind him. Breath that was coming down onto his shaven scalp and neck.

Before he could react, powerful hands grabbed him around the head, completely engulfing it. He felt a sharp twist and heard a crunching sound that he knew had to be the vertebrae in his neck snapping. He dropped to the ground like a ragdoll, unable to move so much as a finger. He heard the pistol clatter to the ground as he lost all sensation in his body.

"This is what it feels like to have your spine crushed," he thought.

He remembered a Discovery Channel documentary on the French Revolution that said when a person had their head cut off by the guillotine, their brain could live for up to three minutes. He thought that had to be bullshit at the time, but now he thought that there might be something to it.

Then he heard the sound of breaking glass and Bosco started screaming in pain. Every fiber of him wanted to go to his rescue, but he couldn't move. Then the screaming stopped as suddenly as it had begun, ending with a wet crunch.

His head lolled to the side. Not of his own accord, so he knew that something had moved him. His head bounced to an angle where he could look down on his body with an odd detachment. He could see two of the monstrosities ripping his clothing and armor away.

Then, there was a surreal moment when they began tearing pieces of his flesh away and eating them. It took a moment for his brain to register what was happening. He was already losing focus and it seemed distant and unimportant. Then something in his brain focused for a final moment and he screamed internally.

"Oh GOD!" he screamed in his mind. "They're eating me!"

Continued in

Apex Predator: Blood Moon

D.A. ROBERTS

Author's Bio: D.A. Roberts

D.A. Roberts is an author of fiction, primarily in the horror/dystopian and science fiction genres. Born in Lebanon, Missouri, he now lives in Springfield, Missouri with his wife and sons. When not writing, D.A. serves his community in Law Enforcement.

Best known for his "Ragnarok Rising Saga," he blends the zombie genre with elements of Norse Mythology. The series has been called "a thinking man's apocalyptic world." This is a unique approach that creates a new sub-genre in Apocalyptic Fiction.

He is also known in science fiction for "The Infinite Black Series." This series is based on the hit video game from Spellbook Studio. Download and play the game for free at www.Spellbook.com.

In November of 2018, D.A. took on the challenging role of C.E.O. of J. Ellington Ashton Press.

In March of 2020, D.A. was elected as the president of the Horror Author's Guild.

Find more about his work at

www.jellingtonashton.com

www.amazon.com/author/daroberts

https://www.facebook.com/DARobertsAuthor/

https://www.haguild.com/

DARK ANGEL
MEDICAL
VITA VEL NEX
WWW.DARKANGELMEDICAL.COM

Printed in Great Britain
by Amazon